LEASHES
IN
HEAVEN

LEASHES
IN
HEAVEN

A NOVEL

JEFF ALLEN

Published by Best Chapter Publishing LLC

For more information, contact: BestChapterPublishing@gmail.com

ISBN (paperback): 978-1-7351810-3-5
ISBN (ebook): 978-1-7351810-4-2

Book design: Christy Day, Constellation Book Services

Printed in the United States of America

Dedication

To my family...

My loving wife Michele.

You were my inspiration for writing *Leashes in Heaven*.

I haven't composed a love letter for you in ages.

Well, here it is—to my love and best friend.

All of my furry children.

Those that have come and gone, and the ones still by my side.

My heart overflows with joy and love thanks to all of you.

Contents

PART 1

Memories

Callings

Sunday mornings are by far my favorite time of the week. I'm thankful to awaken with the love of my life and a few dogs, ready to start a day that's set aside for our little family. Maddie is lying on the other side of the bed, facing away from me. Her beautiful long dark hair flows down the contours of her spine, almost tickling her back dimples. I notice she's making a few subtle moves as she awakens. Rolling on to her back, I hear her take a deep breath in, then release a long exhale, treating her body to a sumptuous stretch. Arms extend overhead and toes point straight out under the covers. Once again, she ends up on her side.

The sun is peeking through the drapes as I bring my arms out from under the sheets. I can't lay still any longer. My fidgeting is going to disturb Maddie; it's almost time.

BeeGee, our beagle mix, is nestled between our warm bodies, sound asleep. I pet, then lift and move her to my other side. This allows me to scoot across the sheets. Maddie's back is still towards me. The closer I get, the more her familiar smell and the warmth radiating from her body soothes my soul. My desire for intimacy with my love has me wrapping my arm around her as I push my knees into the backs of hers. As we spoon, she takes another deep, refreshing breath, grabs my arm and pulls me ever so close, uniting our bodies as one.

"Good morning, sweetie," she says as she leans back and gives me a kiss.

"This is a splendid morning. You know what day it is, don't you?"

I see her forehead pucker as she squints her eyes. Of course, she knows. She's being coy, the same performance she puts on every Sunday. It's our little ritual, and I act as though I believe her. After a few seconds go by, she can't keep the ruse up and, with a smirk on her face she says, "It's Sunday morning, SNUGGLES!"

Our Sunday morning routine is also an alarm for the dogs. With her exclamation, Davy, a husky-shepherd mix, jumps from his bed on the floor onto the foot of ours. Maddie picks up Tramp, a wire-haired terrier who has to be twenty years old, and puts her in bed with us. We're all sitting up now, people and dogs. As I arch my back and tilt my head, I let out a boisterous howl. Davy looks at me, wondering why I'm making that awful noise. Two seconds later, Maddie whoops out an impressive wail. Davy hesitates for a second, then he shows us how it's done—a perfect wolf call. The joyful wailing goes on and on while the five of us sit here, enjoying our happy, foolish moments together. BeeGee stares at us with her head tilted to the side, trying to make heads or tails of what's happening. Tramp is deaf, so she's still snuggling with her mom, not noticing the silliness of Sunday morning snuggles.

As I look into Maddie's eyes, I feel her love for me and our dogs reverberating from her. Everything is right in the world. What's important is right here—togetherness. She leans over to give me a kiss. My eyes close and...

I'm awakened from a wonderful dream, a memory from over fifty years ago, by the cold, wet nose of no other than my sweet little Darla, a cute Jack Russell mix. With all the dogs we've had over the years, I should've been prepared for that wet wake-up call.

Sometimes memories of the life you've lived and of those you've loved and lost seem cruel, but I am thankful for them.

The older I get, the harder it is to get out of bed. Thanks to Darla and the other two dogs keeping me company last night, Buck and LuLu, I only have about eighteen inches of space on my king-sized bed. At least I don't have far to scoot, so I get out with little effort. After sixty years in our enormous bed, I sure appreciate the mere foot and a half my sweet family leaves for me.

This morning there's a lot on my mind, and the bittersweet dream brings back recollections of my lost love. I feel Maddie's strength within my soul. Today I'll need it. Every year I miss her more and more. Along with the aches and pains this old body experiences, my heart aches, too—some days I wish I could just stay in bed. I blink hard, trying to get my vision to adjust so I can find my cell phone on the nightstand. Reaching for it, I traverse the table with my fingers. I find it, but not before knocking my glasses onto the floor. It's 5:30, or at least I think that's what time it is.

It's hard to tell without my glasses. Turning on the light, I see they've landed between two of the four dog beds, all occupied with more dogs.

Darla is the only pup stirring this morning. I don't blame the others; I wish I was back under the covers myself. I can feel a hint of Winter just beginning to cool the air. Time to pull the down-comforter out of the closet. I'm sure their old bones are suffering from the chill just like mine. If only I could turn off the light, pull Darla under the covers, and rub her belly to get another hour of sleep. That's not possible this morning. It's time to get moving; we have a big day ahead of us.

Maneuvering the dogs to one side, I sit on the edge of the bed. I take a deep breath, lifting my shoulders up towards my ears, then rolling them back as I exhale. I follow my breathing routine with a little twisting at the waist, and turning my head from side to side. My earlier yoga days gave way to this modified "seated bed pose," although I see Darla can still manage her asanas as she does her downward and upward facing dog. Doing my bed yoga, I notice the stiffness, grinding, and clicking gets rougher and louder every day. I remind myself those sporting endeavors during my younger years, especially football, were hard on my body.

"Do I chance stepping barefoot in a puddle this morning, Darla? I think not." It's a gamble I've lost more times than I would like to admit, and it's not a pleasant experience. It's especially not something I want to face this morning; I need to keep the positive energy flowing. One of the secret ingredients of Monkey's House, our dog hospice, has always been the Law of Attraction. We've always believed in the power of positive thinking, which is how I'll proceed this morning.

Balanced on the edge of the bed, I wiggle my feet back underneath to find my slippers, right where I kicked them off last night. By squeezing my big toes on the tops to help keep a grip, I drag them out. I slide my feet into the slippers and slowly stand up, hesitating for a few seconds. Over the last few months, I've been getting a slight buzz going from sitting to standing. A few deep, calming breaths while keeping still dissipates the dizziness. The consequences of falling at my age could be catastrophic, so I've learned to proceed with caution.

Now with a clear head, I set my intention on using the bathroom, which is just down the hall, and Darla follows. About to exit the room, I notice the balled-up letter I tossed on the floor last night sitting in the doorway. I hesitate for a moment as my body tenses and face warms. With good aim, my foot slams squarely down on the crumpled paper, which I twist my slipper atop of until it is thoroughly crushed into the floor. I inhale a deep breath; my shoulders straighten and my head sits high as I continue on my journey out of the bedroom and into the hall.

I hear a squelch and look down to find my foot in a small puddle in the middle of the hallway. Gazing down at Darla I say, "Guess I made the right call with the slippers this morning." This is a common occurrence when you live with twenty-five hospice dogs. After taking a moment to clean up the accident, I pick up my speed getting into the bathroom. We don't need another puddle.

When I return to my bedroom, I see all the dogs are still sleeping. Darla's by my side, but then darts around me, entering the room first. It warms my heart, knowing I'm her world. That thought floods my mind. Darla is one of hundreds of dogs we've brought into our home, giving them a loving family.

My gaze falls once again to the scrunched-up letter sitting on the floor. Seeing the government seal gets my heart racing, so much so that I need to catch my balance by grabbing on the doorjamb. We've been fighting this for almost twelve years. Darla senses my pain and runs back to comfort me. I hoist her up into my arms, "Don't worry, those bastards will never close Monkey's House." She gives me a lick on the cheek. I smile, lower my shoulders, and the pounding of my heart lessens.

That dreadful letter spurs on recollections of the dogs that have come and gone. My heart is full: each pup occupies a small sliver, though deep in my soul, I'm aching to be with my family. Especially my love, Maddie. I turn and look down the hall and spot the hanging cord of the pull-down attic ladder. It's been years since I've been up there. Family, and more recently, my cautious doctors advise me to avoid stairs altogether. I had a chairlift installed on the stairway, which makes the second floor accessible. Climbing the attic ladder is out of the question… or is it?

Still struggling to get my body moving, I head down the hall. The pitter patter of Darla's little feet right on my heels reminds me it's time to trim her nails again. It's no simple task. She's feisty. I'll have to remember to ask Holly for help. Darla may love me to the moon and back, but that doesn't seem to matter when it comes time to trim toenails.

At the end of the hall, I reach for the cord until it is in my grasp. My heart is racing as I'm set to pull. Voices in my head are telling me: *don't*. On this day, I wave them off, and when I give it a yank, the door barely budges. "God, am I that old and weak?" I'm on a mission. A deep inhale fills my chest. I raise my other arm and now am clenching the cord with both hands. Pulling with all my might, the door opens, raining down a cloud of dust. While I'm being blanketed with the musty stuff, Darla scoots away, sneezing a few times herself.

With the stairs unfolded, I peer into the dark opening, assuring myself I can do this if I take it nice and easy. One step at a time, I firmly plant both feet on each rung as I ascend. There are only ten steps; *I can do this*. Reaching the second step, I look down. Darla is sitting at the bottom of the ladder. She planted her front paws on the first rung like she's ready to climb up after me. I smile, but am not worried she'll try to go any further. Darla rides the chairlift to the second floor with me every night as she suffers from a major heart condition along with spinal issues. As I look down at her, I notice a worried look on her face and acknowledge her displeasure with me climbing the ladder.

"Darla, I'll be fine. I won't be long, go back to bed." But she doesn't budge. It's no surprise: Darla took it upon herself to be my guardian angel from the first day she arrived at Monkey's House. She's not walking away now. Through the years, we've been their angels, there for them when they needed us. I've learned they have given us so much more than we have ever given them.

On the fifth step now, I'm able to reach the switch for the attic lights. Before turning them on, past memories come rushing back as I anticipate the treasures I may find. Excitement is overcoming me, much like a dog in a game of fetch waiting for the toss of the ball.

As I flip the switch, I notice hundreds, perhaps thousands, of pictures of all the Monkey's House residents from the past thirty years. So many dogs have come and gone, each with their own personalities—loving, mischievous, goofy, you name it—but all willing to give and receive love in their own way.

It's been a long time since I've been up here, and the sheer number of pictures we've accumulated surprises and delights me all over again. I've never forgotten a dog, although I'll admit, some of their names now escape me—but never the dog. Clear plastic drapes over stacks and stacks of pictures. Good planning on my part; I'd forgotten how dusty it gets up here.

I now realize this might not be the best time to continue my pilgrimage into the past. I should have somebody here with me; and, I have to remind myself once again, I have a big day and need to get ready. Reaching up to turn the lights off, I catch something glistening out of the corner of my eye, like stars twinkling in a calm, dark night. I turn towards the glitter and focus. The light is shining off dozens of snaps from colorful leashes strung over a support-beam. They invite me to continue my journey, letting me know not to worry. Loved ones are watching over me.

Almost at the top, I pop my head through the opening. The morning sunlight streams through the attic window, illuminating the condensation from my breath as I exhale into much cooler air. I'll grin and bear it. Since I can't make it down and back for a jacket, it will be a one-and-done adventure this morning. A whimper draws my attention, and I gaze down and see my trusty friend, Darla, waiting for me. Grounding my right foot on the attic floor, I make it off the last step. I walk around the attic, looking for a few particular pictures to reminisce about. Keeping an eye out for low cross beams is critical. My head still wears the scar from one of them which I'd walked straight into. After all, I'd like to avoid adding a concussion to my growing list of ailments.

Years ago, Maddie would accompany me up to the attic. We spent hours flipping through pictures together, experiencing every emotion in the book: happy and sad tears in equal amounts, with a lot of laughter intertwined. We spent our time up here feeling thankful for the opportunity God gave us to have these dogs in our lives.

I notice the billboard Maddie put together for the Monkey's House tenth anniversary hanging on the wall. A collage of pictures shows the beauty of the dogs living life to their best ability at our house. It doesn't show the years and struggles, some between Maddie and me, that we went through to get our little piece of heaven opened.

To this day, I feel a sense of shame. I fought her hard. I wasn't ready to change my life. No way I wanted to open a dog sanctuary. This went on for over a year. Sure, we talked about opening a sanctuary for some time, but I never expected it would come to fruition. She opened it without me, announcing it on social media.

I was not pleased, but I realized how much this meant to Maddie, so I got on board and helped her in all aspects: the long negotiation with the town to exceed the five-dog ordinance; the struggle to get approval on our state's non-profit status and federal identification number, which would make it official; retrofitting the house and property to support all the dogs who were terminal and had special needs. It took over a year, and many more to get things running smoothly. Maddie always called it "organized chaos."

Looking up to heaven, I can imagine Maddie looking down as I talk to her. "Honey, it seems like we're going to lose Monkey's House. I received a certified letter from the courts; they're planning on taking our property. I fought long and hard, fending them off for as long as I could. Over the past thirty years our sanctuary has given me purpose. Thank you for making it all possible."

My heart aches knowing the end is near; it's bringing back heartfelt memories. There's a force pulling me towards the pictures from the early years of Monkey's House. I kneel by a stack from the first few years—decades ago as I can tell by the photo quality, though it feels as though it were yesterday. Flipping through, I savor how many include Maddie. Right on top of the pile is a picture of Maddie with Sora, her sweet and wonderful Sora.

Ask any dog lover: I'm sure they loved all the dogs in their lives, but if you're one of the lucky ones, you'll be blessed with a soul dog. Sora was Maddie's—a beautiful German shepherd she adopted two years before opening Monkey's House. Sora was middle-aged, a perfect dog in every sense. Once we started our sanctuary, Sora became the calming essence within our household. She accompanied Maddie on veterinary appointments, acting as the chaperone, filling the atmosphere with tranquility. Her serenity rubbed off on every living being.

Beautiful pictures of the dogs hang on every square inch of walls in the house. Just like this one, each photo shows thrown-away dogs loving and living their final chapter with us. We ran out of wall space in the house years ago so we'd switch out pictures, displaying the more current dogs throughout the house. Every so often we would turn the clock back, filling the walls with older photos of dogs who had passed years prior. That always brought back such heartfelt memories. Sadly, I haven't done that since Maddie left.

Portraits of Yesteryear

The alarm goes off in the guest bedroom, setting off Jake, who lets out an enthusiastic bark. He triggers a chain reaction throughout the house. It sounds like a grammar school band warming up on the first day of practice. It's 6:30 in the morning, and Kaitlyn is not ready for this. As a San Diegan, she's not used to New Jersey's cold weather, and her internal clock is saying it's only 3:30. She's bundled to the hilt with flannel pajamas and thick winter socks. She battles to wake up, only to realize there's something in bed with her.

Lucille and her buddy Jake made their way into her bed during the middle of the night. Before she can lift her head off the pillow, Lucille gives her a big, wet kiss across her face. Her breath is foul. "Yuck, what have you been eating?" Kaitlyn wipes her face with the edge of the sheets. "Wait, don't tell me... it's better I don't know." She struggles to get the dogs off the covers, but Lucille, a pit mix, and Jake, part lab, are both medium-sized dogs, each weighing in at around fifty-five pounds. Snuggled on each side of her, they have Kaitlyn pinned under the heavy quilt that drapes the bed. She kicks to un-tuck the sheets, trying to escape from under the covers. It's enough to annoy Jake as he jumps to the other side of the bed, allowing her to breathe once again.

Pugsley and Belinda, two pugs, are near her bed, laying on some clean clothes they pulled out of the laundry basket Kaitlyn brought upstairs yesterday. If that wasn't bad enough, Champ found the basket made a nice comfy bed, and laid on the clothes remaining at the bottom. *I should have listened when Uncle Josh said to put my clothes away*, she thinks to herself. Kaitlyn makes her way out of the bed, picks up her clothes and stuffs them in the dresser, leaving Champ undisturbed as he looks too content to move. She's not worried about wrinkles since they're now full of dog hair anyway.

Eyelids heavy and struggling to get moving, Kaitlyn throws on a heavy robe and heads towards her uncle's room, followed by a small pack of dogs. She doesn't notice that the attic ladder has been pulled down at the other end of the hall, nor Darla sitting at the bottom, peering up for her dad.

"Uncle Josh," she calls out entering his room, "it's time to get moving. We have a lot to do before we hit..." Before Kaitlyn finishes the sentence, she realizes her uncle is not in his room. Her forehead scrunches as she sees the flattened, balled-up piece of paper on the floor. It looks like he has stepped on it. She knows her uncle's tidy and wouldn't typically leave trash laying around. Feeling a little awkward once she picks it up, she notices it's his personal mail. Quickly she realizes it's an official letter about Monkey's House. She smooths it out and reads it. Her groggy eyes widen slightly and her the slump leaves her shoulders. She slowly folds and stuffs the letter into her robe pocket.

The dogs in the room look up and charge towards her. They know it's potty time, followed by breakfast. *Where could he be?* she wonders. She passed the bathroom on the way to Josh's room, so she knows he's not in there either. Outside his bedroom door are the stairs to the first floor. Firmly grasping the handrail, which is needed at this hour, she heads down followed by all the dogs—except Darla, who's faithfully awaiting her dad to come out of the attic, though Kaitlyn still doesn't notice this.

As Kaitlyn's foot leaves the last step, her eyes widen and stature straightens instantly after planting the ball of her right foot into a large puddle of pee. It soaks right through her thick wool sock, dampening her toes. "Dammit! Never go shoeless at Monkey's House: I know this, I know this."

Kaitlyn scans the first floor, realizing Josh hasn't been downstairs yet. To avoid wetting the floor further, she shifts her weight to her right heel with soaked toes elevated. A trooper, she is hobbling to the back door, allowing the dogs out into the fenced backyard. She realizes the appointment time is not far off, and hurries back upstairs to find her uncle. In the meantime, Darla is whimpering, wanting to be with her dad. The crying draws Kaitlyn's attention to the fully extended attic ladder. Eyes opened wide, she gasps when she sees the attic light on, the cold draft flowing from above chilling her cheeks. Her frightened, yet stern voice causes Darla's ears to perk. "Darla, is your dad up there? He's not supposed to stress himself." Kaitlyn grabs the sides of the ladder, then freezes in hesitation.

A few years earlier, she had a nasty fall off a ladder. She isn't sure she has the inner strength to climb it to see why her uncle is up there. It isn't a matter of physical limitations preventing her from taking the first step, as much as the mental scars from the accident. Kaitlyn shouts up to the attic. There's no response. Out of options, she slowly ascends the ladder, wet foot and all, muttering anxiously to herself, "This is on its last legs." The next rung makes a cracking sound. "It hasn't been used in such a long time and should have been replaced decades ago." Somehow, she convinces herself to keep climbing. "I simply have to do this; I can't give up now."

Kaitlyn pops her head up above the attic floor and sees a shadow at the far end. Not wanting to spook her uncle, she whispers. "Uncle Josh... Uncle Josh, are you up here?"

"Good morning, Katie." He follows it up with a quote he says on most mornings: "This could be the best day of your life."

Kaitlyn doesn't respond kindly to his positive quote. Also, she's outgrown the nickname her uncle gave her years ago. But what irritates her most is being reminded of the ladder from her past. Her voice is shaking, yet elevated. "You're not supposed to be up here. Why on earth did you pick this morning to do something like this?" Kaitlyn huffs. "I came here to help out, not keep you out of trouble."

Josh seems oblivious to her concerns. "Come on over here," he says, waving her over to the stacks of pictures.

"We are on a tight schedule," Kaitlyn grumbles, emphasizing the word "tight."

Despite her obvious concerns, Josh's demeanor is calm. "Not that tight; we have time. I want to show you some pictures." He coaxes her over with his irresistible smile. At eighty-six years, Josh is handsome for his age. He still has most of his hair, albeit gray. He tries to keep himself in shape and has told Kaitlyn many times she inherited her athleticism from him. Athletic abilities indeed ran in the family, although most surely from her parents. They were both collegiate athletes. Her mother was on the Wisconsin crew team and her father played baseball for Florida State.

Kaitlyn agrees, "Okay, I'm coming over." She pulls herself into the attic and walks in his direction. "It's freezing up here. Aren't you cold?" She crosses her arms, as though she's holding in what little heat she still has under her robe. She rubs her arms with her hands as the chill sends shivers down her spine.

"These memories are warming my soul. That's what matters right now." He extends his arm and grabs Kaitlyn's hand, guiding her across a gap in the flooring. "See these piles here?" He lifts the plastic off a stack and the dust flies. It makes him sneeze as Kaitlyn waves it away from her face. "These are from our early years." He picks the top picture from the pile and shows Kaitlyn. "This one is right before opening Monkey's House." It's a heartwarming photo of Maddie with Monkey sitting on her lap. The two who started it all.

A flood of fond memories comes racing back to Kaitlyn when she sees her aunt with the biggest smile on her face holding Monkey. Her heart aches with sorrow for the woman she loved so dearly. Maddie passed less than a year after Kaitlyn's last summer visit with her aunt and uncle. She's always felt guilty she didn't continue spending those precious summer weeks with her uncle. Sure, she missed her aunt, but that wasn't the reason she stopped. She was growing up, the whole teenage girl thing was kicking in. Now, looking back, she wished she had continued visiting her uncle, as she so enjoyed his company.

Kaitlyn could see great love in her uncle's eyes, but they also contained a hint of loneliness. For the past ten years, Maddie has been gone. "Tell me how you two met."

With a twinkle in his eye he replies, "Who, Maddie or Monkey? You know they were both blind dates." He may be advanced in age, yet Kaitlyn sees he still has his youthful wit.

First Date

When Josh finally relented to the constant match-making attempts from his coworker Rita, he never expected the date to be at a barn. Rita, an accomplished equestrian, has a horse at a local stable, as does the young woman he's being setup with. Josh arrives right after work still wearing his office attire, a button-down shirt and khaki pants, although he changed his shoes to a pair of hiking boots he had stashed in his car. It's perfect weather for a horseback ride this early June evening, with a pleasant temperature of seventy-two degrees. There hasn't been rain for the past five days, so the ground is firm and provides a solid footing for the horses.

Josh is uncomfortable waiting in the aisle, not sure what to do with himself. As Rita notices him, he raises his shoulders with palms face up. She forms a pleasing smile and walks over and starts introducing him to other riders. Most of the riders are wearing riding breeches, a few don jeans. He quickly realizes he looks out of place, and wonders why he didn't pack a change of clothes. Guess that's it: he wasn't thinking. She's late, maybe she won't show. He wonders for a moment if he should just leave.

"Is she going to show?" Josh glances at his watch.

"Stop, she'll be here. She's a visiting nurse's aide and is probably running a little late." Rita appears confident Maddie will arrive soon; besides, she's only fifteen minutes late. "She's here almost every day to ride her horse. She's a big animal lover, too. That's why I thought you two might hit it off."

"What, are you calling me an animal?" Josh snickers as he pets a horse's head sticking out of the stall and nudging at his shoulder.

"You know what I mean... See? Horses like you, too. Throughout your childhood, you've had all kinds of animals, even horses. I have a hunch you two will be a heavenly match."

No sooner does Rita finish her sentence the door to the barn opens and Maddie walks in. Josh's date has arrived. Maddie is a beautiful young woman with big brown eyes, long dark brown hair pinned back by two bobby-pins, high cheekbones and full lips. Like Josh, she is not in riding gear either. She came directly from an elderly client's house.

Rita jumps in and introduces them. "Maddie, this is Josh. Josh, Maddie. Have a pleasant ride. I'll talk to you both tomorrow." Off she flies to get on her horse, Tally, to enjoy a ride herself.

"Well, that was a quick introduction. Very nice to meet you, Maddie."

"Yes, finally. Rita has been talking about you for weeks. Honestly, I'm not into being setup on a date, but when she said you were a rider, I finally gave in," she says with a nervous smile.

He smiles back, "Yeah, being setup is risky. I finally gave in to her constant nagging." He wants Maddie to know he isn't jumping into this date either, even though he is pleasantly surprised by her beauty.

Maddie introduces Josh to Thunder, the horse he'll be riding. Then, she leaves to change her clothes, transforming herself into an equestrian, wearing tan breeches, riding boots and a sleeveless light blue shirt. Jackets aren't needed on this lovely evening. Maddie is grooming her horse, Nosey, while Josh finishes brushing Thunder and turns to cleaning his hooves with a pick and stiff brush in hand.

Maddie notices when he moves on to the feet. "Rita told me you knew your way around horses; it's hard to get Thunder to pick his leg up." Josh smiles inwardly as Maddie appears impressed with his horsemanship skills.

"We had horses growing up. I always found the key is being patient and showing them kindness. They will eventually come around." He goes to the next hoof, pushes his weight into Thunder, and with little effort, lifts his leg. "On getting them to cooperate, leaning into their body to get their weight on the other three legs helps a lot."

Any equestrian worth their weight in salt knows this, and surely Maddie does as well, but she doesn't let on. "You know

I didn't know that; I'll try shifting their weight next time."

On their ride out, the horses are walking side by side. The gentle movement under them is eliminating any anxiety the first date may have stirred up, easing their conversation.

"Rita told me you're in college. What's your major?"

"I'm going for my BSN at Rutgers to become a registered nurse."

"Do you enjoy college?"

"I don't have time to enjoy college life. My social life is non-existent." Maddie is working her way through school, holding down two part-time jobs. Three days a week, she's a receptionist at the local hospital emergency room. The other job has her assisting seniors as a nurse's aide, going on home visits. She takes all the assignments time allows, and spends what little free time she has left at the stable riding and caring for Nosey.

"I've always dreamed of becoming a veterinarian. But my parents, and the lack of finances, steered me into a nursing career." Maddie turns the inquiry on to Josh. "I understand you recently started working with Rita. How do you like working in technology?"

"I enjoy it. It's challenging. I joined there six months ago as a systems analyst. Prior to programming, I was in the military for a period." Josh was a first lieutenant in the Marines. After college, he enlisted and went directly into Officer Candidate School. Next was flight school, where he became a navigator, flying in the F-4 Phantom fighter jet. His hopes of a long career in the military ended when his aircraft went down because of a mechanical malfunction during a special forces mission. In the

incident, he lost the vision in his right eye and received the Purple Heart. After his honorable discharge, he went back to school and studied computer science.

Riding for close to an hour, they learn more about one another, the conversation flowing easily between them. They are both having a pleasant time, hitting it off enjoying each other's company. A couple of miles from the barn, Maddie suggests they get the horses water. She guides Nosey into a small stream, with Thunder right on his heels. They walk the horses into the middle as a swift current brings the water halfway up the horses' legs. Loosening the reins, the horses drop their heads to gulp a cool drink.

Nosey paws at the water, splashing Josh. "Hey, that water's cold." With a twinkle in his eye, he cocks his head slightly while gazing at Maddie. "I think you planned that."

"Nosey might have felt you wanted a drink, too." Maddie's laughter seemed to be the cue to spruce things up a bit. "Are you ready to pick up the pace with a little trotting and cantering?"

"Sure, but remember, I grew up riding Western, so this is my first-time riding English." Josh pushes himself up and down in the saddle with his legs. "Posting is new for me and I'm sure I'll look like a fool. I love to canter, though."

"I'm sure you'll look silly. But you'll be behind me, so no one will see you. Let's go!" Maddie and Nosey canter off across the field. Josh was not expecting her to be playful, at least not on a first date. Thunder is waiting for his command to head off after his friend. With a tap of a heel to his side, they are off, quickly catching up. Josh is captivated by Maddie's spunk and wonders *why he was hesitant about going on this date. He realizes he pushed off Rita's insistence for way too long.*

Back at the barn, they get the tack off the horses and begin cooling them down with a good hosing off. Maddie and Josh get soaked, but they aren't cooling off like Nosey and Thunder. Josh has a warm desire to see Maddie again, and he has a feeling she feels the same way. Walking side by side, they lead the horses around the back riding ring, giving them quiet time to talk. To Josh's surprise, Maddie is in her first year of college. He figured she was closer to graduating. Quickly doing the math, he figures she's five years his younger, but it doesn't seem to matter. He's enjoying his time with her.

The horses finally cool down, and they lead them into a back pasture for the night. Walking back to the barn, Josh takes Maddie's hand in his, which sets his heart pounding like he just finished running a five-minute mile. "I had a delightful time. Can I see you again?"

"Well, that was June 14th, the day I first laid eyes on the love of my life. As they say… the rest is history."

Josh notices a tear running down Kaitlyn's face. He assumes this is not for him or Maddie, but for the love that she herself had and lost. "Katie, you will have a love like this someday. I promise it will happen for you." He puts his hand on her shoulder. "Open your heart and forgive yourself."

Kaitlyn met Carson, the love of her life, at the University of California San Diego her freshman year. An Iowa all-state diver through her junior and senior years in high school, she was reluctant to go that far away to college, but was offered a partial scholarship to join their swim team.

Carson was also an outstanding athlete, a baseball player. They gave him a full scholarship to play baseball for the Tritons, as a relief pitcher. His fastball was awesome and the curve ball was nearly impossible to hit. However, he pitched with such vigor he would tire out after a few innings. Thus, being a reliever was a perfect fit for him.

The two of them became an inseparable couple. Carson's outgoing personality was soon rubbing off on the more reserved Kaitlyn. The once quiet wall flower soon became the watering can, nourishing perfect strangers with interesting conversations. She was blossoming into the young woman her uncle always told her she was, confident and exceeding at everything she put her mind to. Carson majored in pre-law and wanted to follow in his father's footsteps to become a trial lawyer.

At the end of their junior year, Carson was being recruited by professional baseball teams and didn't know where he would end up after graduation—playing baseball or law school. One thing was for sure: he wanted to spend his life with Kaitlyn. He proposed to Kaitlyn, and although she loved him dearly, she asked him to wait until they graduated before they considered marriage.

In a blink of an eye, an accident changed everything.

After some awkward silence, Kaitlyn swiftly shifts the conversation away from herself. "How was Monkey a blind date?" Sadly, she's gotten good at changing the narrative as a way of deflecting her pain.

"Maddie had a habit of bringing dogs home before asking me. She was afraid I would say no. Rightfully so, but she also knew once he was in our house, I would fall in love with him. It took about a week before I was hooked. Monkey was one of those surprises, but when I got home and saw him, there was an instant connection. I picked him up, and it was love at first sight for the both of us."

Josh holds up another picture of Maddie, Monkey, and himself. "Can you see the love in all our eyes? Monkey loved us, but few others."

At the time, the shelter's veterinarian had given Monkey two months to live. With the love and care Maddie and Josh gave him, he lived seventeen vibrant months, loving life. They had talked many times over the years about opening a dog hospice, and after Monkey passed, Maddie felt it was time.

"Your aunt wanted to open Monkey's House after his passing. I wanted to wait a while. Thankfully, Maddie got her way. Soon after, we opened up his house to help other dogs in his honor."

Kaitlyn pulls the letter out of her robe pocket and holds it out toward her uncle. "Why didn't you tell me about this?" Her jaw tightens and eyes squint. "They claim you're not fit to run Monkey's House. That's crap. Close you down and use eminent domain to take your property?"

Josh's head hangs low. Lifting his gaze slowly, looking into

Kaitlyn's eyes, she sees tears welled in his. He braces himself to speak. "I've fought them for years. Battle after battle, I kept losing, but the war was not over. Thankfully, I've been able to give many more dogs a chance at a second life." Josh sighs and shakes his head. "I have the will to fight, but I'm so tired. They drained my bank accounts from fighting all the legal battles. I'm afraid I'm about to lose the war."

"I'm here for you, Uncle Josh."

"Thank you, Katie."

"No. I mean I'm here to help you run Monkey's House. As long as you need me." Kaitlyn gets closer to her uncle and gives him a hug.

She knows they should get moving, but also wants to lighten the atmosphere. Out of the corner of her eye, she spots a picture falling from a pile. "That's a magnificent picture. Who is that, and where are you guys?" The picture is full of joy and love with Maddie, Josh, and a large German shepherd on a beach with the surf behind them.

Kaitlyn notices he's captivated. He takes a long deep breath in, then exhales, not saying a word. The silence lasts a minute or more. Kaitlyn can see in his eyes; he's bringing back that day in his mind. "That's Dozer with us at the Jersey shore." She senses the picture took him way back… back to a day he shared with Maddie and Dozer at the beach.

The Beach

"Honey, you know the pups are going to be mad at us for not taking them," Josh says as he makes his way into the kitchen.

Maddie is packing an old wicker basket they haven't pulled out of the closet since opening the sanctuary. The kitchen island is full of delicacies. There's cheese and crackers, grapes, pears and juicy ripe peaches—all great choices for a picnic. To top it off, Maddie bought a nice bottle of Moscato d'Asti, a fine wine to go with all the light fare and fruit. Josh walks around the island, making his way behind Maddie, wrapping his arms around her waist as he kisses her neck. She turns to face him, running her fingers through his hair and interlocking them behind his neck as their lips meet. To his surprise, she pulls a grape from behind his ear. Maddie had one hidden in her hand all along. She puts it in his mouth as they kiss, and her full lips are even more luscious and tempting with the juice of the grape. He doesn't want this moment to end, but their bus is running outside and Dozer is already on board.

"Sweetie, I need to finish packing this basket so we can get on the road; I'd like to say Dozer is patiently waiting, but I'm sure he's excited."

"He's not the only one," Josh says, pinching Maddie's bottom before he takes a quick step away. Maddie seems to enjoy the flirtation, giving him a seductive look as she continues packing for the trip.

This little outing is for the two of them, and of course, Dozer. A trip for Maddie and Josh always includes dogs, but instead of the six plus dogs they would normally take, today they'll have one. They can focus more on each other by only taking Dozer. It also gives him exclusive alone time with his mom and dad. Today is Dozer's turn to shine.

Dozer, a handsome German shepherd, came to Monkey's House a month ago. He has Degenerative Myelopathy, which is a canine form of ALS, also known as Lou Gehrig's disease. He assimilated to his new environment within a day or two, making new friends quickly with the other Monkey's House dogs and instantly loving his new parents. They wouldn't normally take Waggin' One, their senior dog bus, to travel with a single dog. However, Dozer is not just any dog. Despite his physical limitations, he's comfortable with his bed placed on the floor of Waggin' One, giving him plenty of room. Josh loads his chariot, a large wagon he loves to travel in, with the food Maddie packed and the supplies for the dog. It will transport him to a prime picnic location on the beach.

The hour-plus drive is uneventful, but the excitement is palpable as they approach the beach. "Who's ready to have some fun? I'm talking some real fun?" Josh had the biggest grin on his face as he pulled Waggin' One into the parking lot next to the Brigantine dog beach.

"I'm ready for some fun," Maddie answers. "How about you, Dozer?" He lets out a big woof.

The plan works out with perfect execution; it's 3:00 in the afternoon and the tide is out. It's much easier pulling a loaded wagon during low-tide when the sand is moist and more compact than at high-tide when the footing is mostly soft mounds of sugar-sand.

"I'm going to make it nice and comfy for you, Dozer." Maddie puts another blanket down in the wagon. Josh pulls Dozer out of the bus and places him near the front of the wagon, giving him

a great vantage point of the scenery while also allowing him to keep a close eye on his mom and dad.

Maddie places the picnic basket and a beach blanket into the back of the wagon. Dozer turns his head, sniffing the scent of something superb. "Don't go eating our food, Dozer. Wait until your dad picks a suitable spot near the water." His mouth is watering as the aroma of the bully stick in the basket teases his senses. Josh continues to load the wagon, putting in two beach chairs and a small duffel bag.

"What's in the duffel?"

"Oh, just some stuff." Josh quickly moves to the front of the wagon and grabs the handle to get moving, seemly avoiding Maddie's question.

Maddie knows he's up to something. "Oh, some stuff... interesting," she utters with her brow raised high, slowly bobbing her head up and down.

They have the wagon packed to the gills, and with Dozer at ninety pounds, they struggle to get from the parking lot, traversing along the pathway, up and over the dunes to the beach. It's a rather comical effort, and halfway up the little hill, Maddie picks up the basket, duffle bag and chairs, allowing Josh and Dozer to crest the dunes. It is all downhill from here as they make their way to the water. They find a strategic location, away from what little crowd remains on the beach at this time of day, and stake their claim.

Josh places the chairs a few feet from the remnants of waves washing ashore on this calm sea day. They're alongside the wagon to be sure to include Dozer in on the picnic. Josh puts down the blanket as Maddie hands him the duffel bag.

"That bag is much heavier than it looks. What's in there?"

"You'll see. I'll handle this. You can get the picnic set up."

Maddie is proud of herself for putting together such a beautiful display of food with a nice bottle of wine for their enjoyment. They had dedicated much of the past few years to the dogs, with little time left for themselves. While individually, Maddie and Josh are caring and competent, it's the two of them together that make their relationship and the organization such a profound success.

"Wow, what a spread. It's like something you'd see in a movie."
Josh then points to the blanket—not the array of delicacies she had spread out, but the bully stick on the corner of the blanket. "Is that for me if I behave?"

Maddie chuckles and gives Josh a loving hip check, then heads off towards the water. "I would say yes, but you can't behave yourself. By the way, I don't think Dozer would appreciate you eating his treat."

She eases into the water as the waves gently cover her feet, over her ankles and up to mid-calf. She takes in a deep, relaxing breath, leading to a long exhale. "Come here. The water is so refreshing."

"I'll be there is a minute." Josh stealthily pulls out an old boom box from the duffel bag, popping in a cassette tape with a mix he recorded when they were dating. It contained classic 70s and 80s music they enjoyed during their intimate times together many moons ago. He hits play and quickly makes his way alongside Maddie, putting his arm around her shoulder, and she wraps hers around his waist as they look out across the ocean. The timing

couldn't have been better. Christopher Cross's "Sailing" ballad plays and they smooch, the longest kiss they've had in years.

"I can't believe you still have our music. I don't hear those songs often, but when I do, it brings back such beautiful memories… I love you."

"I love you, too." They stand there kissing, talking about earlier times for what seems like an eternity until Dozer interrupts with a loud "woof". This is his reminder that he needs some loving, too, and this brings them back to earth.

While they enjoy the cuisine, Maddie fusses with Dozer, giving him the bully stick. "Is this what you want? You're such a good boy." All three of them relish in a moment of heavenly bliss.

After finishing the food and having a glass of wine, they decide to take a short stroll up the beach with Dozer in tow. Josh and Maddie walk hand in hand, spellbound with each other, the waves splashing and seagulls gliding in the light breeze. Dozer is especially vociferous with all the new and interesting sights and activity.

Along the walk, stopping often, Maddie picks up a keepsake shell. If they come across a little sea creature still living, she'll gently put it back into the surf. Maddie is telling stories of her childhood and how her family vacationed on the Jersey shore when she was a little girl. She so loved the beach as a child and still does to this day. They couldn't have picked a better backdrop for their little romantic getaway.

⌒⊙

Sensing sadness in her uncle, Kaitlyn gives him a long hug. "Let's go. We do have to get on the road. When we get back, let's figure out what to do with all these pictures. They deserve to be seen and not stacked in a dark, dusty attic."

Josh is fully aware of the struggles Kaitlyn has been through the past few years. Thankfully, she's been doing better the past six months, and it was her parents who encouraged her to be the one to go to New Jersey to help her uncle. She's loved animals ever since she was a toddler. At two years old, she memorized all the Monkey's House dog names featured on their annual calendar. She'd correctly recite each dog's name as her parents flipped through the months. Kaitlyn's parents agreed it would be good for her to be around the dogs. It might help stimulate her desire to pursue her childhood dream of becoming a veterinarian. At twenty-five, it certainly isn't too late.

To lighten the atmosphere, Josh points at her wet sock: he's been there before. "What happened to your foot? I hope it isn't too cold."

Goodbye for Now

The kitchen island is spotless, with a large basket of fruit sitting to one side. It's the one place in the kitchen Josh makes sure stays clutter free. He sits upon a stool parked at the edge, watching Kaitlyn brew a cup of freshly ground coffee. The pleasant aroma is filling the air, masking the remnant odors from last night's spicy tacos and fajitas. He won't be having a home-cooked meal anytime soon, and enjoyed the Mexican fiesta Kaitlyn pulled together.

Kaitlyn pours coffee into a large canister, grabs a banana from the basket, and butters a bagel for the road as Josh looks on. "Sorry, Uncle Josh, here's a bottle of water to take your pills with. You can take a few sips here and there. Okay?" She squeezes his arm gently and gives him a little smile.

"This is not my first rodeo. When you make it as old as I have, you'll know the routine." He gets up and starts making his morning rounds; however, on this day, he's spending precious time with each one of his furry kids. Josh senses Kaitlyn wants to get on the road soon, but she doesn't rush him. A little extra time is spent saying his goodbyes as she waits for him to get through to the last pup. Eventually, he makes his way into the garage with two dogs on his heels. Darla and Rocky, a little black poodle mix, start their morning zoomies. They both scoot their way around Josh, beating him into the garage.

Once Monkey's House became well known in the rescue world, more and more dogs arrived. Early on, it was clear there was a need for more room, so Josh converted the garage and adjacent rooms to support the dogs. Two suites were designed specifically for dogs who had difficulty socializing with the others. They added a dog washing station and an industrial washing machine. This area is also where all the meals are prepared and many of the dogs eat in here as well. It's the operational core, or what Maddie liked to call "the control center," of daily activities. Setting all this up was key in making sure things ran smoothly.

"Good morning, Holly." Josh enters the control center with pep in his step. He elevates his voice as the dogs are getting rambunctious and loud while Holly prepares their breakfast. Darla and Rocky are playing underfoot, making it difficult to move around.

"Morning! How's the 'Machine' today?"

Holly's been volunteering at Monkey's House for twenty-eight years. She volunteered shortly after they opened, and now runs the daily operations. To Holly, Josh is a machine, a multi-tasker getting more things done in a day than an average person would do in a week—and he did it all efficiently and accurately. While she christened him with his "Machine" title, Josh, in kind, nicknamed her "Mini-Machine." She's a workaholic herself and wonderful with the dogs.

Josh often wonders why he didn't become an engineer; he'll admit he's an efficacy nut, likely enhanced because of his time in the Marines. He can drive volunteers crazy, but not Holly; she comes from the same ilk, which is why they've been able to work well together through the years and still get along. They understand each other's quirks and demands.

"The Machine is slipping a few gears. I'm hopeful the doctors will get me fixed and running efficiently again. Get me back to 75% and I'll be happy." Josh loves his nickname, although he knows he's not the same old machine of yesteryear. Nevertheless, he appreciates the endearment from Holly.

"In my office upstairs, you'll find all the Monkey's House binders. They contain everything needed to run the back-office operations. Instructions on donor management and fundraising, such as our t-shirts and calendars campaigns. You name it—everything is up there."

"Thanks for reminding me, but you'll be back before we need to flip through those. Besides, heaven forbid we get them out of order." Holly gives Josh a look with an impish tilt of her head, raised brow, and silly grin.

Pointing his finger at her and raising his eyebrows, he smirks and says, "Hey, watch it."

Kaitlyn comes out of the house into the garage, where she exchanges pleasantries with Holly. They'd only met a couple of weeks ago when Kaitlyn first arrived. Holly has been showing her the ropes and, to no one's surprise, Kaitlyn's a quick learner. Rocky and Darla turn and run, barking at the door leading to the parking area. Two cars pull up the driveway, and within minutes, two more volunteers, Tracey and Bob, walk in.

"Hi guys," Josh shouts out over the barking dogs.

"Hi Josh," Tracey replies, as she slides her feet across the floor with Darla and Rocky jumping at her legs. "I want to say hi to your dad," she says as she pets their heads. Once she finally makes her way over to Josh, she gives him a big hug.

Before Josh can catch his balance, Bob is shaking his hand, patting him on the back with his other hand. "Morning, Josh, and don't worry about a thing. The crew will take care of everything." Bob is a recent retiree who loves dogs and, equally important, tinkering around the little farm Monkey's House sits on. He's taken on most of the upkeep. At Josh's age, he doesn't know what he would do without Bob.

"I know Monkey's House is in excellent hands, and I can't thank you all enough." Josh realizes they haven't met Kaitlyn yet. "Tracey and Bob, this is my great niece, Katie. She flew in from San Diego to lend a hand." Josh hesitates for a moment. "Sorry, she likes to be called Kaitlyn. I still think of her as our little girl we spent summers with." Kaitlyn appears a little uncomfortable with the awkwardness of her uncle correcting her name, although she appreciates his effort.

"Besides being the prettiest member of the family, she's also the smartest and an outstanding athlete," Josh brags. "She was once short-listed for the Olympics." Upon hearing her uncle's praise, Kaitlyn cuts off eye contact and her posture folds as she looks downward.

Kaitlyn graduated with honors from UCSD with a BS in biology. Her dream was to become a veterinarian, but fate intervened with other plans for her. She was a powerful athlete who outrivaled her competitors in diving in the three-meter springboard event. She qualified to try out for the Olympic diving team and her coaches encouraged her to take part.

The competition was shortly after graduation, and she was excelling in the trials. By the last day of the event, she was fighting for the top spot on the roster. On her third dive, Kaitlyn hit the board on the way down, injuring her shoulder. She shrugged it off and continued competing, knowing she only needed average scores on the last two dives to make the team. All was going well. She skillfully executed the next dive, able to keep pressure off the injured shoulder. Confident she would get a spot on the team, she felt adrenalin streaming through her body.

Kaitlyn saved her best dive for last and knew she didn't need a high score. On her last trip up the ladder, with only one more step to reach the board, her shoulder gave out. Losing her grip, Kaitlyn came crashing down, suffering a grievous spinal injury to her first and second cervical vertebra at the base of her head.

Over a year, healing and physical therapy restored most of the mobility to her neck, but the tragedy didn't end there. Sadly, the opioids prescribed to manage the excruciating pain ravaged her life for years to come. Kaitlyn ultimately kicked the dependency, but she still had a broken heart. The diving accident changed everything.

Tension filled the air. The volunteers had often heard Josh talking about Kaitlyn's story. It was tragic, and they knew Kaitlyn was not where she had hoped to be a few short years ago. Josh didn't sense it as he loved Kaitlyn for who she was—who she is today, and who she will become tomorrow. To him, she could accomplish anything. It's no surprise: he always saw the positive side of life, in everything and everybody.

Breaking the uncomfortable silence, Kaitlyn pointed to a picture on the wall. "I didn't notice this picture. It's cute. Who's the dog wearing the blue bonnet?"

"That's LA. She was such a sweetheart," Holly replies. Time was passing, and they needed to be on the road thirty minutes ago. "You'll have to ask your uncle about her on the trip. I'm sure he can tell you a lot of stories—he does like to talk," she said with a big smile and a wink at Josh.

As Josh and Kaitlyn ready themselves to head out the door, Josh kneels down and says goodbye to Rocky and Darla. He gives his baby Darla a little extra attention, knowing how much she'll miss him while he's away.

Halfway out the door, Josh turns and shouts. "This could be the best day of your life!"

The Storyteller

A thin sheet of ice covers the windshield. Kaitlyn is shivering as she attempts to get the car started. It grunts and groans, but finally cranks over. While the engine warms, waiting for the defroster to work its wonders, Kaitlyn grips her coffee tight in her hands to garner whatever warmth she can from the outside of the canister. It appears Josh doesn't mind the cold; in fact, he seems to relish in the crisp, fresh air.

"Beautiful," he says, as he moves his arms back and forth, like he's on some sort of exercise equipment. Kaitlyn gives him a strange look.

One year after Josh and Maddie were married, they purchased their first house. Like many first-time homeowners, this stretched their budget, making money tight. They scrimped and saved for their down payment. Once in their little abode, keeping up with their mortgage payments and living expenses left little discretionary income. To help save on utilities, Josh talked Maddie into turning down the heat at night to the high fifties. He bought a down comforter, making their bed nice and toasty. But if you ventured out of bed, you felt like a popsicle.

Josh gazes at Kaitlyn. "Aunt Maddie was like you, going to bed in flannel pajamas and heavy socks. I would be in my skivvies." He chuckles. "She would be in bed like a flash. I would walk around, getting ready for the next morning. Before I would get into bed, I'd stand by the edge and swing my arms." Josh swings his arms again. "She considered me a little odd and would yell, saying my swinging created a cool breeze as she pulled the covers over her head." As he settles into the passenger seat, Kaitlyn sees him staring into space with a smile on his face; she assumes he's reminiscing about the funny moment with Maddie.

Kaitlyn, who likes to ease into her day with a few cups of coffee before she gets moving, giggles. "Are you sure I'm not adopted? I can't be your great niece." Conversely, her uncle's day kicks off from the minute his feet hit the floor.

Just before Kaitlyn puts the car in gear, she grabs her cell phone and inputs their destination's address into the navigation system. With traffic, travel time is a little over an hour. She knows it won't be a boring trip, as her uncle is indeed a talker. Her grandmother, Josh's sister, would always say he'd have made a great salesperson. That's not the path Josh chose, though. He worked for thirty-five years in corporate America, moving his way up into middle management where he was happy leading a small global technology team. It was during this employment that he and Maddie started their nonprofit. It was fresh, exciting, and something completely new, requiring unique skill sets. Josh loved it, but most of all, it overjoyed him to help Maddie fulfill her dream. He enjoyed most aspects of running the organization but found genuine delight specifically in promoting Monkey's House.

In his new role, he honed his communication skills, eventually becoming an impressive storyteller. He even penned a few books about the dogs at their hospice, one of which became a bestseller.

Heading out of the driveway, Kaitlyn jumps right into it. "Okay, what's the story with LA, the dog in the picture with the blue bonnet? It sounds like it might have something to do with Los Angeles." Her mission is to keep her uncle's mind off the day ahead. Besides, she loves to hear his stories and is curious about the dog with the funny blue hat.

"You're spot on. Let me tell you about LA, a sweet yellow lab, pittie mix and how she got her name."

LA's Story

They board the plane, pleased to be taking two plush seats right at the front of the cabin. This is the first time Maddie will fly first class. Although she's not a fan of flying, she is excited to be taking a trip with her sweetheart. Josh flew often for work, with most flights being international. On those long flights, he sat in business class with perks like fine cuisine, airline pajamas, and a seat that folded out into a flat bed. Quite a unique experience versus being in coach, and Josh always wanted Maddie to experience it at least once in her lifetime. He used frequent flyer miles he accumulated over the years to upgrade their seats so this trip would be special in every aspect. Prior to take-off, the flight attendant offers them two small glasses of champagne, which they happily accept.

Maddie lifts her glass to make a toast. "Here's to a glorious trip, a great husband, a noble life." They clink their glasses and both take a sip.

"I can't agree more but I'll throw in a well-deserved congratulations. I'm so excited they invited you to talk about Monkey's House with Oprah. Not to mention receiving an award from her."

"The biggest benefit is we get to spend a few days together. The show's great and lets us get our mission out to the world. But spending time together is what I'm looking forward to." She leans over and gives him a gentle kiss.

It is a long, uneventful flight from Philadelphia to Los Angeles. They talk for hours, mostly about each other, how they met, loving and funny memories through their forty plus years of marriage. They steer clear from talking about Monkey's House and the dogs. For these few days, besides the appearance on Oprah, it's time to reconnect, to deepen their love for one another—rekindle the flame.

The car service pulls up at the airport and they quickly load their luggage and head to the hotel. Maddie asks to take a scenic route to the hotel, passing by any sights of interest along the way. Their driver, Quinn, is a delight. She becomes their personal guide, transforming their ride into a wonderful, albeit brief, tour of LA. To their delight, they cruise right by Universal Studios and the famous Grauman's Chinese Theatre, bustling with fans snapping photos of their favorite star's footprints or handprints in the cement.

The thirty-minute car ride feels like just a few moments, the iconic LA landmarks captivating them. The hotel is a pleasant vision, allowing them to relax after their long trip before their *special night out. Their hotel is conveniently located a few blocks from the studio where the taping with Oprah will occur. Originally, the show booked a standard room, but once again, Josh used his reward points for an upgrade to a lovely suite with a terrific view of the city.*

Walking into the hotel room, Maddie's eyes widen and she's at a loss for words, standing in such a luxurious suite with red roses on the living room table. She pulls Josh in for a hug. The backdrop of LA shines through their floor-to-ceiling window as their silhouettes stand together in a passionate kiss.

After some rest, the couple gets ready to head out. Sally, the producer of the Oprah show, invited them to dine with her at a swanky restaurant in Beverly Hills. Josh walks out from the bathroom and sees Maddie, staring at herself critically in the mirror. She pulls at her dress and then rifles through her suitcase again to look for accessories that could possibly match the extravagance of a Hollywood producer, but doesn't find anything. Everything she owns screams country bumpkin from south Jersey. Josh thinks she looks exquisite, but he senses her tension and does his best to put her at ease.

"You're so beautiful," Josh says as he zips up the back of her dress. The black dress highlights her luscious curves, further enhancing her beauty. She'd just gotten her hair done before coming on the trip, and its shiny waves are her crowning glory. With a touch-up here and there, it looks as though she just stepped out of the salon.

"You look handsome too," she says, straightening the collar of his blazer. It really doesn't need any adjustments; it's her way

of taking care of her guy and stealing a little kiss and hug. The embrace, however, is short-lived as Josh's cellphone rings.

Josh answers the call, which is from Sally. It's a short one and as he hangs up, Maddie's asks, "What's up? Everything okay?"

"Sally can't make it, but she wants us to have a good time. She sent a car to take us to the restaurant. It will be here in fifteen minutes."

At first, Maddie thinks she should be disappointed, but it's no surprise she's not. What an unexpected pleasure for the two of them to have a romantic evening alone. Even more exciting, they'd be dining at a restaurant with an influential 3-star Michelin rating, the ultimate hallmark of culinary excellence. "Wow, I'm sorry she can't join us, but thrilled the two of us get to have a nice dinner together."

At the restaurant as they walk to their table, they hear a gentleman call out, "Excuse me, aren't you Maddie from Monkey's House?"

Shocked anybody would recognize them, they stop, and take a step back to see who is speaking. Wary of strangers in a big city, Maddie eyes up the well-dressed couple sitting at the table. "Yes, I'm Maddie. This is my husband, Josh. We are the founders of Monkey's House."

The gentleman stands. "I'm Robert. This is my wife Monica and we're dog parents. We have a boxer mix named Carlie and a little Pomeranian named Bentley. We follow you every night on social media, and fall in love with all your dogs. Your mission is dear to us."

Monica sits higher in her seat as her eyes widen and a smile forms. "I volunteer at a shelter here in the city and we have a dog named Old Lady that was recently surrendered. She's in dire need of a Monkey's House type facility."

"Would you like to join us for dinner and share some thoughts on Old Lady?" Robert gestures with his arm waving across the table.

Josh glances over to Maddie; she's struggling to find the right words. This is supposed to be their special night, and she doesn't want to share her husband. "As followers of Monkey's House, you know we seldom get the opportunity for some alone time."

"Of course," Monica jumps in. "We understand."

Although this trip is for them, Maddie still wants to hear about the dog and help, if possible. "We're here for a few days; I'm scheduled to be on Oprah's show in two days, but we have tomorrow to tour around. I'd love to see Old Lady while we're here if possible." Maddie gives Monica her cell number and asks her to call or text in the morning to make plans. Monica's all smiles hearing Maddie will give her advice.

After the unexpected interruption, they sit down at their table. The restaurant has excellent ambiance, the right amount of lighting, a candle burning on the table, and a classical pianist playing softly in the background. "When's the last time we've experienced dining like this?" Josh asks.

"We've eaten at a few upscale restaurants, but never this fancy. This is definitely the place to come for a romantic dinner." Maddie kicks off her shoe and gently touches her foot to Josh's thigh with a seductive look. They both laugh, knowing they aren't the same frisky love birds of their younger years, but the depth of their

love has only grown as the years passed. Maddie and Josh enjoy a bottle of wine with their exceptional meals. But what they savor the most is each other.

Back at the hotel, after some tender moments in the bedroom, they emerge into the suite. Maddie goes through her notes, making sure she is prepared for her appearance on the show.

"*Honey, does something seem odd to you?*"

"*Are you kidding me? Of course, something is off. We have no dogs with us.*"

"*We should have asked your new friend Monica for a couple of loaners.*" *Josh smirks.*

"*Don't laugh. Years ago, after we lost Maggie, and Buster was at vets overnight, the house felt so empty. I almost called up Teresa to borrow a dog. I hate being dogless.*"

Maddie's phone pings, receiving a text. "*Speak of the devil. Monica just texted me. She can get together tomorrow morning so we can meet Old Lady.*"

"*We have an open day tomorrow. Text her back. We can meet at the shelter at 10:00 in the morning. Get the directions and info on the shelter. We'll meet Old Lady and start our LA adventure from there.*"

The next morning, they enjoy breakfast at the hotel, then make their way over to meet Monica. As they arrive, Monica is waiting with Cathy, the shelter director. She's excited to introduce them to Old Lady, the dog she fell in love with.

"*Hi Maddie, hi Josh, this is Cathy, our shelter director.*" *There are smiles all around except for Cathy.*

Cathy's eyes sharpen as she tersely mumbles, "*Hello.*"

Maddie's gut tenses. She's dealt with many shelter directors; most loved their jobs, and more so, the animals under their care. She doesn't get a good vibe from Cathy. From her demeanor, Maddie knows Old Lady has little time remaining. Cathy appears ready to take the dog into the back of the shelter, never to be seen again.

"Can you bring Old Lady out of the shelter so we can see her in a peaceful setting?" Maddie asks Monica. She has no desire to go inside after meeting Cathy. Based on the leadership, she knows the environment would be stressful and doesn't want to get upset over something she has no control over.

Monica points to a large fenced-in yard with a big shade tree in the middle, with a couple of benches underneath. "I'll meet you guys in the yard. Old Lady is friendly. Go on in and have a seat. We'll be there in a minute."

Cathy announces, "Looks like Monica has this under control. I have work to do," and storms into the shelter, slamming the door behind her.

"Someone's having a bad day, or maybe an awful life." Maddie's hackles raise; she sure doesn't trust Cathy.

Josh puts his arm around Maddie. "Put her out of your mind. You're here to give Monica some advice on Old Lady."

Monica enters the yard with a large dog. Well, a large framed dog, that is. She appears to be a yellow lab-pit mix. Old Lady looks as old as dirt, and is nothing but skin and bones with lumps and bumps everywhere. Maddie, however, looks right past the neglect and abuse this dog has endured—all the things an average person would notice. While Monica reads off a long list of Old Lady's medical aliments, Maddie's gazing into the dog's eyes, right into her soul.

In an unwavering voice, Maddie states, "This dog is coming to Monkey's House." Monica's eyes widen as big as a full moon on the evening's horizon, tears welling up. Old Lady will finally have all the love she so deserves in her life.

Josh doesn't express dismay by Maddie's declaration, even though it came so quickly. In a few days, Old Lady will head to New Jersey, a new member of their family. They'll need to figure out the logistics of a three-thousand-mile trek and the wrangling it will take to get a dog with medical issues across the country safely.

Suddenly Josh says, "Maddie, I have an idea. Let me make some calls. Monica, let nothing happen to Old Lady… you know what I mean."

The next day, Maddie's appearance with Oprah is a tremendous success. She's a natural at the interview, and engages in a little banter with one of the other guests, George Clooney, a dog lover himself. They immediately hit it off. He too adores senior dogs and even adopted one, named Einstein. Maddie has George blushing when she tells Oprah they have a freezer at Monkey's House named George Clooney. When Oprah asks how they came up with George's name, Maddie replies, "What else would you call such a great-looking freezer?"

Even with Oprah presenting Maddie with her "O" award for exemplary service for animal kind, neither Maddie nor George was the big star this day. It was Old Lady. Josh's salesmanship and perseverance convinced Oprah's producers that having a dog on the show with Maddie would be an audience grabber. This wasn't any dog, but a dog rescued from an LA shelter living out the rest of her days at Monkey's House.

During the show, Oprah and Maddie both agree the name "Old Lady" isn't right for her and Oprah suggests changing it to LA. After all, she's an angel from the city of angels. In a thoughtful, generous expression of her support, Oprah arranged for Maddie and Josh to fly on her private jet, allowing Maddie to comfort LA and care for her needs. She's heading to New York City, and a quick stopover in Philadelphia wasn't far out of her way.

"Wow, Uncle Josh. I knew you took in dogs from surrounding states, but never as far as California. Thanks to Oprah, no less. How did I miss LA's story growing up?"

"I'm so glad we jumped through hoops to get her into our family. LA was such a sweetheart and all the volunteers loved her. She was one of my favorites."

Josh always has a smile on his face when he reminisces about their pups. With LA, just like the other dogs, Josh always focuses on the precious time the pups spent at Monkey's House, living their best final chapter. He never gives a second thought to their lives prior to coming into their family.

"LA loved to lie on the front porch, even during the winter. She especially liked the sun on her face. If I found her laying there when I got home, I'd give her a big hug, help her up, and guide her into the house. There are many ways dogs show their appreciation and I believe hers was greeting me on the porch. It was her way of thanking us for giving her a loving family."

Kaitlyn can see Josh's thoughts shifting behind his eyes and he begins fidgeting in his seat. "Katie, how long before we reach the hospital?" She can tell he's nervous and is glad his story telling has distracted him so far.

"Not too much longer. We'll be there in about thirty minutes. Do you see my banana? I want to eat it before we get to the hospital."

"Here it is." Josh is holding the banana and smirking. You might even say he's laughing tenderly.

"Okay. What's so funny about the banana?"

"Hooch is what's so funny."

"Guess I'm in for another story. Right?" She snatches the banana out of her uncle's hand. "Who is this Hooch character?"

"With a grab like that, you might be related to Hooch."

Hooch was one of the ten cocker spaniels they've had over the years. He came a few years after opening Monkey's House, the only chocolate cocker they ever had, and boy was he a handful.

"I've always said cockers have a mind of their own. An attitude." Josh says with a smile. "Maddie labeled it 'Cockertude.'"

Josh holds his right hand out and points at the meaty part of his palm with his left index finger for Kaitlyn to see.

"This little scar is Molly's signature, our first cocker. It was actually my fault, as I tried to lead her by the collar to take her outside. She pulled away, and as I went to grab her again, Molly said, 'No thank you, I don't want to go outside' with a nice nip to my hand. It taught me a valuable lesson: always lead a dog with a leash, not by the collar."

"Come on, cocker spaniels are beautiful dogs. You loved them all."

"There are a few dogs I miss terribly, and for as mad as I would get at Hooch, I still miss him immensely... especially his spunk and antics. Your grandmother was here when he came to Monkey's House. The two of them quickly bonded. He was calm the first few weeks and blossomed in our environment. Perhaps 'blossom' is not accurate because he certainly wasn't a delicate flower, more like a bull in a China shop."

"My grandmother loved dogs. She always had chocolate labs. Maybe his color was what connected her to Hooch. Plus, her dogs were very active."

"Even missing half his foot didn't slow him down a bit. He was all over the place. To say he liked food was an understatement. If you weren't careful, Hooch would steal food right off any plate. It happened to me more than once."

"Wow, he sounds like he was a ball of fire."

Josh points to her banana. "Hooch became obsessed with those."

Kaitlyn's eyes squint and head pulls back. "Bananas?"

"It all started one day when he got into Aunt Beth's pocketbook. Setting anything edible on the kitchen counter was not a safe place with Hooch around, given his surfing abilities and his keen sense of smell. Banana aroma was too tempting for Hooch. He couldn't resist going in for the snag. Nobody saw him take it; they only noticed him eating it. The entire banana, along with the peel and sticker."

"Are you telling tales, Uncle Josh?"

"Swear to God, it's all true. Hooch stole a couple more bananas off the center island over time. He became a great surfer, albeit a counter-surfer. Then, somehow, bananas ended up in places more convenient for him to find."

"I wonder how?" Kaitlyn giggled, seemingly enjoying the stories and the fact that her uncle was keeping his mind occupied.

"Guilty as charged." Josh laughs, recalling one special outing. "On one of our beach trips, I took a banana along and hid it in the sand with the tip sticking out. I made sure Hooch would stumble upon it. He was so excited and woofed it down in a few seconds. Bananas and the beach were his favorites."

"Wait a minute, when I was a little girl, I vaguely remember my mother having a shirt with a dog on it surfing on a banana. I loved her shirt, that wasn't..."

"Yep—Hooch."

Monkey's Leash

Within ten minutes of arriving at the hospital, Josh's eyelids droop and eventually close, as his chin finds a resting spot on his chest. Rhythmic vibration lulls him to sleep when he's in a moving vehicle, and not busy telling stories.

Kaitlyn pulls into a parking spot at the Hospital of the University of Pennsylvania garage next to the elevators. She gently reaches over and jostles her uncle's arm. "We're here. Wake up. Are you ready to go in?"

"Sorry, I must have dozed off. Wow, a nap without a dog on my lap. I don't know the last time that's happened, nor do I like it. It's always better with a warm little pup curled up on me." Josh takes in a few deep breaths as he rounds his shoulders. He's collecting his things when suddenly his forehead furrows and his eyes narrow. He hastens his actions and Kaitlyn notices his breathing escalating.

Kaitlyn's forehead scrunches. "What's wrong?"

Without saying a word, Josh rushes to get out of the car. He opens the back door and frantically shuffles the clutter around on the back seat. "I think I forgot my lucky charm. I can't go through this without it." Five inches of Monkey's leash is Josh's good luck charm.

"Uncle Josh… don't worry. I have it right here in my bag, along with your letters." She pulls it out, holding it up high so Josh can see she does indeed have it. "You asked me to bring these, remember?"

"Thank you. I'm going to need it today." His eyes soften and his breathing normalizes.

They enter the hospital, and after registering at the front desk, someone promptly escorts them to surgical prep as they're behind schedule. Kaitlyn notices Josh is not concerned about being late, and doesn't seem worried at all. On the other hand, she's experiencing tightness in her chest, overrun with apprehension. This is a reasonable reaction, as it was only a few years ago when she herself spent months in hospitalization and rehab, recovering from her broken back.

Kaitlyn will never forget falling from the ladder at the Olympic trials, the incident that destroyed her future plans and the life she so loved. Once she arrived at the hospital, she received a thorough examination and was quickly transferred to the ICU. The specialists there stabilized her spine, and she was eventually moved to a step-down unit where she spent most of her stay, fighting to heal and desperately hoping to walk again.

The lead Orthopedic Spinal Surgeon advised Kaitlyn they considered the location of her break as one of the most severe of all spinal cord injuries. The effects from injuries such as these vary depending on the extent of the damage. In the end, her break was not as bad as it could have been, and she avoided permanent paralysis of her arms and legs. Over the months, they worked to stabilize her spine, and she did have extensive muscle atrophy due to the restricted body movement. Thankfully, the six months of intensive rehab restored her head and neck movement close to normal.

Being back inside a hospital, even though it's for her uncle this time, is overloading her senses. The sights of scrubs, various medical alarms, and the aroma of antiseptic has her body trembling. The notion of a hospital is bringing back frightening memories.

Carson was there for Kaitlyn through her lengthy hospitalization and rehab. However, the unbearable pain on her broken vertebra required pain killers. Opioids were the only way for her to get relief. However, the drugs changed her personality; she became angry and distant, pulling deep within herself. Unfortunately, her dependence on them and the changes they brought out eventually drove Carson away. Kaitlyn was in hell—experiencing a horrible cycle of knowing what they were doing to her life and her relationship with Carson, but she didn't see a way out of the nightmare loop.

Her life was a catastrophe for a couple of years after the accident. Even though she eventually became drug free, her shame was too much to bear. She could not forgive herself, let alone muster the strength to reach out to her love and best friend. This left a permanent hole in her heart and her life.

Despite an urge to run, Kaitlyn courageously pushes those reflections aside and thinks to herself, *I can do this. I can be strong for Uncle Josh.*

Betty, Josh's pre-op nurse, is prepping him for surgery after weighing him in on the way to his bed. She takes his basic stats, blood pressure, pulse, and temperature. All are within acceptable limits. They satisfy Josh. Maddie had always told him to take an interest in his health, including knowing what the stats should be. He still follows her advice.

"My wife worked here years ago on 6-Main, a pulmonary floor." Josh tells Betty. "Is it still pulmonary?"

With an understanding smile she replies, "Your wife was a nurse here? She must have been a very special person. Pulmonary moved to the third floor and 6-Main is now dedicated to cardiac patient care. You'll be recovering there for the next few days." Josh eases back into the bed as his body relaxes. It seems he's garnered a bit of solace, knowing he will be on Maddie's old floor.

Josh pauses for a moment, then tells Betty, "She was an extraordinary person and an exceptional nurse, too. Back in the 90s, they honored her with the Nurse of the Year award. When she left nursing, she cared for our dogs until about ten years ago… when she journeyed to meet up with them at the Rainbow Bridge."

Betty consoles Josh, "I'm so sorry. I see you have your niece here though and can tell she surely cares about you."

Josh smiles. "She's my great niece." He then remembers his good luck charm and gets it from Kaitlyn, holding it out to Betty. "This needs to be sterilized. It's going into surgery with me."

Betty's face scrunches up. "I'm sorry, Mr. Kelly, whatever that is, it can't go into the operating room with you."

"It's Monkey's dog leash. He's the inspiration for Monkey's House. It always brings me good luck. I need this with me in surgery."

"I'm sorry, it's against all operating room policies. Let's give this to your niece."

It was at this moment Josh's cardiologist, Dr. Sena, stopped by to consult with him before the operation. Having overheard the conversation between Betty and Josh as he approached, he quickly intervenes: "How are you feeling this morning, Josh?"

"Hi Dr. Sena, I was doing fine, but there seems to be a misunderstanding." Holding up Monkey's leash he continues, "You and I discussed my good luck charm a few weeks ago, and you agreed I could have it in surgery with me. Betty is telling it can't go into the operating room."

"Dr. Sena, this is highly unusual. Even if we allowed it, I don't believe there is time to sterilize it," Betty maintains.

"Betty, Mr. Kelly will not be heading into the O.R. for another ninety minutes. We have enough time. He's been my patient for over thirty years and I worked with his wife, Maddie, when she was a nurse here. She was one of the best nurses I've ever had the pleasure of working with."

Dr. Sena turns to Josh. "Please give me your leash." He takes it from Josh and puts it in his white coat pocket. He looks over Josh's chart, asking a few more questions. Then, with a comforting pat on Josh's shoulder, accompanied with his signature calming smile, Dr. Sena assures Josh all will be fine. As he pulls the leash slightly out of his pocket for

Josh to see, he stresses, "I'll take care of this. You'll see it again in the O.R."

Over the years, Dr. Sena has become much more than a doctor to Josh. He is a connection to Maddie in the outside world and feels like a dear friend Josh can always count on, even though Josh only sees him during his visits to the hospital. Every checkup is much more than the series of blood tests, X-rays, EKG, and Echo, followed by Dr. Sena combing through the results and listening to his heart and lungs. In the hospital with Dr. Sena, the halls where Maddie spent so much time brought back a part of her to Josh on each of his visits. The order of tests at his typical appointments were always the same: first stop was the phlebotomy lab with drawing of blood, and the last finishing up with a consultation with Dr. Sena.

On Josh's route from the lab to the next station, he always got sidetracked and a little weak in the knees, not from the prick of the needle he received, but from what lined the walls of the hall. There were plaques hanging as far as the eye could see, etched with the names of hospital employees who received awards for their excellence over the decades. One was for the Nurse of the Year, and Josh would always stop by and find Maddie's name. He'd rub his finger over the brass plate, feeling the impression of each letter with his index finger, beaming with pride for her achievement.

Over the years, the staff learned to delay his arrival time for the next station. It wasn't uncommon for him to spend thirty minutes there, as memories of his love flowed through his mind and heart. Dr. Sena also held a special place in his heart for Maddie, as he was acutely aware of what a kind and giving person she was—another key reason Josh liked and respected him so.

Kaitlyn, who had been quiet through all of this, speaks up. "Dr. Sena must think the world of you. It sounds like taking a good luck charm into surgery isn't allowed, or at least it's highly frowned upon." Kaitlyn is once again looking to keep Josh occupied on something besides his surgery, knowing he's going to be in pre-op for some time. "You know the holidays aren't far away. Before you know it, they'll be here."

Josh doesn't respond right away to Kaitlyn; he's gazing across the room. He appears mesmerized by a Franky Ferret figurine sitting on a cabinet opposite his bed.

The last Majestic World trip Maddie and Josh took differed from the ones they'd taken many times before. Earlier trips brought out their inner child among all the magical wonders of Majestic World, and they always rushed to take in as many sights, rides, and attractions as possible. Their last trip, taken less than two years before Maddie's passing, was different... almost relaxing. There was no hurrying from park to park this time; besides, they'd seen most of the rides over the years, so simply enjoying each other's company in a fun, familiar setting, was the perfect plan. The special trip took place between Thanksgiving and Christmas, when Majestic is less crowded and they deck the parks to the nines in holiday cheer.

On previous trips, they enjoyed visiting the various resorts within the Majestic properties, and Maddie fell in love with

Majestic's Floridian Grand hotel. Subsequent trips would include taking the monorail and stopping at the Floridan, to stroll around and take in the ambience. One evening, they found a choice spot in the lounge overlooking the Majestic Kingdom. As they sipped their drinks, the nightly fireworks lit up the sky over The Majestic Castle, shrouding the rest of the kingdom behind a brilliant curtain of sparklers, rockets, and pinwheels.

Christmas with Franky

Recalling previous visits to the park prompts Maddie to say, "Remember, this trip is not at all like the others. We're past hurrying from ride to ride. This week is for us to relax, enjoy some alone time, and rejuvenate our bodies and souls. Holly will have everything taken care of back home, so there's no need to worry."

"You got it." Josh raises his hand up to his head and flips an imaginary switch. "I've turned off my 'A' personality. I'm now as 'B' as I can be."

"Yeah, right." Maddie giggles. "That will never happen, but I know you'll do your best. That's all I can ask." She walks over and gives him a big squeeze. "I can't believe we're finally staying at the Floridian Grand. What a spectacular view."

Together on their balcony, Maddie's arms are still around Josh's waist. Romance is in the air as he moves even closer, embracing her. They gaze dreamily at The Majestic Kingdom across the lake. After a tender kiss, their week together kicks off.

They hadn't been to Majestic together in well over a decade, although Josh was down a few years ago for a writers' conference. Maddie wasn't able to attend, so she arranged for Kaitlyn and her brother Max to join him for a few days so they could enjoy the parks with their uncle. Now, as Maddie steps off the monorail onto Downtown America, it's so familiar to her, as if she had just been here last week. Visiting Majestic around the holidays is a first for them and the festive decorations are everywhere. The holiday theme appears to be inspiring a cheerier disposition for everyone at the park. Not that Majestic's ambiance doesn't do that already.

Majestic during the holidays is living up to all its hype. The first two days, they tour The Majestic Kingdom and Future Land at a leisurely pace. They enjoy jumping on a ride here and there, watching a couple of shows and basking in the warm December sun Florida offers. However, spending time together is what they treasure the most.

As they go to leave the Majestic Kingdom, they happen across Gabriel's Flight. Maddie pulls Josh into the entrance of the ride. "Sweetie, we have to do this ride. This was the first ride we took on our first visit to Majestic, over thirty years ago." With all the rides Majestic World offers, most would not be impressed with this ride. Many would walk right by. To Maddie and Josh, it's not just a trip down memory lane. The ride itself is symbolic of their lives. "If you dream it, you can do it." They snuggle close, and Maddie leans her head on Josh's shoulder as their car flies over Paris.

They get back to their room shortly before the fireworks show begins. They amble out onto the balcony, which overlooks a large lake called the Majestic Seas Lagoon. Josh nudges their lounge chairs closer together, and sitting next to one another, they wait for the colorful fireworks of brocades, pistils, willows, and occasional comets shooting high into the sky. As they recount how much they loved their day together, the atmosphere invites them to relax. The moon is shining brightly across the water, making the façade of The Majestic Kingdom resemble a 3-D panorama, like those in some rides. The fireworks are spectacular—a perfect end to a perfect day.

Tomorrow, they don't have plans to go to any of the theme parks. Instead, they'll tour the various hotels within the resort. Maddie wants to enjoy all the distinctive holiday decorations selected for the uniqueness of each hotel. They'll cap off the day at the Horse Shoe Revue, one of Josh's favorite attractions.

It's another beautiful sunny morning as the monorail approaches. "Maddie, here it comes. Hurry."

She briskly makes her way over to Josh. "So, where did Mr. 'B' go? I seem to be standing here with the old Josh." Maddie chuckles as she pokes him in the ribs.

"I may be old, but I lost the 'A' guy the day we arrived at the resort."

"How did all the planning go? I assume you have all the hotels mapped and numbered in order of sequence?" Maddie rolls her eyes.

"Nope, we're going by the seat of our pants."

"Who took my husband? I could get used to this new guy."

"Don't," he jokes, "You have four more days, then the old Josh will be back."

Traveling by monorail, ferry, bus, and their own two feet, they visit all the major resort hotels, each beautifully decorated. While at the Animal Preserve, they enjoy an exotic lunch in Africa. Once back to the Floridian, they snuggle, taking a brief rest, delighted once again to have a little alone time.

Lying in bed, Josh turns to Maddie. "Merry Christmas," he says as he hands her a little box.

"It's not Christmas yet and you know we don't exchange presents anymore." Maddie's eyes sharpen as she examines the box.

"I know, both are true, but I wanted to get you a little something to let you know how much I care about you." Maddie is all smiles as she accepts his gift and gently shakes it.

"Okay if I open it now?" She can't imagine what's inside and removes the wrapping paper before Josh can even answer.

Josh laughs. "Sure, but I guess it doesn't matter what I say at this point."

Maddie pulls a gold necklace out of the box, which has a heart-shaped pendant attached. "I love this. It's so pretty." As she inspects the pendant, tears well in her eyes and roll over her cheeks. She senses Sora's presence, her soul dog.

The pendant is a composite made from strands of Sora's fur. When Josh laid Sora to rest years ago, he took some hair, knowing someday he would do something special for Maddie with it. He found a jeweler who specialized in incorporating a loved one's hair into custom jewelry.

By now, Maddie is holding Josh tightly as he proclaims, "As your heart told you, they made the pendant with Sora's fur. I know she's always in your heart. I thought this would be another reminder of the love you two shared." They hold each other a while longer, reminiscing about Sora before catching the water taxi to their evening date.

The Horse Shoe Revue dinner and show does not disappoint. Franky and Goofball make appearances, weaving between the tables, entertaining both small and big kids alike. Goofball has a special place in their hearts, as they often referred to Bullwinkle, a Treeing Walker Coonhound they rescued years ago, as Goofball.

"Here comes Bullwinkle's twin." Josh chuckles. "He was a lovable character, for sure."

"Yeah, but I'm not sure Bullwinkle could control himself with all this delicious food around. I think he was part Food Hound." Maddie laughs. "I remember hiding treats all around the house and him using that enormous nose of his to search them out."

"Oh, I can guarantee he found them all with that schnoz."

Among their notable adventures over the next few days, Maddie and Josh traveled around the world at Future Land and even became movie stars in Movie Reel Park. On their last night, dinner at the Red Fox was delicious. On their stroll back from the restaurant Maddie puts the red rose Josh purchased for her up to her nose. She takes a deep inhale; the fragrance brings a smile as her eyes soften glancing at Josh.

Their love has evolved from the day they first fell for one another, their wedding day, and spanning the decades. Much like the beauty of a rose, from bud to fully blossomed pedals, it's beautiful: It's all love, just different layers of love.

෨

Josh's eyes focus back onto Kaitlyn. "The holidays are bittersweet for me, and I know they're no different for those missing a loved one. My good luck charm, Monkey's leash, is what Maddie gave me on our last Christmas together. She told me it would always lead me in the right direction."

A tear trickles down Kaitlyn's cheek. She didn't know Maddie gave her uncle Monkey's leash. Obviously, Maddie knew he would need enormous strength to carry on without her.

Josh notices her sadness. "Let's say we head to the shore house, Paws & Relax, after all this? You always loved the beach when you were younger."

"I would love to." Kaitlyn's face brightens up, knowing the beach holds many significant childhood memories.

PART 2

Togetherness

ELEVEN YEARS EARLIER

Sunsets

"Is your crew ready to go?" Josh asks, as he's leashing up Parcel, Randy and Lilly. The anticipation of their walk on the beach has the pups jubilantly wiggling about as Josh tries his third attempt to snap the leash on Randy's harness. Finally, they're all hooked up. "I'll meet you outside as soon as these knuckleheads stop tying me up in knots," he shouts over their enthusiastic barking. He gets the last leash untangled from around his leg and readies to head out the door.

"I need to get Ariel into her cart. We'll be right out." Maddie maneuvers the little pup into position. This white miniature poodle is missing her right back leg and has a mere stump from her knee up on the left side. Her life before Monkey's House was hell, but it changed the day she made her way into their arms. Maddie is talking to her now, telling her all about the great walk she'll be having as she lowers the top support of the cart, securing all the clips and buckling the front strap around Ariel's tiny chest.

Maddie and Josh always look forward to spending time at their charming little getaway, Paws & Relax, in North Cape May, New Jersey. They purchased it years ago, after Maddie had been searching for a place for the two of them to enjoy a little down time. It didn't take her long to convince Josh this was where they could dash off for a few days. It wasn't far from their home. The beauty of Paws & Relax is its location. It's a little north of Cape May, the southernmost tip of New Jersey, where the Delaware Bay meets the Atlantic Ocean. It's also a perfect little town for dog lovers, whose pets have access to the beach all year long, with a few restrictions during summer. They're not allowed on the beach between 11 am and 4 pm. Dog parents are fine with this stipulation as mid-summer days can be extremely hot, and many times humid. So, it's better for parents and pups to stroll early in the morning or later in the evening. In Josh's case, he liked to take the dogs out both morning and evening.

"All set?" Josh is being pulled in every direction as he continues his attempts to get them organized, and into a forward motion so they can head to the bay. "Ariel's blinding me with all that sparkle."

"She's is revved and rolling in her blinged out cart. You better put your sunglasses on and get your crew moving or Tiggy and Chase will run you over." As usual, Maddie has her cohorts in-line and motoring right along.

Maddie is comfortably walking a large pack of dogs, keeping them well aligned and untangled. If, by some chance, they get their paths crossed, she's adept at getting them back in sync without a fuss. Josh prefers to walk a maximum of three dogs. He's handled more, but doesn't have patience with the occasional cross-walker tangling up the entire crew.

They treasure their little oasis where the walk to the bay is only a block away. They pass well-kept cottages and bungalows, each with bright paint colors and landscaping which was unique to each home. Josh would often comment how this reminded him of the Florida Keys. Before they know it, the entranceway to the beach is footsteps away.

"You go first." Josh lets Maddie enter the ramp so he can make sure Ariel's wheels don't get caught up in the dune grass along the narrow, winding path. "Besides, Randy and Parcel won't wait once we hit the beach." They're like a bunch of kids, all wanting to be the first to discover all the wonders along the shoreline.

Maddie looks over her shoulder with a smile. "I wonder who they take after? Like father, like sons."

The beach is a different world for the dogs. Even though they've been here many times, it never disappoints them. As soon as their paws hit the sand, they are all over the place, smelling seaweed and driftwood, and confronting the occasional sea creature. In this area of the bay shore, the remains of horseshoe crabs litter the beach. Those prehistoric looking arthropods have been around for over 450 million years, making them even older than dinosaurs. During the spring, horseshoe crabs cover the beach laying their eggs, but now, in late August, you'll only see an empty shell here and there, washed up from a storm.

Josh reaches over to hold Maddie's hand. She switches the leashes to her other hand and spreads her fingers wide as they interlace with Josh's. Gleeful grins—this is their favorite place on earth. Strolling hand in hand, the ocean breeze provides a little relief from the warmth of the sun. They walk without speaking, intuiting one another's steps and motions. With the sunlight glowing down on them, they exchange a knowing glance—their hearts are full.

They turn around and head back after walking about a dozen blocks. Josh picks up Lilly and puts her into a little canine backpack. She's reached her limit, and it's time to give her a ride back home. The pups are enjoying their adventure, but there will soon be naps all around, dinner, then more excitement for an evening walk. Occasionally, the pups take a moonlit stroll under the stars during a full moon.

As they approach their house, a man exits a parked car and meets them before they make their way onto the front porch. "Mr. Kelly, Ms. Kelly." He hands Josh an envelope. "You've been served." He quickly turns, gets back into his car, and takes off.

"Sweetie, you said this may happen sooner or later." They make their way back into the house. Maddie wipes tears from her eyes as she struggles to unleash her dogs.

Inside, Josh quickly opens the envelope. A cursory review of the document reveals it's exactly what he's expected. "Dammit. They have no right to take our land," Josh says—red faced with his carotid arteries bulging, the subpoena makes him feel ready for a fight. They didn't commit their entire lives to Monkey's House, only to find themselves in this turmoil. Sadly, the dogs they rescued were discarded from their homes for whatever reason. In Maddie and Josh's case, being evicted to enable greedy investors to replace it with a high-end development felt like the same thing happening.

Josh hugs Maddie as tears roll. She pulls Josh in close, and he gently caresses her hair. "We'll work through this. We'll get a tough lawyer to fight them." According to the letter, they'll have until December when their hearing date is scheduled, to prepare.

They've been dreading this moment. For the past couple of years, developers have harassed them to sell their property. There's a large parcel landlocked behind them, and the land Monkey's House sits upon is the only way to access the property. Maddie and Josh have no desire to part with their sacred oasis. The developers have offered prices over market value, but still, they refuse to sell. Not only is it their dog's final resting place, the two thousand acres behind them is a nature's paradise. Developing this wilderness would change the entire region, impacting the wildlife they and so many others love.

They try to put this out of their mind as they have a special guest coming tomorrow. "What time are you picking up Kaitlyn?" Maddie says with a tilt of her head and a smirk. Josh is the planner of the two and never late: he knows she's egging him on.

"Really, you're asking me about planning my trip? That's hilarious. So, I'll be leaving for the airport at eleven. We should be back here in plenty of time to get her settled as long as her flight is on time. I'll grill up chicken and vegetables for dinner. Of course, afterwards we'll take the dogs for a walk at sunset on the beach. You know how much Katie loves the sunsets here on the bay."

"You know Kaitlyn is turning into a young woman. She's not a little girl anymore. I think she tired of being called Katie a few years ago."

"She'll always be my little Katie; I couldn't imagine calling her anything else."

"Fine, but when you introduce her, use Kaitlyn. She'll appreciate it." Maddie gives Josh a little love tap in the ribs. "Stop by the grocery store on the way home? We need a few things to make all of Kaitlyn's favorite meals."

Maddie and Josh realize this might be one of their last summers with Kaitlyn. She's been spending part of her summers with them since she was nine. Turning fifteen soon, she'll be transitioning into high school, a teenager whose life is blossoming. The little girl they adore is becoming a woman, ready to find a whole new world. They're excited about all the adventures and opportunities her life will soon unveil. Even though they'll miss having their summers together, their philosophy for themselves, as well as the dogs of Monkey's House, is to live in the moment and they intend to do it by having a great time with Kaitlyn on this visit—making memories to last a lifetime.

All is on schedule and Kaitlyn's flight arrives on time at Philadelphia International airport. Josh meets her in baggage claim, and after loading the car, they hastily make their way on the road back home. They need no radio on the drive back to Cape May. Kaitlyn, happy to see her uncle, is a little chatterbox and, of course, Josh does his share of talking.

They're both excited about sharing family time together over the next few weeks.

After spending a beautiful afternoon together, Maddie and Kaitlyn are finishing cleaning up in the kitchen. "Hey gals, let's get ready. It's only twenty minutes to sunset." Josh scours the house, gathering up leashes.

Maddie's more relaxed style meant she was okay with missing a sunset now and then; however, if Josh is around, they're never missed. He's figured out exactly how long it takes to leash the dogs, walk to the beach, and still have plenty of time for a relaxing stroll along the bay shore as the sun dips below the waterline, creating the most beautiful sunsets. Even as the sun melts away, amazing colors in an artist's palette paint the heavens before the velvet color of dusk dims the waning splendor.

"Katie, who do you want to walk?" Even though it's been a year since she was in New Jersey, Kaitlyn knows all the dogs like she's been here all along. She never misses a single post Maddie puts on social media, virtually meeting and falling in love with all the new dogs welcomed into Monkey's House. Many of the dogs at the house have been with them for over a year, so Kaitlyn's happy to reunite with those.

"I'll take Randy and Lilly. They seem to remember me, and I always enjoyed walking with them." Josh hands her two leashes, and she hooks up the pups.

Josh and Maddie each take two of the other dogs and they all make their way up the road and onto the beach. They walk as the sun is dropping towards the bay. Josh and Maddie, hand in hand, are in the lead, with Kaitlyn slightly behind as Randy fixates on a ghost crab digging his way into the soft sand.

"Aunt Maddie, Uncle Josh, I'll never forget these sunsets."

Maddie turns towards Kaitlyn, "They are spectacular, aren't they?"

Josh adds, "Even as the sun sinks below the horizon, the magnificent colors in the sky never seem to fade." They all stop, absorbed in the moment's beauty, thankful for all they have together.

"I imagine this is what heaven looks like, with the colors representing the overflow of love," Maddie says as she squeezes her beloved's hand.

The dogs are tugging on their leashes, trying to get to the next clump of seaweed for a sniff, so they resume walking. Kaitlyn falls back again. This time it's Lilly holding her back. She's fixated on a clump of mussels. Looking up at her aunt and uncle, Kaitlyn sees their silhouettes against a backdrop of color splashing across the sky. "I agree… this might be heaven. At least what I imagine heaven might be like. I'll never forget our summers together; I love you both."

Over the years on her visits, Kaitlyn took on more responsibility, watching dogs alone while Maddie and Josh went on an occasional date like a night out to a tasty restaurant in Cape May; but this summer, they had big plans. Maddie put a lot of consideration into what she is calling, "Our Cruise Adventure." Reservations made, their itinerary has them boarding the Cape May–Lewes Ferry in the morning with the return trip, putting them in the middle of the bay at sunset. They'd be back to Cape May in time for a late dinner. She even confirmed dogs are welcome on the ferry in specific areas of the boat. They had to be leashed and well behaved. That takes Chase off the list as he causes a ruckus in public.

On the morning of the adventure, Josh and Kaitlyn wake early and take all the dogs down to the beach for a walk. The plan is to get the pups worn out, both physically and mentally. Tired dogs are often better behaved. Tiggy and Randy would be on the adventure with their parents. Kaitlyn's job is to watch over the others back at the house. She won't be comfortable taking all the dogs down to the beach, especially with Ariel in her cart, so this was their only chance for a beach walk today.

Their house is a block from the beach, but it takes longer to get there this morning. They take a detour to Josh's favorite coffee shop, "Top of the Morning." Giving in to the tempting aroma, they grab two fresh cups of coffee and bagels to go, then continue their trek towards the beach.

Approaching the trailhead, Josh notices a bench overlooking the bay. "Let's take a seat here and relax a bit. We'll be able to sip coffee and eat our bagels without our arms being jerked about by the pups. I've worn my coffee more times than I'd like to remember."

"Sounds like a good plan." Before Kaitlyn can take a seat, Randy and Chase hop up on the bench. "Come on guys, there's plenty of room. Move over a little." She dips her shoulder and nudges them towards Josh with the side of her body.

Randy and Chase remain hugging close by Kaitlyn, eyeing up her bagel. The other dogs on the ground are looking up, hoping for a few crumbs. No, make that praying for some major droppage. They know that almost never happens, but hey, can't a dog dream?

"You guys are not getting anything. You had your breakfast, fresh and healthy, no less. I won't give you junk food. Besides, your mom would kill me."

Josh agrees with Maddie's philosophy of feeding fresh food. This therapy has worked wonders on the Monkey's House dogs. Never the less, he'll put the blame for "no treats" on their mom every time.

"Katie, are you looking forward to high school? It will be a big, exciting change from middle school."

"I am. Yeah, the school has a LOT of kids. It will be much different."

"What classes are you taking?"

Kaitlyn is an excellent student, much like her grandmother. "I'll be taking college prep; mostly advanced level classes. I do well in math and science which will help in becoming a veterinarian."

"Wow, you have big plans. Someday you might care for the Monkey's House dogs." Josh knows Kaitlyn would be a great veterinarian. She's gifted and can accomplish anything she puts her mind to.

Turning towards Josh, she says with a big smile, "Wouldn't that be cool, caring for these pups?"

Finishing up their coffee and bagels, Kaitlyn sneaks

Randy and Chase a morsel. Josh gives her the *never let your aunt see you sneaking treats*, look.

Kaitlyn laughs. "Who's going to tell her?" she says and gives her uncle a wink.

"Not me," Josh grins. "It will get us both in trouble." Changing the subject, he says, "Let's get the pups onto the beach so they can have some fun. Turn right. It will take us back to the house. We need to get home soon so I can get ready for the cruise adventure Maddie planned."

As they head up the beach, Kaitlyn hands her dog leashes to Josh and jumps into a handstand, springs into a flip, followed by tumbling across the beach. She's been in gymnastics since she was five years old.

Josh lifts his eyebrows and nods, proud to see his niece's talent developing. "I see you're still chasing your dream." Kaitlyn always aspired to be on the US Olympic gymnastics team.

"Not any longer. You never see five-foot-ten girls at the high levels of competition. It's a sport better suited for shorter frames." Over the past year, she had a growth spurt, adding quite a few inches to her height.

She didn't sound sad about it at all, which surprised Josh. "Are you taking up any other sports in high school?"

"My school has a strong swimming team; I'm going to try my hand at diving. I've heard many gymnasts have transitioned into diving and have done well."

Josh hands Kaitlyn Chase's and Randy's leashes back. "You'll do great," he says—and soon, they make their way home.

The ship's air horn blows, the launching of the voyage. Randy's ears perk up and he tilts his head, wondering what that noise could be. Tiggy doesn't move, staying curled up on Maddie's lap. Being deaf sometimes has its advantages, especially during fireworks. Ferry boat horns are now added to the list. Randy and Tiggy are well behaved in public, and although they have major medical issues, the day shouldn't be stressful for them. However, Maddie is always prepared and has a backpack full of supplies, both for medical emergencies and comfort, just in case they're needed. Cell phones work on the ferry, a must for Maddie. If Kaitlyn is having any issues with a pup at Paws & Relax, or Holly at Monkey's House, she'd be reachable and able to consult with them.

Maddie appears a little jumpy, inviting Josh to put his hand on her knee. "Everything will be fine." He leans over and kisses her cheek. "I'm looking forward to this little adventure you planned."

With his words, she exhales, her shoulders lower, and her body eases into her seat. "I know. It's time for me to concentrate on us and our day together."

Crossing the mouth of the Delaware Bay takes about ninety minutes and departing on the 10:30 a.m. ferry will have them in the Lewes, Delaware port around noon. Shortly after leaving Cape May, Maddie falls asleep. Tiggy, who is content on his mom's lap, joins her. Josh notices Maddie is tired, and sleeping on a boat is unlike her. She loves being on the water, especially out in the ocean. Josh, not so much. He's known for getting sea sick in choppy waters. He's thankful the bay is smooth as glass today.

An hour into the trip, passengers on the port side of the boat are pointing into the water. Curious, he gets up from his seat, scoops Randy up into his arms, and goes over to the side of the ferry. Not twenty feet away, they see a small pod of dolphins. Josh counts five as they would crest the surface and dive back into the water. He knows Maddie would love to see them, so he quickly returns to their seats, gently patting her shoulder to ease her awake.

"Wake up. Come with me. I have something to show you."

Maddie opens her eyes, lifts Tiggy from her lap, and follows Josh. She can only imagine it's something exciting. "What is it, a whale… dolphins?"

Leaning against the side railing, Josh puts his arm around Maddie and pulls her close. "You guessed it, a pod of dolphins. Isn't this exciting? We haven't seen them in a while."

"Wow, it is. The other day, I asked when we last saw dolphins. I'll bet you see more out here in the open water than in the bay near our house."

The seventeen-mile trip is ending, and as they pull into the dock at Lewes, they decide their windbreakers are no longer needed. There's a noticeable difference in temperature on the water: at Lewes, they found it had warmed to eighty degrees with a pleasant breeze.

The first line of business is to get the pups to the dog relieving area. Next, a little stroll along the bay. The beach is much like their beach in North Cape May, however, there's a greater variety of shells. Lewes is closer to the Atlantic

Ocean. Josh widens his toes and scrunches his feet into the sand, grounding himself on a solid foundation. His body was at attention on the water, muscles compensating for the rocking boat, but here on the beach, his muscles loosen. The dogs enjoy sniffing shells and seaweed. Maddie loves any beach; you can tell by the huge smile that remains frozen on her face for the duration of the stroll.

After a short stretch break, it's off to their lunch date. The aroma of seafood fills the air as they exit the Uber and Josh opens the front door to let Randy out. Susan, the Uber driver, thankfully loves dogs. When Randy made his way up into the front seat, she designated him as the co-pilot.

They head up the walkway into the Big Oyster Brewery. Since it's such a beautiful day, they choose to eat alfresco on the back patio. Seated at a table for two under a cheery red and white striped umbrella, they have a marvelous view of the surrounding farmland and vineyard next door. Maddie is not much of a beer drinker, but since she's at a craft brewery, she tries one. She opts for a beer called Marshmallow Dreamsicle, which has a little sweetness to it. Josh is more daring and selects a Golden Stout called It's Complicated. He thinks the beer may help to disentangle the many demands he puts upon himself, if even for an afternoon. Meanwhile, Randy and Tiggy are lapping fresh bowls of water the server brought out for them.

Alongside the beers, they order one of Maddie's favorite shore staples, a bucket of steamed clams—a perfect combination. Josh pauses his indulgences to take in the moment with Maddie. "Beer and steamers, nothing goes together better at the shore."

Giving Josh a big smile, Maddie slips her sandal off and extends her foot under the table until her toes meet Josh's thigh—her signature move, which he still loves after many years of marriage. Raising her eyebrows she says, "I know two things that go better, you and I."

After devouring a pair of fresh salads, they cap off their date by sharing a decadent slice of cheesecake. Susan had given them her number on the way there, so with a quick call, she is taking them back into town with co-pilot Randy barking directions. Once on Main Street, they meander like the tourists they are on this day.

Crafty shops line the streets of Lewes, and they spend time exploring a local pottery store, cute boutiques, and several shops carrying ocean themed knickknacks. They planned to take turns waiting outside with Randy and Tiggy, but the store owners cheerfully welcomed the dogs inside their stores. Maddie ended up buying an adorable plaque featuring a dog on the beach, while Josh scored an old boat oar. He had the perfect location in mind. A narrow section on the family room wall. He's searched for years to fill that gap and is delighted with his find. For the past seven years, they found Kaitlyn the perfect trinket to remember her time with them. Josh recalled her saying she wanted to be a veterinarian, so they couldn't resist the plaque they found engraved with "Good veterinarians talk to animals. Great veterinarians hear them talk back."

The adventure is living up to all their expectations, even surpassing them. Once back on the ferry, making their return crossing to Cape May, fatigue sets in for all of them. They take their seats inside as the breeze picks up, making it a little chilly on the outer decks. Tiggy and Randy both curl up in their parent's warm laps, eyes closed, and fall asleep. About an hour into the trip, the ferry horn bursts, alerting the passengers the heavens are ready to meet the bay, the majestic sunset on the water. Randy gives out a little bark as Maddie and Josh snap awake.

Gathering the pups, they head to the outer deck on the starboard side, the best place for viewing. Josh stands behind Maddie with arms wrapped around her. They've never seen a sunset from the water. The sky has three different cloud formations—cirrus, cumulus, and stratus—sparsely spread from horizon to horizon. Their vantage point from the ferry provides a stunning view of the sun, which dips into the bay as the clouds take on every color of the spectrum.

"I love the sunsets almost as much as I love you," Josh whispers into Maddie's ear as he gives her a tender kiss on the neck. They both have smiles of contentment, knowing they are with their soulmates. Even after forty years of marriage, they have never been more in love.

Back at the car, Josh is ready to drive into Cape May for a quaint dinner, but Maddie is slumped in her seat with drooped eyelids; the adventure seems to have drained all her energy. This isn't normal. She's usually full of vigor, but then again, they did have a full day of activity.

He knows what he needs to do. "I'm pretty tired. This was such a great day you planned. Would it be okay if we picked up takeout? We'll call Katie and see what she wants." Kaitlyn is leaving in a couple of days and they are going to miss her, so he would love for them to eat together.

Maddie buys into it. "Great idea. I didn't want to say anything, but I'm pooped. I'm a bit surprised I'm this tired."

"Takeout it is."

It feels good to be back with Kaitlyn and the dogs. At dinner, they tell Kaitlyn all about their excursion. How they saw a lively pod of dolphins, Randy's becoming an Uber driver, and how much they enjoyed their time together. Maddie hands Kaitlyn a gift bag. "This is for you. We love you."

Kaitlyn's eyes widen as she pulls out the plaque and reads it. "I love this. It's going to hang in my veterinary office someday."

"I have no doubt you'll hear animals talking back to you," Josh adds.

The next day is like the past few weeks: precious time spent together, walking dogs on the beach, and even some paddle boarding in the bay. The evening approaches, and Kaitlyn is preparing to head home in the morning. After dinner, Josh gets a raging fire going in the firepit. It comes as a big surprise for the girls; he has all the ingredients for s'mores, and in no time they are toasting marshmallows by the fire. The flames take the chill out of the air as they sit in the Adirondack chairs positioned around the pit. The full moon is illuminating the yard and the glare of the fire lights up their faces. No need for the backyard floodlights.

Josh lifts his lemonade glass as a parting gesture to the evening and the time they enjoyed together. "To good s'mores, a loving family, and splendid memories."

Spending a few weeks with Kaitlyn fills their souls with joy—she is so much more than a great niece; she's the child they were never able to have. When Maddie and Josh started to contemplate having a family of their own, Maddie was in a bad car accident, crushing her pelvis. Sadly, they were informed Maddie would never be able to bear children, which may have amped up their love of animals and them having a large furry family.

They would see Kaitlyn at family gatherings, around the holidays, or the family trip back east, but her summer visits were the pinnacle of the year for them. They'd dread the day she'd leave to go home. They always want the best for her, but they will flat out miss her energy, her youth, and, mostly, her love. It would be wonderful if she continued her summer retreats with them, but they have a hunch it's coming to an end. This makes the last night with Kaitlyn at the beach even more special.

Scrooge

Maddie leans over the banister and shouts up the stairs, "When you get the decorations out of the attic, be sure to bring down the Christmas outfits for the dogs."

Ready to pull down the attic stairs, Josh rolls his eyes, knowing that request is no small feat. There are only a few boxes of decorations, however, there are tons of clothes for the dogs—likely close to ten outfits per dog. He exhales a loud huff.

"I heard that," Maddie shouts up the stairs. "I want the volunteers to pick outfits for the dogs. They will be here tomorrow. We have our photos with Santa event next weekend. Remember?" Adding a little sass she continues, "Look for your Scrooge outfit while you're up there. Although it sounds like you are wearing it already."

"Hey, go easy on me. I ate way too much Thanksgiving dinner. The extra piece of pumpkin pie was over the top." Josh slowly makes his way up the ladder, hesitant to go too quick. As he steps from rung to rung, the ladder creaks and moans.

"I'll be up in a minute. You can hand the boxes to me." Maddie finishes up in the kitchen and heads upstairs, followed by no less than five dogs. She's carrying Foxy, a little Cairn Terrier who has mobility issues.

Each December, Maddie, Josh, and the volunteers hold the pinnacle event of the year shortly after Thanksgiving. All the dogs get decked out in their holiday attire and have Christmas photos taken with Santa. They set aside the day for dogs that not only live at Monkey's House but also dogs living with their foster families and "Imposters." The latter is an endearing term Maddie and Josh give dogs the shelter veterinarian declared terminal; but with expert veterinary care, a healthy diet, and of course love, they find they are not in need of hospice care after all. These imposters, lucky enough to get adopted into their own forever families, are invited back to attend the Santa gathering. The event has become an annual family reunion of sorts.

It's the same routine every year: the day after Thanksgiving, Josh goes up to the attic to bring down decorations, commencing the start of the holidays at Monkey's House. Josh is getting out of breath, carrying the boxes of decorations over to the entrance. He takes a seat on the attic floor, dangling his feet from the opening of the pull-down stairs to catch his second wind. Glancing back at the stacks and stacks of boxes full of clothes, not theirs mind you, but Christmas outfits for the dogs, he cries out, "Ah. Come on," as he shakes his head in disbelief. There are over a dozen boxes in the far corner.

Maddie has made it upstairs and is ready to help get the boxes down. Josh glances through the opening and sees Maddie below. "Honey, which containers of Christmas clothes do you want for the dogs?"

"What do you mean, which?" Laughing, she spreads her

arms as wide as possible. Her Italian-American grandfather, who emigrated from Italy, would have been proud of his granddaughter's hand gestures. "All of them, of course. The aunts want to make sure they pick the perfect outfit for each dog."

With a baffled look on his face, he quips. "Didn't we donate a bunch of clothes last Christmas?"

"We did. We donated half of our outfits to Tiny Paws and Happy Tails rescues after our last Santa visit."

Maddie hears Josh grumbling to himself, "These dogs have more clothes than I do," as he heads to the far corner to grab the first container.

Maddie shouts up, "I heard that! Maybe they're a lot cuter than you." This is normal banter as they love ribbing each other. The back and forth always ends with Maddie having the last word. It's never clear if she outwits him or if he lets her deliver the last zinger. Whatever it is, it works for them.

With the boxes out of the attic, Josh's foot hits the floor, coming off the last rung. He retracts the ladder back into the ceiling. Maddie's eyes focus, scouring up and down the hallway. "I hate to do this… but I believe you forgot Sandy's Christmas tree."

By this time, Josh's pace has slowed, and his breath is strained. He feels he doesn't have the energy to head back up. Yet, he knows the importance of the tree, especially to Maddie. So, once again, he pulls the ladder down and heads back up. A short while later, Maddie is helping him guide down an oversized box containing the tree and ornaments.

Sandy is the Monkey's House groomer extraordinaire. She's been making the pups look adorable since they started their sanctuary. A few years ago, she surprised them with the Christmas tree as a gift. The tree is scrawny, but treasures hang from its branches: over two hundred glass Christmas ball ornaments, each filled with clippings from dogs they rescued over the years, and later made their way to the Rainbow Bridge. Brown, black, red, golden yellow—there is every color imaginable from their dogs she groomed, making it the most memorable Christmas tree ever. It's become the Tree of Monkey's House and sits proudly in the family room every year during the holidays.

Maddie makes sure Tequila's ornament is always front and center. His blond hair not only fills the precious glass globe, but he also fills their hearts with wonderful memories and love. He was a cocker spaniel, missing both his eyes; he lived with acute heart disease, and eventually developed cancer. His owners dumped him like many of the dogs they rescued. They were moving into a new home and didn't want to take an old dog. He ended up at a local kill shelter and was scheduled to be euthanized within hours. When Maddie laid eyes on him, she couldn't imagine the fear and betrayal he experienced.

For Tequila, like so many other senior dogs at shelters with medical issues, he didn't stand a chance. It was hard for Maddie and Josh to conceive that being old, neglected, and slightly imperfect carries a death sentence. They provided loving care to the last breath. Maddie, as a nurse, and the both of them with their sanctuary, couldn't imagine parents deserting their own furry children because of age and illness.

One of Tequila's favorite pastimes was sitting on Maddie's lap, giving her kisses day and night. Once he curled up, he would turn into butter, melting into her chest as he felt the beating of her loving heart. When he wasn't with his mom, he loved to walk his dad. The lack of sight made no difference to him, for he wholly trusted his dad to lead him down the right path. Their frequent get-aways down to North Cape May would find Tequila with his nose poking out of the window, seeing the world in his own special way. Tequila walked along the beach by faith, not sight. Josh understood this firsthand, with the lost vision in his right eye. Thus, they both understood having a disability didn't mean inability, so they always loved their walks on the beach together. Tequila seemed to enjoy the sunsets as much as his parents did.

Everything they wanted from the attic now lines both sides of the hallway. As Josh weaves between boxes, making his way to Maddie, he puts his arms around her and whispers, "Maybe we could start our Christmas celebration a little early." He gives her a gentle kiss and they make their way into their bedroom, closing the door behind them.

Shortly after the caressing and kissing begin, they hear banging on the bedroom door. They ignore it until the howling becomes unbearable. Josh opens the door and almost gets bowled over by half a dozen dogs charging through the doorway. Jasper and Faith jump into the bed as Josh lifts the remaining pups to join them. Amidst all the activity, Maddie leans over and opens the nightstand drawer, pulling out a small box wrapped in Christmas paper, topped with a little red bow. Josh doesn't notice as she tucks it under the sheets.

The dogs are congregating around Maddie, taking up most of the bed. "Hey, come on, guys. Let me get in there next to your mom." Josh slides under the covers, creating a mini tidal wave, as he raises the bedspread. It rearranges the dogs, giving him a split second to take his righteous place beside his beloved.

"We sure know what it's like to have a bunch of kids, albeit four legged ones." Maddie laughs as they assume their favorite position, spooning. Maddie wiggles her way down in bed. Josh rolls on to his back and she rests her head on his shoulder, holding her tight. The dogs find every available nook and cranny around their bodies, snuggling their parents as close as possible. Maddie's secret present is still tucked by her heart under the covers.

Pulling the little box into view, she places it on his chest. "Sweetie, this is for you." Josh rocks himself side to side, trying to prop himself up. It isn't easy with dogs lying on both sides of him, but he finally makes his way up slightly.

"Hey, last year you gave me heck for giving you the necklace. I thought we didn't exchange Christmas presents anymore." He says this, but his bright gaze toward the box reveals his true feelings. The box rises and lowers with each breath. He is eager to discover what is inside.

Jasper and Faith inch closer and closer, assuming the

mysterious box is for them. They would've torn into it like Hooch on a banana, had they gotten it first. "It's weeks early, but this seems like a great time to give it to you."

Josh opens it slowly, first removing the bow and ribbon, then slowly rips off on the paper. His pace is not only driving Jasper crazy, but also Maddie, who is eager to see his reaction. Finally, opening the top of the box, he pulls out what appears to be part of an old dog leash. At first, he thinks it's a little strange since it's only four, maybe five inches long. The leash has a brass snap, about an inch of actual leash remaining, and a worn leather handle. It's so familiar to Josh: he slips his hand in the handle, trying to place it, studying it for some time. A lone tear trickles down his cheek accompanied by a rewarding smile forming on his face.

"I love it. It doesn't surprise me you had Monkey's leash tucked away for over twenty years." Josh runs his fingers through Maddie's hair, both of them with welled up eyes.

"I told the cobbler to make it into a key chain. I couldn't tell him to make a lucky charm out of it; he'd think I was crazy," she says squeezing him tight, "but that's exactly what it is: your good luck charm. If anything could bring you luck, it would be Monkey."

"Sweetie," she continues, "you've guided me since my first year of nursing school. In the last two decades, you've led hundreds of dogs from hell to heaven." Tears dribble over her cheeks. "When you need it most, Monkey will lead you." Maddie closes his hand with Monkey's leash inside, cupping both her hands around his. "He'll take care of you always."

"I love my present; I love my life… I love you." Josh gives Maddie a kiss, then she rests her head back on his shoulder. He kisses her on the top of her head, taking them both back to their younger days.

Maddie reaches up and holds onto her Sora pendant, reminded of her good luck charm from a previous Christmas surprise. They both seem to have similar emotions upon receiving their unique gifts, something special to remind each of them of a loving companion.

Josh prefers to stay lying next to Maddie, but it's already been close to an hour in their twisted bundle of love, and he knows they need to get things organized for the Christmas outing. When he kisses Maddie's cheek, it's his way of telling her they have to get up. She opens her eyes as he bends closer and their lips meet. "A little longer, five more minutes," she begs.

"I'll give us ten, but we do have to get back to work." Harvey, a little beagle who is wedged between their legs, gives a sigh of relief for a few more precious moments curled up with his parents. After a short period, Josh sneaks out of bed, leaving Maddie smothered in dogs and still grasping her memories of Sora. Maddie tires easily lately, so Josh lets her get a little more rest. He has a helper, though; Jasper jumps off the bed and follows him out of the room.

The week flies by: volunteers try the holiday clothes on all the dogs, acting like a bunch of schoolgirls, picking out the perfect outfit to match each pup's personality. Once labeled with the dog's name, they'd throw it into a large stack by the front door for the big day. Maddie even sneaks a Scrooge sweater in the pile with a label identifying it as belonging to Josh.

The morning of the big event, Maddie seems drained. For the past couple of months, she's been rundown, not herself. It's no surprise: she's up all hours of the night caring for the dogs. Although she's normally able to get her stamina back in a few hours, lately she doesn't seem to snap back. It's concerning to Josh.

Josh sits on the edge of the bed and holds her hand. "You okay? You look exhausted." He kisses her cheek.

"I'll be fine. Give me a few more minutes of sleep and I'll have my second wind."

Josh fears she has been holding back. He wonders if she's not only hiding it from others, but more so from herself. Her life revolves around the dogs. They need her, and she'll do anything to be there for them. Maddie is always taking care of the dogs, but sadly, not herself.

"We'll have the volunteers here soon. Rest a little longer. I'll have them get the dogs ready and loaded onto the bus. I'll come get you when we're ready to head out."

It takes some coaxing, but she agrees. "Okay. Get me if there are any problems. Don't forget. Shadow rides in a volunteer's car and Pepo is not well enough to go see Santa. Aunt Marcia is going to stay home to keep him company." She closes her eyes and falls back asleep.

It's 8 a.m. and the atmosphere at Monkey's House is joyful and full of anticipation on this special day—the most exciting day of the year for the pups. They can sense something magical is about to happen this morning. The weather is ideal for the first week of December. Clear skies with temperatures in the mid-fifties are forecasted. Josh finished decorating Waggin' One. The bus has a wreath hanging on the front grill, and this year, Josh had decal magnets of elf hats made. He places them on the heads of the dog images lining the sides of the bus, and soon, each dog is wearing its own unique holiday topper.

The aunts and uncles are arriving. Josh makes his way back into the house to ensure everything is going as planned. It's time to get the dogs dressed in their holiday outfits for their visit with Santa. Aunt Tracey and Aunt Terry are dressing the dogs as the other volunteers bring the dogs over one-by-one. A week ago, all those clothes were up in the attic. Josh now realizes why Maddie wanted them all down. It is joyous and magical to have a sea of dogs in their holiday best.

Once all the dogs finished getting their outfits on, Aunt Tracey calls to Josh, "We have one sweater left."

Josh is baffled: all the dogs are on the bus and look great wearing their holiday gear. "That can't be. We're getting ready to head out. You guys will have to figure it out. I have to run upstairs to get Maddie."

As Josh heads towards the stairs, Aunt Tracey picks up a sweater and holds it high. "Well, well. Guess whose name is on this? Josh!"

A fast U-turn takes Josh back to Tracey. Approaching her, he can now see she's holding a Scrooge sweater that looks like the character in Dr. Seuss. Grinning, he knows Maddie has played a prank on him. He decides he's going to one-up her. Grabbing the sweater, he makes his way up the stairs, and pulls on the ugly sweater, heading over to Maddie.

Josh spins in circles, making sure Maddie notices what he's wearing. "What do you think of my new Christmas attire?"

"I got you, didn't I? I didn't think you'd actually wear that ugly thing. Go take it off. I'll meet you downstairs."

A short time later, as Waggin' One pulls into the parking lot of Red's Garden Center, there are twenty plus aunts and uncles waiting, ready to escort the dogs onto Santa's lap. Thankfully, the brief rest recharged Maddie. Santa is sitting in a sleigh on a large platform with a beautifully decorated Christmas tree in the background, making the perfect photo opportunity. As the aunts and uncles walk the dogs up to meet Santa, Maddie and Josh stand on the corner of the platform, as they do every year. They watch as each dog has their own magical moment sitting on Santa's lap, asking for a special treat or toy: "Click", another beautiful memory captured.

Midway through the photo session, Josh brings a little levity onto the stage as he unbuttons his shirt, revealing Scrooge, front and center, on his chest. Maddie's smile turns into tears running down her face. "Is everything okay, Maddie?" Josh takes her hand in his.

She is silent for a moment, then a smile appears as her eyes soften. "They were all scheduled for euthanasia. Now they are loving life and sitting on Santa's lap. Maybe for the first time, they're truly loved." Maddie turns, looks into Josh's eyes and squeezes his hand. "I feel truly loved."

Josh has mixed emotions; he clearly knows the over-whelming love between them. However, there appears to be a sense of fear in her eyes, a fear she doesn't want to burden him with. "I will always be here for our children and, of course, you."

All alone back at the house, a sense of serenity overcomes the family. The visit with Santa has worn the pups and their parents out. Dogs are spread across the room in comfy beds, dreaming of treats Santa will bring them soon. Josh is sitting at the end of the couch; Maddie is lying back with her legs across Josh's thighs. A few dogs join them up on the sofa. The sounds of Lucy and Mr. Peebody break the tranquility of the silence, snoring as they snuggle.

Lucy and Peebody are a bonded pair of hunting beagles who aged out of favor with their owner. They didn't know being dropped at a shelter would be like winning the lottery. It was their third annual visit with Santa, and they never had to sleep in the cold again. The way they're always cuddled so close, you might think they're cold, but they're merely inseparable, much like Maddie and Josh.

Josh throws out one of his witty quotes: "Snoring from a person is deafening; yet snoring from a dog sounds like a well-played symphony." He squeezes Maddie's foot.

"How true. I love the sound of content, snoring beagles."

After a few minutes of listening to various sounds coming from tired, content dogs, Maddie begins an uncomfortable conversation. "As you know, I've been exhausted lately. I have some health concerns and made an appointment to see Dr. Janesko, our family doctor. I also scheduled a few tests, which I can cancel if she doesn't think they're needed. As a nurse… well, you know I've seen it all and like I said, I have concerns."

Josh's hands freeze from caressing and massaging her feet. "Concerns? What do you think is going on? I should have known something was up. You seemed tired when Katie was in this summer." He releases her feet, reaches for, and now holds her hands. "What's making you so tired? What can I do?"

"I don't know. Hopefully, we'll get answers quick. My appointment is for Tuesday afternoon." She looks deeply into his eyes. "Just be here for me."

Josh leans in and gives Maddie a kiss and deeply hugs her. "I love you."

Sharks

Maddie's stomach is in knots, her legs trembling as she gazes up at the large pillars sitting atop the steps of the county courthouse. Roman columns jump into her head. She's wondering if they are heading in for their slaughter. The cold, freezing weather goes unnoticed with all that's on her mind this morning. Josh meets back up with her after parking the car. She quickly grabs her warrior and hugs him tight.

Wrapped in their long winter coats, Josh points his elbow out. "Are you ready for this?"

"Not really. But I need to be for our family." She loops her arm within Josh's and they ascend the marble steps.

They look ready for the occasion. Maddie found an old gray pant suit in the back of the closet from decades ago. The style came back around, and it still fits. She has a white blouse and a deep purple scarf highlighting her beauty. Josh wears a navy-blue business suit with a red power tie.

Two-thirds up the steps, they stop for Maddie to take a breather. "I'm worried about Toby." She clenches her jaw and tightens her grip on Josh's arm.

"He'll be okay," Josh reassures her. "Tracey will monitor the little fellow."

"It's not okay." Maddie's heart is racing. "We shouldn't even be here. Our place is with our family." Her eyes soften as tears well up. "Toby's heart is fragile. He needs me with him today, fighting for his life." She wipes the tears with her glove as her eyelids narrow. "Not fighting off damn lawyers and developers."

"You're right, Honey." Josh puts his arms around Maddie. "Let's go give them hell. Fight for Toby and the rest of our pups."

Inside the halls of the courthouse, they meet their lawyer's assistant, Judy. They make their way into a conference room located just outside the courtroom. Inside is their lawyer, Dennis Katz. They say their pleasantries and get down to business. Maddie can't help but notice the room is not much bigger than a walk-in closet. She feels pressure pushing against her chest as Dennis describes what's about to happen in the hearing. Josh is sitting next to Maddie, holding her hand, squeezing it when she appears to tense up. They are in this battle together.

Dennis tries to put their nerves at ease. "You guys look great, very professional." He points out supporters of their cause are arriving: the environmental expert from the Pineland Conversancy, a handful of other rescues, and concerned neighbors.

As Dennis paces the room, he emphasizes to Maddie and Josh that this is a preliminary hearing. Final judgement will not be made today. This hearing is to determine if this case has merit to continue on.

"I have to tell you the truth. There's a very good chance the judge will rule in favor of the plaintiff—the developers." Dennis stands behind them and rests a hand on each of their shoulders. "If it goes forward, there's a lot we can do to push it off… for years, if it comes to that."

Josh and Maddie are basically fighting city hall. The developers don't mind it getting caught up in the court system. They have deep pockets and know the Kellys will eventually run out of money. Not their ideal situation, but the developers fallback plan is to financially ruin the Kellys so they will eventually have to close Monkey's House. Then, they will take their property.

Looking down at the floor, Dennis says, "Don't be surprised if the judge is favorable to the plaintiff's lawyers. Judge Ash is golfing buddies with their lead lawyer, Melvin Goldmann."

Josh jumps out of his chair. "Golfing buddies!" He quickly sits back down and turns to Maddie. "Sorry, honey, I don't want to stress you out." Looking back at Dennis he replies, "You know this is a golf community they want to build, right?"

"I do. I addressed my concerns to the court already. Judge Ash informed me he can be impartial in this hearing and would not recuse himself."

Maddie's skin tone pales. "I need to visit the ladies' room."

Judy shows her the way, then makes her way back to the conference room. Maddie needs a break already. Standing at the sink, gazing into the mirror, she sees a calm, collected woman reflecting back. Yet, she knows deep down inside she's barely holding it together, not sure how she will get through the day. But she knows she has to be strong for her family and the future of their sanctuary.

Bending over, she has the water running and dampens a paper towel, putting it up against her cheeks. The coolness is refreshing as she takes a few calming breaths.

A loud noise startles her. As Maddie's head jerks up, she sees a thick manila folder sitting on the sink next to her, and a well-dressed woman staring at her through the mirror. Maddie notices her beady eyes and taught stature.

Maddie asks, "Who are you? What do you want?"

"We just want you to be aware. Your medical history is an open book." The woman flips open the folder, scanning through the documents. Maddie gasps as she notices results from her most recent doctor's visits.

"I don't know who you are or how you got those. It's illegal to steal medical records." Maddie grabs for the folder.

The woman grins, "Oh, you can have those. But it wouldn't matter: we have electronic copies. It's our insurance policy if needed. To prove you're not capable of managing Monkey's House." At that moment, the mysterious woman quickly exits.

Maddie is stunned and takes a seat on the couch at the edge of the room. Tears flow. She planned not to let the news from the doctor, given just a week ago, affect her today during the trial. But now, it's impossible; everything is crashing down, and she knowns she needs to get back to the conference room as the hearing will start soon. Frozen on the couch, she can't muster the courage to face anybody.

As time passes, Josh and the others are worrying what's taking Maddie so long. Judy goes to see if everything is alright, but quickly ends up back in the conference room. "Josh, you need to come. Maddie needs you. Something happened and she won't discuss it with me."

Upon entering the room, Josh sees Maddie crying, holding a folder. "Honey, what's wrong?"

"See this?" She holds up the folder. "They have my medical history and will use it against us."

"They won't be able to. It's against the law." Josh's jaw tightens, but he quickly transitions with a smile. "They are just trying to intimidate us."

After a few minutes of Josh's presence, Maddie's tears are gone. A quick touch up of her makeup and they are off to the courtroom—ready for the sharks.

Taking a seat on the left of the room, Maddie and Josh appear outmatched, at least by the sheer numbers of the legal teams. They have one lawyer in Dennis, along with Judy. The plaintiffs have seven sitting at the lead table and directly behind. The Global Animal World Alliance (GAWA) has a representative on hand. Not surprising, it was rumored the developers made a handsome donation to the organization. However, Maddie is pleased at the support sitting behind them: those wishing to save Monkey's House and the environmental oasis behind their property.

Maddie turns to Dennis. "You know the GAWA is the

biggest scam. Eighty-five percent of their donations go towards administrative costs. Real non-profits spend eighty-five percent or more on their causes. Like we do."

The bailiff calls out: "Big Pine Country Club vs. Josh and Maddie Kelly and Monkey's House, Inc. All rise."

Judge Ash enters the room and shortly after, he calls the lead lawyers up to the bench. Maddie can see the friendship, clear as day, between Melvin Goldmann and the judge. After the conversation, the entire courtroom can hear Judge Ash say he is looking forward to the next golf outing with Melvin.

These proceedings differ from a trial. Judge Ash instructs the courtroom that this is a hearing to determine if the complaint has merit to move forward. In a hearing such as this, the judge asks questions of the legal teams. The evaluation is based on the answers, and the judge will make the overall finding. The finding will be delivered in three weeks.

Judge Ash looks at both tables. "I've read the affidavits and accompanying documents." Turning to the stenographer he says, "Let the record show this is an eminent domain case. The township wants to seize the Kelly property and provide compensation without the Kellys' consent. Eminent domain is to allow for the development of a golf community and the Kelly's land is needed for access to the property."

The plaintiff is asked to provide the merits of a golf community. Their team immediately goes to the financial benefits. Their accountant has charts and graphs going out for twenty years and claims that Big Pine Country Club would bring in well over a million dollars a year in tax revenue. They claim the new community wouldn't put any additional burden on the township services as the Big Pine development would be self-sufficient.

The plaintiff's team goes on with estimates of increased business for local establishments, such as restaurants, landscapers, and construction. Melvin Goldmann jumps in, "This would be a big win for the township financially as well as local businesses." He then jokes with the judge, "And a great place to play golf. We just need two more."

Dennis quickly stands and addresses the court. "Golf is played in foursomes. The two more comment means the plaintiffs lead attorney and you will be looking for two more golfing buddies. I object."

Judge Ash interjects, "This is not trial. I explained that already so 'objections' are not treated the same here. Besides, we were just joking around."

Maddie's blood is boiling at this point. Yet she realizes this is only the first question. She needs to keep calm. It will be her turn to speak shortly and she needs to stay focused, be direct, and convey the Monkey's House mission. Josh reaches under the table and puts his hand on her thigh, squeezing lightly. She realizes he's letting her know they are in this together.

Now, it's the defendant's turn to provide the merits of Monkey's House. Maddie gives a very emotional view inside their organization over the past twenty years—saving over four hundred dogs from euthanasia that they rescued, providing them a wonderful life till the end.

Judge Ash interrupts, "You're a hospice, correct?"

"Yes, we rescue dogs with terminal diagnoses."

"Then why not let them be euthanized? They're hospice. What kind of life can they have?"

Maddie's knuckles turn white. "A wonderful life, sir. What all living beings deserve in our final months, weeks or days." Maddie goes on explaining their philosophy on food therapy and veterinary care, getting the dogs in the best condition to live their lives to the end, how dogs that were given weeks to live are with them years later. She talked about their field trips, visits with Santa, and on and on. It looks like the judge wants to cut her off, but he lets her continue.

The next question isn't a question at all. The judge sets it up on a silver platter for the plaintiff. Judge Ash states, "There is a world-renowned animal rights organization represented in court today. Ms. Clark, please provide your expert analysis on the Monkey's House organization." Ms. Clark is Vice President of animal welfare at the GAWA.

"Judge Ash, Monkey's House is a tiny organization whose impact on the canine rescue community is miniscule. They have a horrid adoption success rate, which is how we rate a rescue organization. In fact, ninety-eight percent of all their dogs die at their facility. The GAWA would give them an 'F' rating because we have nothing lower to rate them at."

Dennis raises, "I would like to have my client address these accusations."

"Ms. Clark, thank you for your analysis. You may sit

down." Judge Ash looks over to the defendants. "Who would like to rebut her analysis."

Maddie stands, a little wobbly on her feet. "Monkey's House is a hospice, as you even noted. We don't adopt out. The dogs live out their remaining lives at our home, not in a facility, as Ms. Clark claimed. We may be a small organization, but our impact is huge to the dogs we take in, not to mention the hundred thousand plus Monkey's House families across the globe. There are thousands of small rescues across the world. Any one of those organizations is doing more for dogs' welfare than GAWA. Less than fifteen percent of donation to GAWA actually go to helping animals. Unlike small rescues, I believe their philosophy is to see how much their CEO and leadership can steal out of the coffers."

Judge Ash cuts Maddie off, "I've heard enough. I have the information to comb through and make my decision."

Dennis addresses the court. "Judge Ash, the defense has environmental experts, neighbors, as well as other small rescues to provide their insights."

"Again, this is a hearing—for me to gather the facts and decide. We're finished here."

Dennis interjects, "I object. How can you make an informed decision without hearing from all the impacted parties?"

"Bang, bang, bang!" Judge Ash slams down the gavel with a red face. "I said this hearing is over. Not another word!"

The banging, on top of the stress of the hearing is too much for Maddie. Her health was waning way before today.

As she stands to exit the courtroom, the walls close in on her as she blacks out, hitting the floor hard. Josh and Dennis rush over, along with one of the plaintiff's aides. Melvin Goldmann quickly escorts the aide away, as they walk right past Maddie.

Friends

Prior to the court hearing, Maddie had many doctor appointments and tests to diagnose her lack of energy and sudden weakness. The blacking out in the courtroom resulted from restrictive cardiomyopathy, which was the doctor's conclusion about her health. The diagnosis was not good—they saw specialists in Philadelphia and New York City with their hopes dashed at each avenue they turned, looking for a positive resolution to her condition.

The twenty-plus years of caring for hospice dogs still didn't prepare them for what would lie ahead. Maddie seemed to find more urgency in getting things in order so Monkey's House could continue to meet the needs of terminally ill dogs. Josh understood her desire to ensure her absence would not impede the dogs' care, but she, too, deserved to live the final chapter of her life with peace, joy and comfort. They had dedicated their lives to ensuring the end of each dog's life was just so, and now, all Josh wanted was for her to be afforded the same attention. Now was the time for Maddie to live her final chapter, and he was going to do his best to make it happen.

Maddie's New Year's Day tradition started while she was in her twenties. On the first day of the year, she took part in an activity she strived to continue throughout the year. Back then, it was loading her horse onto the trailer and meeting up with friends for a long trail ride at Wharton State Forest. Meandering down sand roads and through slow, winding streams filled with brackish water in the New Jersey Pine Barrens was tranquil. For Maddie, it set the theme for the year: no resolutions for her. She wanted to live that lifestyle all year long. Shortly after noticing how one-day's tradition had such a positive impact on Maddie's attitude, Josh started his own tradition of mountain biking with friends each New Year's Day.

Over the years, they were true to their annual traditions, but once they began Monkey's House, their annual rituals merged with a different, but equally important focus. Maddie no longer had horses, and many of Josh's riding buddies focused on growing family commitments. They realized enjoying this day hiking in the park with each other, their dogs, and volunteers—this was now their greatest New Year's Day tradition yet. It was not only setting the path for their lives but also setting it for every dog, and hopefully their volunteers. Their intention was set: enjoy every day—live in the moment.

As this New Year's Day draws closer, Josh informs the volunteers the walk-in-the-park would be delayed for a few weeks. Even though Maddie wants to go, she's not up to it. The new medication she was prescribed last week hasn't made an impact yet. Dr. Janesko is hopeful it will help her feel better and give her strength to tackle a short walk with the crew in the coming weeks.

Josh advises her of the delay, but knows, somehow, he can find a way to keep up the tradition. So, he and Holly put their heads together and concoct a grand scheme to make sure Maddie won't miss the yearly ritual she loves dearly.

A small recliner is wrangled out of the garage and hauled alongside the bus. Momentarily bewildered, they wonder how to get it through the door. They both realize how silly they are, forgetting the bus has a hydraulic lift. In Waggin One's former life, the lift brought wheelchair-bound people on board; now it's used to help load large dogs with mobility issues. "It a good thing The Machine is here to show you how it's done."

Holly laughs, "Wait, we thought of using the lift at the same time."

"Yeah, but you learned that from me, Mini-Machine."

Holly goes inside the bus, raises the two bench seats, making room for the chair in the middle of the bus. She engages the lift as Josh stands outside, ensuring the recliner won't rock off as the lift raises slowly. Holly notices the wheelchair anchors on the floor and realizes they could hold the recliner in place. "Slide the chair over the anchors. That will let me get the strap around the frame and secure it to the floor."

"How's this?" Josh asks as he maneuvers the chair directly over them.

"Perfect." Holly weaves the strap between the frame, extending it from one side to the other to create a solid connection to the floor anchors.

Josh has both hands on the recliner, rocking it back and forth. "This isn't going anywhere, thanks. We'll surprise Maddie. I hope the swans are in the front bog today."

The recliner will make the day special for Maddie. Josh has another little thoughtful touch up his sleeve. Last week, he transferred his old tape mix to a CD, and now, he pops it into the bus's CD player. Waggin' One has never had a CD in it since the day they bought it. He's relieved when it plays. All is ready to take Maddie and a dog to the old cranberry bogs for a special day in the state forest—a noble attempt to save their unbroken New Year's Day streak. Josh, along with Holly's help, has everything set for the little adventure. He's eager to surprise Maddie, yet he still needs to convince her to go, so they can set the tone for the year.

Josh goes upstairs to meet Maddie. Quietly entering the room, he sees her curled up in bed with her back facing him, and hears soft whimpering. Gently lifting the covers, he makes his way into the bed and holds Maddie. "This is the first year I haven't done my New Year's tradition in over fifty years." She kisses the back of his hand and pulls him in closer. "I'm so sorry you and the dogs are missing it, too."

"Please don't fret over it. We'll do the tradition in a few weeks. If you're still not ready, I'll get the volunteers to organize it and we'll get the dogs out for their adventure. Besides, you're not breaking our tradition." Josh gets up and pulls a set of her clothes out of the closet and lays them on the bed. "Here's something warm and comfy to throw on. Don't take long. We have somewhere we need to be."

"But I'm really not…"

"I'm taking you to one of our favorite places where we have some friends to see."

"You know my body is not up to this… but I trust you know what you're doing."

Josh guides Maddie out the front door and over to the bus. At first, she cocks her head, confused. Then, a shift behind her eyes—she realizes what he's done for her and a quiet smile forms on her face. Holly is there to help her get aboard and sit comfortably in the recliner. "This chair is comfy; where are we headed?"

"It's a surprise." Josh hurries off the bus and grabs little Bandit out of Holly's arms and carries him over to Maddie. "You're not heading anywhere until you get a pup on your lap."

After driving along the highway for ten minutes, they turn off the primary thoroughfare onto a dirt road that looks as though it's a part of the Fort Dix Army artillery range. It's peppered with potholes as far as the eye can see. Maddie is not sure where they're headed. The recliner is sitting low on the floor which makes it impossible to see out of the windows. Josh is doing his best to keep their destination a secret.

Suddenly, Josh lets out a warning. "Hold on to Bandit. It is going to get rough." He's carefully weaving around the potholes until they're impossible to avoid. Maddie has a good grip on Bandit. The little mixed breed's eyes are as big as his little six-pound body. The cute little guy is fully alert, ears perked, uncertain about the rocking and rolling.

"We are going to the bogs, aren't we?" Maddie figures it out. They are heading to their favorite place to see the Pine's waterfowl, where they would often walk the dogs.

Once through the maze of potholes, the road narrows, barely allowing the bus to pass; the occasional pine branch reaches out as though its needles are petting the dog images lining the bus. The road finally opens up into a small field filled with clumps of tall grass and scrub pine. A large tree, spectacular in its day, sits right in front of the overgrown cranberry bogs filled with water and life. The old tree has petrified black and gray bark. Its branches stretch far and wide, creating a majestic silhouette against the blue sky, with its reflection coming off the water.

"We're here honey." Josh positions the bus as close to the water as possible with the wide doors of the hydraulic lift facing the water. If Maddie isn't up for taking a stroll along the sand road leading out to a magnificent lake, they can stay on the bus and witness the wonders of their little corner of paradise from Waggin' One.

The recliner needs to be moved to see out the side door. Josh leans in close. "Let me undo this strap and push you back to the door so you have a better view." He releases the strap and, using all his might, pushes against the recliner until the chair glides along the metal floor.

"Stop here," Maddie shouts, as a smile grows upon her face. Decades of enjoying time in the Pine Barrens rush through her mind. Trail rides through the forest with her horses, Zeus and Olympus, her all-time favorite mounts.

Nursing is an extremely stressful profession, and those rides were her ultimate stress reliever. After the horses were gone, her love of the Pines never faded, they simply changed from horseback riding to walking dogs with her love.

Maddie takes stock of the bog and points to the far-left corner, about fifty yards away. "There they are." The excitement brings energy back into her weakened body, opening her eyes wide and forming a blissful smile.

After noticing her joy, a smile grows on Josh's face. It's like those days when they walked hand-in-hand on the beach. The Tundra swans, along with their Canadian geese counterparts, are on full display. Josh does a quick count, as he always does. "There are sixteen swans and ten Canadians; I don't see any mallards today." The cool breeze flowing toward the bus brings a collection of harmonious avian clatter.

Josh squeezes his way into the recliner with Maddie and Bandit. Together, they're enjoying the peaceful sounds of nature, feeling the slow movements from of each other's breathing, and knowing this is where they both belong—in one another's arms.

Maddie's eyes harden as she hugs Josh tight. "We need to keep fighting for our property and Monkey's House. But more so for the dogs: for our family, and those in need of love in their last chapter, for years to come."

"Honey, I'll fight to the end for our pups." Josh squeezes Maddie. "Don't worry, I have a lot of fight left in me." He gives her a gentle kiss. "I'll do everything in my power. Let me worry about this. I want you to enjoy the moment."

Time passes, savoring one another in the tranquility of their natural oasis. After a while, Josh gets up and heads to the front of the bus. "I'll be right back; I have to get something." He grabs a little package as he pushes play on the CD player. "To Love Somebody" by the Bee Gees is playing as he walks back towards Maddie, who notices a small square box in his hand.

"Oh no, one of us won't be crying again, will we? Tears flow when we hand each other gifts. You even upped your game with one of my favorite songs."

"Yeah, but they're happy, loving tears, aren't they?" He twists and turns, slipping his body back into the chair alongside Maddie once again. "New Year's Day has always been special to us. I've always loved sharing this day with our family, but especially with you. You always said, do something to set the tone for the year."

Josh hands the box to Maddie. "I believe this started your tradition." She has the biggest smile her weakened body can muster. Her hands are having trouble opening the box and the anticipation of what's inside is making matters worse. "Here, let me help." Josh gets the top open and lets Maddie take over from there.

Maddie removes the tissue paper and pulls out a clear Christmas ball filled with long, coarse blondish hair. Tears stream down her face. She knows the hair is mane from her soul horse, Zeus. Although he passed over thirty-five years ago, her love for him never diminished. Not able to speak, staring into the ball she's holding, she reaches up with the other and grasps her Sora pendant. In her mind, she's riding Zeus down the sand path she was gazing upon earlier. By her side, Josh is riding his horse, Brit, with Sora trotting alongside.

"This is so special. I love it... I love you." Maddie turns her head and gives Josh a kiss. "On New Year's Day, I have everything I could have ever wanted. You, Sora, and Zeus, my three soulmates. Is this heaven?"

One of their all-time favorite movies is *Field of Dreams.* The famous line from the movie "Is This Heaven?" is a phrase they would catch themselves asking each other often. They cherished their lives together and were thankful for the opportunity to be part of all the dogs' last hurrah. They loved their family.

"Feels like it, but I believe it's New Jersey. You may be tired, but I see you still have your sense of humor," Josh says. Relaxed and content being in each other's arms, their eyes close.

Josh awakens from the unplanned nap by the loud engine noise of a diesel truck. It pulls right alongside the bus. He wriggles his way out of the recliner, waking Maddie as he gets up. There's seldom anybody out in the Pines. If there are, they give others a wide berth. Josh's face twists into a worried grimace. "I'll see who it is. Stay calm."

The intruders turn out to be their good friends, Butch and Teresa. Teresa is one of Maddie dearest and oldest friends, her trail riding cohort from years ago. They have a lot in common with their love of horses. Teresa took a similar path as Maddie, helping dogs on the other end of the spectrum. Years back, she began fostering puppies from Georgia. They are transported up each month. She'd have three to five puppies from each trip, and by the time the next caravan brought her a new batch of puppies, she would've already adopted out her previous fosters into loving homes.

Maddie and Teresa are experienced equestrians. Growing up, they both took part in Pony Club, an organization much like 4H for horse lovers. They were in different clubs, yet took lessons from the same riding instructors. Although they were the same age, Maddie would always tease Teresa for being younger. She never mentioned it was only three months.

Butch is retired, but he always has side gigs. He was the pro at a local golf course and continues to rent out his fleet of carts to courses around the area.

"Hi Butch, hey Teresa." he shakes Butch's hand and gives Teresa a big hug. "What brings you guys out here?" Butch is pulling a trailer with two golf carts aboard. "I can't imagine anywhere out here you would deliver these to."

Butch explained, "Holly called us a few days ago and told us about your surprise, so we wanted to help make Maddie's annual tradition a little extra special. These carts will handle the sand fine. We brought two as Teresa and I would love to join, if you don't mind?" Teresa had made her way onto the bus and the two of them were already chattering away like teenagers. Josh is smiling once again, knowing the surprise visit is exactly what she needs—to focus on the here and now.

Butch and Josh get the carts off the trailer, all the while hearing the Pony Clubbers reminiscing, laughing and enjoying each other's company. The Pines is Maddie's favorite place on earth. It boosts her energy, but the addition of seeing Teresa makes her believe everything will be okay. Josh and Maddie make their way into one cart. Teresa places Bandit in Maddie's lap, then joins Butch in the other cart. Josh takes the lead, driving carefully with his precious cargo. As they serpentine their way around the bogs, through stands of tall pine and oak trees, they come out to Josh's favorite location in the Pines. He pulls over to let Butch bring his cart alongside.

In front of them is one of the largest lakes in the Pine Barrens. Jaws dropped and eyes widened, they see hundreds of swans, geese, and ducks covering most of the lake. Josh walks a couple of dogs here every week. "The migrating Tundra swan population had been decreasing over the years. Ten years ago, I'd count a hundred swans. Over the past years, the number dwindled to thirty. Seeing this many is a thrill."

Teresa can't sit still and jumps out of her cart, making her way over to Maddie. This is her first visit to this lake. She migrated from the United Kingdom as a child, lived in the states for over sixty years, yet you can still hear her thick English accent. Maddie would tease her about some words she used. She loves her dear friend's familiar accent; it's calming her heart.

Teresa exclaims, "There are hundreds of swans and Canadian geese, and look over there." Her arm is waving as she points to the far left of the lake. "Look at all the mallards. Maddie, your friends came to see you today."

Tears stream down Maddie's face; she's at a loss for words. The tears are not tears of sorrow, but tears of solace. At this moment, this is right where she needed to be. With Josh, her friends, and with God.

In the Moment

Sun is shining brightly through the front dining-room windows. It's void of dining room furniture; they moved it all into the barn. Now, the room is sparse, with the basics needed to support Maddie and their life together. It contains their king-sized bed, nightstands, dresser and a reading light sitting alongside a small rocking chair. The furniture came from their upstairs bedroom. The movers tried to convince Josh maneuvering a king-bed down the stairs would be difficult and suggested bringing down the queen-bed from the spare room instead. However, he insisted on the larger bed, explaining it wouldn't just be occupied by Maddie and him, but would include an unlimited number of dogs as well. So, they grudgingly muscled the king-bed downstairs.

Close to a hundred pictures line the walls throughout the room, pictures of their lives together. Josh even found a picture from their first date where they went horseback riding. Rita snapped it as they rode out of the barn on their trail ride. Josh had it enlarged and touched up as much as possible. Even though it was still rough and grainy, it was fitting for an older couple's memory wall.

There's a room in The Cottage Maddie calls the Healing room. Besides its obvious purpose, it's also where she takes dogs nearing the end of their lives. To Maddie, this space is spiritual. The south wall of the room is lined with windows and a door leading into the yard. Bright sun illuminates the room where one absorbs the power of its rays and the restorative force it emanates being in this magical space. Outside in the front yard, Nemesia and Pansies overflow in decorative pots, wind chimes sing in the breeze, and a yard flag with the saying "Who Saved Who" waves. The white picket fence encapsulates the beauty within this little yard.

The healing power of the mind and soul is experienced inside or outside The Cottage. When in the Healing room, comforting a dog, Maddie and Josh know there is something larger at work, much more than themselves alone. They always felt the sun rays beaming in on the dogs was the Rainbow Bridge shining down to let the pups know they were welcome "home" whenever they're ready.

Josh and Maddie agree she can no longer navigate the stairs safely. His initial plan was to put their bed in the family room, turning it into their living space. It's where all the dogs hang out, and where they watch an occasional movie on the big screen, covered in dogs. They already spend a fair amount of time there, yet there's one problem: it faces north. Although sliding glass doors line the outer wall, the room doesn't get direct sunlight. However, it provides beautiful views of the backyard and farm pond. Gazing over the back field, recollections of pack walks come to mind. Magical walks were taken through the years, where souls of dogs, cats, horses, goats, and even a goose named Hootie, united as one. It has the best views by far, bringing back significant memories, but lacks the sun Maddie cherishes. So, the dining room was the better option, with its windows facing the south. Besides, they never had a formal dinner once they started Monkey's House. They were too busy. Even if they had the time, they figured their guests wouldn't like twenty plus dogs circling the table.

The Christmas tree sits between the two large windows in the room. It didn't matter it wasn't Christmas; it fit right in with the Spring flowers blooming outside the window. Day after day, Josh would sit with Maddie, and they soon established a sweet little routine. He would go to the tree and bring Maddie a Christmas ball filled with the hair of one of their babies. He'd hand it to Maddie and beautiful stories would flow, each taking turns reminiscing about the dog. Loving, funny, happy, all wonderful memories they loved recalling about their fur babies.

One globe contained hair belonging to Hannah Bear. When she arrived, Hannah Bear was a pathetic little Pomeranian, full of cancer and hairless from her neck back. She was lethargic with a slim chance of making it through the first few weeks, but she fooled everybody, especially their cat, Sammy. After food therapy to get her well enough for extensive surgery, she had the cancerous mammary masses removed. Within a short period, Hannah's energy and spunk emerged. As her healing continued, her hair grew back, and she soon developed the most beautiful, thick, and lustrous coat ever. Once she felt better, Maddie realized Hannah's favorite pastime became chasing Sammy, whenever she wasn't sleeping or snuggling with her mom.

Their new routine goes on for weeks. Every day for about an hour they share stories when Maddie has the strength. On this evening, Maddie appears extremely tired. Josh isn't sure if they should play their little game, but thinks it may cheer her spirits. As he makes his way to the tree to fetch a ball, Maddie calls out, "Come, lie next to me."

He assumes his place alongside Maddie in their treasured position. She's becoming weaker and even more exhausted every day; her body is worn out. Josh takes in her warmth, her aroma, her love. He can't imagine life without her, and rearranges the dogs, allowing him to drift across the bed. He gently wraps his top arm around her, bending his knees as he slides them up against hers. Cuddling up to Maddie always feels so right—like a pair of well-worn leather gloves that fit perfectly when you put them on. You know they'll protect you from the elements, and you dread the day they wear out.

More dogs make their way onto the bed, scooching as close as possible to Maddie. Their little heads rest upon Maddie's body, consoling their mom. Josh tears up with a lump in his throat. He waits a bit, then whispers into Maddie's ear, "You're loved by so many."

With a weak voice, almost a whisper, she replies, "I'm the luckiest person on earth."

These are her last words.

A week earlier, they took one of their favorite little adventures, a pack walk around the backfield. Even though

Maddie was riding in a golf cart, the walk resembled the journeys they'd taken together over a thousand times before. While Maddie remained quiet on their excursion around the perimeter of the field, a slim smile was on her beautiful face. She was clearly living in the moment. This is exactly what she'd always said about the Monkey's House dogs: they were living their best finale possible.

Every dog at Monkey's House was out on the walk, each accompanied by one of their aunts or uncles, their loyal, loving volunteers. Dogs with mobility issues used their carts while a few were pushed in strollers. Even Big Ben, a gentle old Saint Bernard, sat in his wagon while being chauffeured by one of their younger volunteers, Uncle Tony. The only one strong enough to pull the big boy around the field. Blind dogs have no problems on walks. Aunt Trish was guiding Leo and Wanda. Bugsy and Peanut were off leash, running and tumbling across the field. You'd never know these dogs were in hospice. This walk was a grand celebration of their mom and enjoyed by all, none more than Maddie herself.

In the cart with Maddie and Josh was Fifi, who made her way to Monkey's House after her person passed. Pets ending up in the shelter system after a deceased parent is an occurrence Maddie and Josh witnessed way too often. It's such a tragedy. They couldn't imagine one of their babies ending up in the shelter. Being witness to this far too many times spurred them on to make it part of their mission, to educate pet parents on including plans in their wills for their beloved furry family members.

Fifi, a sixteen-year-old white poodle, was surrendered to a kill shelter. Thankfully, a friend alerted Maddie of her urgent situation. Fifi, on the brink of dying, arrived at their house lethargic, covered in blood and urine. She's diabetic and at the time of her rescue, was suffering from diabetic ketosis-acidosis (DKA). Although things looked dire, Fifi didn't seem to be suffering. However, Maddie sensed she was dreadfully missing her mom as her head drooped sadly in depression. With extra tender love and care, things improved.

Early on, they discovered FiFi loved hugs, the type of hug which expresses true love. She would wrap her front legs around their necks and pull herself in close. They could tell FiFi's person loved her dearly, one of the few dogs who had a great life full of love before making their way to Monkey's House. On that day, she was simply enjoying the ride with her mom and dad.

Rounding the last turn in the backfield, they headed for home with bright sun shining down on Maddie's face. With her dogs and friends by her side, she touched Josh's arm and asked him to stop the cart by the bank of the pond. Geese and ducks churn up ripples in the pond that are slapping upon turtles basking in the sun atop a fallen tree: Maddie is hypnotized. The sun's warmth was no match for the flame of love for animals and people. She was not just living, but also loving her life with those who meant so much to her.

The little adventure gave Maddie her second wind. Resting in bed afterward, she sat up and grabbed her writing pad and pen. The couple of weeks prior, she had little strength for writing her "goodbye" letters, as she called them. The list of dear friends was long. She had most written, but not Josh's letter. That night was for her soulmate's letter. The walk energized her; she felt better than she had in months. This gave her confidence to compose the most important, yet difficult, letter of all.

Maddie took a deep breath in… held for a few seconds, letting out a calming exhale and began writing.

To my love Josh,

As I lay here surrounded by the warmth of our dogs, their comfort is dwarfed by the love within your heart, your soul. For over fifty years, you have been my best friend, the love of my life. Never saying no to my dreams, you were always there to give me guidance. You've been my rock and encouraged me to go for what I felt in my heart, my passions. For all of it, I am grateful.

You said your favorite thing in life was to walk with me. We'd tune out the world with nothing but the two of us and a few of our furry babies. It was our time without phones or the internet. The two of us reminiscing about the past, planning exciting future endeavors, but mostly living in the moment. Looking back, I now realize our walks hand-in-hand were my favorite as well. Whether a stroll on the beach, a hike in the forest, or a lap around the backfield. The sun setting across the field, or those spectacular bay settings, was always a beautiful sight. But was even more so when my hand was within yours. Often, I turned down your offer for a walk. I was too busy. Life had its grip on me. Only now do I realize life consists of those special moments together with the one you love. Please forgive me and know whenever you're walking the dogs, I'll be right there alongside you.

We were both so young when we first met. It impressed me when you took the reins of your horse and rode off. To my surprise, Rita set me up with a closet equestrian and a quite handsome one, I might add. You know I loved riding Zeus and Olympus in the Pine Barrens. But even more so when you sat upon your trusty steed, Brit, walking beside me on those twisting trails, cantering on the sand roads, or wading through a brackish creek. From the ride on our date, to our last trail ride together, to these last moments. I have no regrets but one.

Josh, I've had plenty of time to ponder our lives. Mostly your life. I'm sorry you completely changed your life for my passion, Monkey's House. You couldn't love the dogs more; you're the perfect father to each one of them. However, I fret my hunger to make a difference in dogs' lives made a difference in yours, and maybe not for the better. I've diminished your own passions – biking, skiing, traveling, and so much more. For that, I am truly sorry.

You don't have to live my passion anymore. I know you'll love and care for the pups at Monkey's House now, but you don't have to continue rescuing new dogs. You'll figure out what's best... please make it what's best for you. I just want you to be happy, to enjoy your life.

I will wait for you at the Rainbow Bridge with all our children. Looking forward to the day we are once again together.

Walking hand-in-hand amongst our furry angels and seeing the most magnificent sunsets, painting the sky bright with every color of the rainbow.

All My Love,
Maddie

Maddie left out any mention of the legal battles they were having to keep Monkey's House. She already knew Josh would do his best to fight the good fight. Much of it was out of his control, and she didn't want to put an additional burden on her love.

After wiping away tears, Maddie finished stuffing the letter into the envelope, moistened the glue and sealed it tight, addressing it "To My Love". The timing couldn't have been better. Josh stepped into the room after finishing up the dishes. Maddie's writing material was spread all over the bed amongst the dogs. Melvin, a little chihuahua, was rolling around in the bed, scratching his back on the paper, making a mess of everything.

"Wow, it looks like you had a productive writing session, or maybe I should say Melvin did." Josh collected the paper and envelopes and put everything back into the writing box sitting on her nightstand.

"I did… Melvin helped me smile through it," she said with a grin. Maddie patted the bed. "Come here. I'd love you to hold me tight." The moment became a more solemn one.

Josh moved Melvin to the side and snuggled in close to

Maddie, sharing their warmth and love. As quickly as the pack walk energized her, it drained her, and she faded fast. Josh squeezed her tight. "You had an eventful…"

"Shh" Maddie held her finger up to Josh's lips, stopping him from talking.

Maddie's eyes were watery as she handed Josh an envelope. "I don't want you to open this now." A tear ran down her cheek. "You'll know when it's the right time."

Josh got choked up; he hesitated to take the letter. He knew by the time he read it, she'd no longer be by his side. "I… I don't know what to say."

"That's hard to believe." She said with an anxious smile. "You're the best storyteller I know, never at a loss for words."

Josh's throat was dry as he struggled to speak. He loved her so much. "I love you." Holding up the envelope, he continued, "I don't want to read this… I know I'll be without you. I'm dreading the thought of being without you."

"You'll never be without me. I'll always be by your side. Remember that." Maddie put her warm hand on Josh's face, her loving touch. It's no surprise, throughout her life she's comforted people and animals alike. She didn't know any other way; she'd do it until her last breath.

Josh slid closer to Maddie, if that was even possible. They hugged, both so thankful for the years they shared and the journeys they embarked on. Especially their mission, which brought hundreds of dogs into their life. They felt blessed.

Leashes in Heaven

Through the years, Monkey's House has cultivated a large social media family, followers supporting their mission from around the globe. They fall in love with dogs they've never met, willing to give a piece of their hearts sharing in each dog's journey. Like a grandparent following their grandchild from afar, they are emotionally connected. Joyous in the littlest of accomplishments, laughing at their crazy antics, praying for those brave pups fighting through struggles, and yes, tears for those who make their way to the Rainbow Bridge. But most of all, their following witnesses the smallest victories day in and day out and cheers them on. At Monkey's House, it's all about dogs living their lives to the fullest of their ability.

On most days, Maddie would do the evening post, providing updates on the dogs while educating on the many aspects of caring for senior dogs with medical issues. Occasionally, Josh would write the post, keeping it light and uplifting. They had different styles, which thoroughly complemented each other. Followers, or what Josh liked to call the Monkey's House family, would often fall in love with specific dogs, most likely those with qualities much like their own, or a dog they had loved and lost.

Hundreds, if not thousands, of "Likes", "Love", and "Caring" emojis are a daily occurrence on their social media accounts.

A prayer request would go out when the dog was nearing the end. They wholly believed in the "Law of Attraction," and the prayers brought positive energy into the house, providing strength to the ailing pup. Maddie also wanted to make sure their family was aware when a dog was approaching their time, taking them on their final journey. During those last hours, the dog would lie on a loved one's lap. They would be told how much they were loved and would be missed. Afterwards, though devastated and broken-hearted, Maddie would fight through the tears to inform the family of their passage by crafting a beautiful memorial post. It would be full of pictures showing them enjoying their life as a member of their little sanctuary. She had a gentle way of letting everybody know by opening her post with, "We are sad to say we have a Tissue Alert."

Josh and Maddie kept their personal lives private, at least as much as possible. Their mission was about the dogs, not the struggles they may encounter in their own lives. Josh wanted to let their extended family know of Maddie's condition when given the bad news, but she preferred to keep it between them and a few close friends. Eventually, there was compromise when, a couple of months before her passing, Josh posted mentions of Maddie battling through a major health issue and all their prayers were surely welcome. The day Maddie made her way to the Rainbow Bridge, Josh wasn't sure how to go about sharing his sadness with the Monkey's House family. He remembered how gently Maddie informed them, so "Tonight, we have a Tissue Alert." The news is crushing for the friends of Monkey's House. Maddie was not only an angel to the dogs but also their hero. Once the news breaks, a group of followers reaches out to Aunt Carrie, a volunteer, for guidance. They want to do something special to honor Maddie and support the cause. It is a given that Maddie will go straight to the Bridge, and therefore, Carrie posted a special request out to the Monkey's House family. They could send a leash in one of the colors of the rainbow or a donation. If their hearts speak to them to do so, they can write a letter expressing the impact Maddie had on them and their furry best friend.

A few weeks go by in a home without the positive energy that is normally present. Josh has lost the spark that ignited the passion in their mission. He sees it in the aunts and uncle too. Even the dogs seem weary. The dogs continue to get their needs cared for, but their spirits are crushed.

The answering machine is no longer accepting messages as it's full. Josh rarely answered the phone for the past few weeks. It is just too hard talking about Maddie. On this morning, somebody is feverously trying to reach him. It rings three times in one hour, yet it's as though he doesn't even hear it, not even a flinch upon the first ring. However, on the fourth attempt, Josh feels an urge to answer. He reluctantly picks up the receiver—a brief conversation. Josh goes out to the garage and sees Holly is cleaning up after breakfast.

"The post office called to let me know the Monkey's House post office box is overflowing. I haven't been there, well, since Maddie passed." Josh's posture slumps as he looks down. "I guess I'm avoiding talking to anybody, or in this case, reading cards people may have sent. They are bringing the mail to the house today."

Josh helps clean up, then enjoys a short walk with Tank and Lulu. After they finish a cruise around the backfield, he puts them into The Cottage yard and heads into the house.

Holly shouts out, catching him halfway in the door. "Here come the postal trucks."

Josh stops and quickly spins around. "What do you mean, trucks?" As the words come out of his mouth, Josh notices not one, nor two, but three small USPS trucks coming down the lane.

Josh walks down the driveway to meet the lead truck. He has a confused look as the driver rolls down her window. "Hi, I'm Becky. We're here to drop off your mail. I'm a dog lover and part of your Monkey's House family. I'm so sorry for your loss." Apparently, she isn't the only one who feels his pain. The trucks are full of boxes and letters addressed to Monkey's House.

Becky swings her truck around, backing it close to the garage door. Along with her colleagues, Rich and Dolores, she starts unloading the trucks. Somehow, they deliver not just mail, but also Maddie's spirit, straight back into the house, Monkey's House. It invigorates Josh and Holly, seeing them unload the first few bags. Josh gives in to his curiosity, seeing what's being delivered. He opens one of the mail bags, reaches his hand in and feels around, pulling out a letter. Walking over to The Cottage yard with letter in hand, he sits down on the bench and is joined by LuLu and Tank. He shows them it's not a treat, but a letter postmarked Boise, Idaho from Patricia.

Dear Josh,

I started following Monkey's House fifteen years ago when my little guy, Chester, was diagnosed with cancer. A friend of mine suggested I check out your organization. She said you offered expert advice for parents of terminally ill dogs. Maddie's guidance gave me precious extra time with Chester, time I wouldn't have had otherwise. There were difficult times, but we fought through them and enjoyed so many special moments together. I am forever grateful for her support.

Over the years, I could see the special bond between the two of you. Notably the love you had for Maddie. Your posts together, your books, and your videos all conveyed a special loving relationship. As we tuned in each night, getting our updates on the dogs, we not only loved the likes of MLBob, that little beagle reminded me so much of my sweet Chester, but it was clear there was love everywhere, especially between you and Maddie. It felt good to know true love exists, and not just for the dogs you rescued.

Maddie is with all your babies at the Rainbow Bridge. I see it was not only dogs like MLBob, touching hearts in every corner of this world. It was the two of you working together to make better lives for your dogs and making a wonderful life together. The genuine love you and Maddie had for one another and your dogs expressed love in its purest sense.

I found a piece of myself in your journey with every dog you rescued and transformed. The two of you worked together to make every dog's last days so special. I'm sure you did the same for Maddie. She had the heart of a warrior, fighting for the dogs long after the battle was supposed to end. I believe she did the same for herself because of the love you two shared. She didn't want to leave a life perfect beyond her wildest dreams.

Your love gave Maddie the will to live, and it also assured her it was ok to go.

Sincerely,
Patricia

Reading the letter takes the wind out of Josh. His heart is broken missing Maddie. The sentiments in Patricia's letter are more than he can bear. He makes his way back into the house and lies down on the couch, in Maddie's spot. He's seeking to be close to her, to pull on her strength. With tears forming, he calls the dogs around him for support, lifting a few up onto the couch with him. They sense his sorrow and snuggle up to provide comfort. Josh can't concentrate: memories of his love are spinning through his head. He quickly falls asleep holding a dog in each arm. Little over an hour later, he wakes and pulls himself together. Outside, he wanders to investigate the mail bags further. To his surprise, Tracey and Claire have joined Holly in the driveway. Bags were piled all around them as they picked through the mail.

Tracey notices Josh's forehead scrunch and eyes squinting. "Holly called and said we had to get over here as soon as possible. People are sending leashes, donations, and letters to Maddie." Josh's jaw drops, noticing what appears to be over a hundred mail bags covering the driveway—bags filled to the brim with boxes and letters, but mostly, love.

Claire can barely speak, her eyes bloodshot from intermittent tears. "I've read a few messages that were sent along with a leash. They loved Maddie and are sending a piece of their hearts. There are leashes in every color of the rainbow. And letters, so many letters." She hands Josh a box containing a red leash wrapped around a letter.

Josh sees this is emotional for everybody. "Why are we getting these? What's with all the leashes?"

Holly came forward. "It's because of Carrie's post. Asking followers to send leashes in colors of the rainbow, in memory of Maddie." Holly was the only one willing to let Josh know of the request. Communication is Josh's responsibility to ensure the proper message gets delivered in-line with their mission.

Josh's eyes squint and forehead wrinkles. "Why leashes? Why in every color of the rainbow?"

Tracey speaks up, "Leashes in heaven. Maddie needs a lot

of leashes in heaven for all the dogs. What could be better than the colors of the rainbow?"

Initially, Josh's eyes gleam as he clenches his teeth. He quickly softens his jaw, and his eyes light up as he forms a smile. "She'll need a lot of leashes, that's for sure."

He knows the impact Maddie had on the dogs. Yet, he never realized it was not "just about the dogs" but about the community she built over the years. Looking at the letter in his hand, he is taken to that evening—the evening Maddie handed him the letter addressed "To My Love." The letter he's yet to open. Josh pictures her last breath, lying there with her. Even after she left this world, he held her close. Josh takes a breath and blinks, bringing himself out of a trance. He opens the letter Claire handed him.

Dear Josh,

I'm so sorry for your loss. My thoughts and prayers are with you and the Monkey's House aunts and uncles.

I've learned so much from Maddie. She'll forever be in my heart, my hero. When my little Buddy was in his last month, she gave me the knowledge and confidence needed to fight for him. Maddie gave me hope for better days, and there were many better days... wait, not just better days, but great days I could share with Buddy on our little adventures.

Whatever the cost, emotionally and financially, I'm grateful I found Maddie to guide me with Buddy. Please accept this red leash, Buddy's favorite color.

Along with walking the Monkey's House pups, I hope Maddie meets Buddy. Maybe she could include him on her walks among the stars. He loved his walks.

Love overcomes all, even in death.

Sincerely,
Jessie

As Josh inspects the leash, he notices Jessie had it embroidered with Buddy's name.

It took weeks to go through all the bags, even with the help of the aunts and uncles. In the end, there were 2,349 leashes, close to $1 million in donations and 4,164 letters sent. It took Josh over a year to read all the letters, but he was adamant about reading every one.

Maddie never wanted a funeral; her ashes were to be spread over the farm along with the animals she loved throughout her life, whom they buried on their property. However, Josh planned a memorial service. They donated most of the leashes to other shelters and rescues in Maddie's name. He also swapped out old leashes at Monkey's House with those sent in memory of Maddie. Josh stored multiple sets of leashes in every color up in the attic. He'd bring them down when others eventually wore out. However, Josh kept a few sets of leashes in every color of the rainbow for her memorial to celebrate her amazing life.

The sky was bright blue on the day of Maddie's life's celebration. Josh had an inkling there would be a big turnout for her memorial, so he reserved the largest Catholic church possible. This was excellent planning as well over a thousand are in attendance, some from as far as the west coast and a few from Canada. Even Clive, an adamant supporter from the United Kingdom, is here. He rearranged his business trip to coincide with the memorial so he could express how much Maddie had meant to him.

Over a hundred pictures of Maddie line the viewing room, and dozens of videos play. Of course, all are of Maddie with animals, mostly dogs, and many with Josh by her side. Leashes hang over every doorway, arched like rainbows, as well as next to the altar.

Ashley from Tiny Nose Prints Rescue gives a heartwarming eulogy. Ashley and Maddie had become close friends over the years. Many of the dogs of Monkey's House came through Ashley's non-profit as they were ill-equipped, nor experienced enough to care for dogs with challenging medical conditions.

There are other heartfelt eulogies but none compare to Josh's.

As Josh walks up to the altar, he gazes upon those who loved Maddie. Many never met her in person, but bonded with her through their combined love for dogs and her dedication to those forgotten, when they needed their person most. Tears well up in his eyes; he struggles to fight them back. It's difficult. He's witnessing pure love in front of him. After a deep breath, he composes himself and has the wherewithal to take in the essence of this moment. Living in the moment, as Maddie always put it.

A Lover's Tribute

"There's a quote by Josh Billings. 'A dog is the only thing on earth that loves you more than he loves himself.' I can say Maddie loved the dogs more than she loved herself. She was committed to saving and caring for them. Everything else was secondary. She strived to give them the best life possible, no matter their ailments."

"I should have known early on animals would surround us throughout our lives. Our first date was on horseback. After our wedding vows, we stepped out of the church and into a horse-drawn carriage. Within a year, we adopted our first dog together, Davy, followed by a pair of cats, Larry and Darrel. Next, a horse named Bourbon joined our family."

"Throughout our marriage, our family comprised horses, goats, geese, ducks, chickens, cats... and did I mention dogs? I learned within the first year of Monkey's House, Maddie had a special connection with every dog, knowing when to fight and when to let go. I questioned her about this when we adopted Daisy Mae, a little chihuahua who was extremely ill. After a few weeks, anybody else would have given up on her, including me. Not Maddie, she said, give her time, she'll pull through. Daisy Mae did recover to enjoy over two years with us. I never questioned her again. From then on, I was no longer surprised when Maddie worked miracles time and time again."

"Simple things in life matter. Like a walk on the beach with a leash in one hand and the other arm wrapped around the love of your life. Maddie was the love of my life; there was nothing better than a barefoot stroll along the sand together. No words

needed, just togetherness, the true essence of love."

"I want to leave you all with thoughts about Maddie's favorite poem 'The Dash', by Linda Ellis. For those who aren't familiar with this poem, I suggest you not only read it, but live it like Maddie did."

"Basically, it states: The engraving upon your headstone will contain your birth date and the day you pass, separated by a dash. What matters in life is not the birth or end dates, but the dash – how you lived your life. Maddie felt the same about Monkey's House dogs. We know little about their previous lives, let alone their birth dates, and of course, we never contemplated their end dates. Our mission is to make their 'dashes' the best they can be."

"We're honored to have shared in the dashes of hundreds of dogs. Dogs like Dozer, the German shepherd, with a lack of mobility. It never diminished his thirst for life, befriending the other dogs of Monkey's House and unconditionally giving his heart to Maddie and me."

"Tequila, the handsome cocker with no eyes. He wouldn't let the lack of sight stop him from having the day of his life strolling the beaches of Cape May. At the end of the day, he loved nothing better than curling himself up on Maddie's lap and falling fast asleep."

"Hooch, the Philly street dog. He didn't let cancer stop him from counter surfing and scoring bananas while capturing all your hearts."

"Ariel, who despite her body missing back legs, loved flying around in her cart, enjoying a walk wherever her mom traveled."

"LA was one of the oldest looking dogs we've ever seen, with lumps and bumps everywhere. The Hollywood star loved sunning herself on the front porch and awaiting my arrival home."

"Monkey, the guy who inspired it all. A little mutt we fell head over heels for, and in whose name we started Monkey's House."

"And last. The love of my life, Maddie. The woman who gave up her life so others could have one. Giving life and love to homeless dogs with terminal illnesses. Those discarded by the ones they trusted the most, when they needed them most. She gave them a loving family."

"Maddie lived her dash more than anybody else I know. She would tell you to 'Live your dash' by helping others live theirs."

Josh weakens from the magnitude of losing his love. Reciting her eulogy brings it all home. He takes a few moments and a sip of water as he composes himself. "Maddie, I miss you; I'll always love you. You are with our children now, give them a hug for me. God brought you home to care for our family. There's an outpouring of love for you." Lifting a bunch of leashes in every color of the rainbow high above his head. "Honey, you'll need these leashes in heaven for all our pups."

Just three days after the memorial, the lawyers once again set their sights on Monkey's House. Maddie and Josh held them off the past year, but this time, they come after Josh with vigor. The vultures launch a new attack to acquire the property. Eminent domain is still their goal, but they now claim that, without Maddie, the canine hospice expert, the dogs will suffer so the sanctuary needs to be closed and the dogs sent to local shelters.

Over the past months, they garnered connections with state politicians, donating into their political campaigns. The developers are building a larger contingency of experts and political muscle to challenge Josh and Monkey's House.

Josh and Maddie gave their lives together to the dogs of Monkey's House. Getting it off the ground took years, despite many struggles and setbacks. But they pushed forward, never giving up on their dream and their mission. Josh will fight to the ends of the earth to protect his dogs. Right now, this has to take a back seat. Maddie occupies his mind.

After a few days, Josh musters up strength to do what he must. Preciously holding the love of his life—Maddie's urn in his hands—he walks out towards the back field with a set of colorful leashes draped over his shoulder. Those close to him never asked where Maddie's final resting place would be. Josh knows the ultimate place. It's in heaven with their family. As for her ashes, they would remain on their little farm, among family.

For over twenty years, Josh had buried the dogs of Monkey's House on the farm, their home. Even before their non-profit, it was a given all their animals would live forever on their little farm. Friends, aunts, and uncles all knew spreading her ashes was something he would do alone, not unlike the burial of every dog. It was his time to say goodbye. One soul saying a last farewell to another. He found the burials peaceful, his ultimate connection with each one. In the heavens, he'd gaze, praying for God to take care of them. He would ask Monkey to show them the ropes in heaven. Conversely, he assumed the pup crossing the Bridge would fill their furry children in on how their parents were doing and all the shenanigans going on at Monkey's House.

The dogs' resting place overlooks the pond and their house. It's off the final turn home from the pack walks they took in the backfield. As he walks to the hallowed grounds, he stops, looking at the graves, and in his mind, he sees Maddie with every dog. He drops the leashes and keeps walking past them to the back of the field where their horses are buried. Bending to his knees over the grave of Zeus, her soulmate steed, he sprinkles a handful of ash. "Maddie, I can imagine you and Zeus riding into the waves on the beach, or weaving your way through the sandy roads in the Pines."

Eyes welling up, he hears birds chirping in the trees. Looking into the hedgerow, he witnesses a sign, like he has many times before when saying his precious goodbyes. Today, the sun shines on the most vibrant chest of a bluebird, a more vivid blue than he's ever seen. Resting on one knee, imagining they are once again together, riding on a sandy trail, the flitter of the bird's wings brings him back to earth. He now makes his way over to Brit's and Olympus's graves and takes some ashes in his palm and as he slowly wiggles his fingers releasing them. "Thank you for all you've given me."

Making his way back towards the house, at the edge of their magical field, he's once again standing upon Monkey's House holy ground. This is where hundreds of dogs are peacefully resting. Josh digs a small hole in the center of the graves, grabs the leashes, folding them a few times so they will fit. He realizes the red one has Buddy's name on it, the very first leash he saw the day the post office delivered them. Once finished patting the dirt down on top of them, he picks up the urn and slowly walks between the rows, spreading her ashes, ensuring Maddie will be eternally with every dog. "Lord, please take good care of Maddie and my family. Monkey, I know you and the others will be excited to see your mother. Tell her I miss her so… take care of her. I'll be with you all again someday soon."

Coming Home

It's been a while since Maddie passed, and the letter she wrote Josh in her last days sits on his bedstand. To Josh, it's hard to believe it's only been a little over a year since she's been gone, the anguish of missing her is making time creep by. The appearance of the letter and envelope seem to align with his perception of time: they appear ancient from the constant handling. He reads it every night to feel close to Maddie.

It sat there, pristine for the first month after her death, though he desperately wanted to read her words, to hear her voice in his head. Yet, the idea hurt so badly, wrapping him in knots. Josh feared once he opened it, she would be gone once and for all. He was thankful he finally gave in as it seemed to bring back a part of her. The hair Maddie stuffed in the envelope, from dogs lying by her side that night, brought back heartfelt memories—from Sora's pendant, to the dog's Christmas globes, even her horse, Zeus's mane. He knew Maddie hoped it would ease his pain.

It's been a struggle without Maddie by his side. She was the one person in his life who really knew him, his love and lifelong companion. Josh's heart aches night and day, but it especially hits home after the last dog is walked for the evening and all the volunteers have gone home.

How could a house full of dogs and love feel so empty? Those thoughts swirl inside his head every evening. Josh is extremely lonely without his best friend by his side. Besides missing her so deeply, he also feels he may be failing her with his lack of medical knowledge. Maddie's canine medical expertise was vast, while Josh's only scratches the surface. The argument the developers asserted in their legal challenge to close Monkey's House sits deeply in the back of his mind.

The added stress of fighting to save their sanctuary over the past year weighs heavily on his heart. He hates the fact that a majority of the donations in Maddie's name for the dogs had to be used for legal fees. With the economy in shambles and the onset of another great recession, those funds could've made a difference in dogs' lives. He's hopeful the state of the economy will at least put a hold on developing the luxury golf community. But mostly, he despises them for consuming any of his attention at a time he could have been reminiscing about his love.

His self-doubt occupies every major decision affecting Monkey's House residents, and he wonders if he can continue to make such a difference in the dogs' lives. He's lost a fair number of dogs to their illnesses, and although it happens every year, he worries if any were his fault. Despite his concerns, he continues to take in hospice dogs, giving his all to make sure the time they have remaining is special.

Josh starts losing interest in activities he once enjoyed. It's taking a toll on his health as well. He's lost weight from skipping meals due to lack of appetite. The constant thought of being inadequate in caring for the dogs leads him down a path he had avoided all of his adult life, drinking. Josh drinks alcohol every evening, hoping it will dull the yearnings for times past and to rid himself of the loneliness. Losing Maddie left a dark hole in his heart. First, it was a couple of beers to help relax, which escalated into hard liquor. Some nights, two drinks turn into three, four or more. He loathes that he's becoming like his parents—"five o'clock alcoholics"—the label he gave them as a teenager.

The model family, that's what most from the outside would believe of the family he grew up in. His grandfather, a first generation American, started a successful business through hard work and determination. Josh's father joined in the family business after serving in the Korean war, taking over upon the death of his grandfather. His mother was a stay-at-home mom caring for Josh and his two older sisters. His oldest sister, Vicki, excelled in both academics and sports. The other sister, Debbie, mastered breaking all the boy's hearts.

The Kelly family was perceived as upstanding in the small blue-collar town of Roebling, New Jersey. Josh's father was a member of many of the town's business organizations and, along with his mother, was well known in social circles. However, perceptions can deceive and alcohol was the demon that twisted itself into all hidden aspects of their lives, leading to a secretly broken family. Childhood memories haunt Josh to this day. A verbally, abusive father, triggered by alcoholism, was a nightly occurrence manifested by drink after drink upon his arrival home from work. Fear would run down Josh's spine as he would hear the clanking of the plates and silverware being pulled from kitchen cabinets and drawers, a sign dinner would be served soon. The old cuckoo clock set him into a trance waiting for the little door to open and hear the bird chirp six times. Dinner at the Kelly house was a tinderbox, always ready to blow. The trigger could have been a meal not cooked to his father's liking, Vicki receiving any grade other than an "A," or Josh's chores not being completed to his father's expectations. Josh especially hated his assigned seat alongside his father, who not only decided what he would eat but if he should even add salt, pepper or any other condiments.

He despised his father for creating nightmarish recollections of his childhood instead of wonderful memories. He longed for experiences like those in Norman Rockwell paintings of years past, with a dad and son playing catch, building a tree house, or going fishing together. Instead, Josh still sees a little boy with nerves wrenching his stomach into tight knots—just a child, crouched down in one of his hiding places, in his bedroom closet or under the vanity in the bathroom. Making himself invisible never seemed to mask the shouting that went into the night.

Josh justified his few drinks, even though he feared it was turning into a habit, the demon he despised—the five o'clock alcoholic. He consoled himself: *Who is it hurting?* he thought, confident it wasn't harming anybody except himself. He'd sit at home, not drinking and driving. Daily chores were done around Monkey's House, posts went out on social media, fundraisers continued, and of course, the dogs were well cared for.

Yet, despite telling himself all was okay, it was also eating at his soul. He hated his drinking, night after night, which seemed to bring back those dreadful childhood memories haunting him. Even worse were the thoughts of him becoming his parents, which many times led to yet another drink to cloud his recollections. In the end, it was his need to escape the pain of missing Maddie that drove his desire to continue drinking. Much like the perception of the Kelly family in their small town, Josh's façade was deceiving to all except himself.

This dependence went on for a year after Maddie's passing until tonight and the near death of Tootsie, a beautiful Irish setter, which opened his eyes. At nine o'clock in the evening, Tootsie has a major seizure and needs to be rushed to the 24-hour veterinary hospital. However, at this late hour, Josh is in no shape to drive. In a panic, he calls several volunteers until he finally connects with Holly, who agrees to drive them to the hospital. They arrive in the nick of time, within mere minutes of losing Tootsie.

A few hours later, Tootsie is comfortable, lying on a cushion by the foot of Josh's bed, recovering. Sober now, Josh falls to his knees, elbows on the bed, with his hands folded in prayer. He can barely breathe—the events of the evening is the spark, lighting every bit of kindling, the emotions built up within him since the day Maddie died. "Lord, help

me. I can't do this myself." The room is quiet. The dogs
had been asleep for a couple of hours. "I can't run Monkey's
House on my own. I need Maddie. Tell me everything will
be okay." He rests his head in the palms of his hands and
breaks down, sobbing.

Josh sees a vision of Maddie walking alongside Matt in
a rolling field of wildflowers. Matt was a beautiful yellow
Labrador retriever they rescued shortly after opening their
sanctuary. Memories of Matt fill his soul as he realizes his
life is not about him, but about how to serve others, what
he's been doing for so many dogs. He recounts every detail
of Matt's time with them. It's like he's meant to relive Matt's
story from close to thirty years ago.

He recalls Matt coming to them after one snowy evening
in January. Maddie received a phone call from Sergeant
Allison Clark, a Burlington County SPCA humane officer.
Sergeant Clark and her partner were called by the police to a
vacant residence a few towns away. The police stumbled upon
an animal neglect case and needed help to remove five dogs
found living in the abandoned home. There was no electricity
or running water, nor a sign of any dog food. The place was
in shambles and all the dogs were in poor health, especially
Matt, who needed emergency veterinary care. They rushed
him to a veterinary hospital and had emergency eye surgery;
the result was the removal of his right eye. The other dogs
went to the shelter to recover. Sergeant Clark's call was to
ask Maddie to foster Matt back to health while they built
a case against the owner. The next day when Matt arrived,

they could see he'd been through the ringer. He was filthy, severely underweight, and unable to walk. Matt's horrible journey brought him to Maddie and Josh, a home completely opposite of the horrendous conditions he had lived in before his rescue. He had a new life now; he was part of their family.

After living without food for a long period, Matt was thirty pounds underweight and needed a custom meal plan designed for him. Multiple small meals throughout the day would slowly bring his weight back to a healthy level. Matt now had one other major health issue to address; he couldn't walk on his own. His body had been getting nutrients from anywhere it could, including his own muscles. They purchased a special harness, allowing Josh to lift him. In this way, with the harness supporting most of his weight, he could toddle along.

Matt also received physical therapy; an underwater treadmill helped him walk with the aid of buoyancy from the water. Over time, Matt was happily walking again, playing with his favorite toy, a tennis ball. Within a couple of months, he gained back those much needed thirty pounds; once again, he was a proud, handsome yellow lab. He enjoyed his new life on the farm and loved his walks with Maddie or Josh around the property. For the first time in his life, he was a cheerful dog. Experiencing genuine love. Matt sure loved being the farm dog.

The SPCA humane police were building a case against the owner, who was now inquiring about Matt and wanting to see him. Although Maddie didn't want her anywhere near Matt, sadly, the law tends to not be on the dog's side; most states consider them to be property. They were ordered to allow the owner to see Matt, which was an upsetting experience for both Matt and Maddie.

Matt loved his life at Monkey's House, as he made many friends, big and small, even befriending their resident cat, Sammy. Everything was falling into place when Maddie noticed a few changes in Matt and took him to see their veterinarian. They diagnosed him with bone cancer, and movement of any kind eventually became excruciating for him. When it was time to be released to the Rainbow Bridge, the "owner" would not consent. The Kellys pursued legal channels to release Matt's soul from his broken body. It took time, time Matt did not have, as he was in agony. Maddie and Josh fought hard for Matt and finally won. Those who loved him, humans and dogs, surrounded Matt as he gently made his way to heaven, wrapped in a prayer blanket.

As if losing Matt was not bad enough, the nightmare with this "owner" continued when she decided she wanted Matt's body back. At Monkey's House, ALL their dogs live there forever. Their spirits go to the Rainbow Bridge, as their bodies remain on the farm. This demand was heartbreaking. It felt like they let Matt down when they had to give up his body.

The day before Thanksgiving, six months after Matt's passing, Sergeant Clark contacted Maddie. After a long court battle, the owner reclaimed her living dogs, but left Matt behind in the shelter's freezer. Josh jumped into action, called the shelter, and told them he was coming for Matt.

He hopped into his car and raced to the shelter. Their love for Matt never diminished and, in his heart, he knew Matt was living his best life at the Bridge. When he got to the shelter, the staff had prepared Matt for his final journey. Josh gently put him on the backseat and headed home. As he drove down their country road, reaching their little farm, it lifted a tremendous weight off of his heart. Matt came home to be with his family.

The vivid story of Matt that came to him tonight has him realizing... he, too, has finally come home. For a year, he's agonized every moment over losing Maddie—it's too much for him. "Heaven help me." There's a touch on his right side... then on his left. Angels have sprung upon him, the ones with fur and paws. After a few deep breaths, wiping away tears, he sees Randy, Tiggy and many other dogs surrounding him, providing him solace. He realizes God has reached out to him and now understands this is not the first time he's been touched.

Throughout their lives together, caring for God's creatures, Josh and Maddie have been doing his work. In the past, Josh could push through challenging times, knowing there was a guiding spirit. Times may be harder without Maddie, but he knows he's not alone. He needs to ask for help; he needs to pull from within, but mostly from above, asking for guidance through the difficult times. It's at this point he fully understands the mission must go on. Josh gathers a pad and pen and sits back in bed with his pups. He's finally writing a letter to Maddie.

The words to the love of his life seem to come easy; no rewrites or edits are needed tonight. After finishing up, he wipes the lone tear running down his cheek and hugs Randy, who made his way over to Josh, and now lays across his lap. Josh's life with Maddie flows through his mind like a movie reel. The scenes are in no particular order, sporadically reinforcing the wonderful times they shared—life's journey filled with love, laughter, and even sorrow. In each vision, they are together.

Josh is afraid he won't be able to get to sleep tonight. He wants to be breathing in Maddie's scent and the warmth of her presence, to tell her how much he loves her and the difference she's made in his life. He folds the paper and slips it into the crumpled envelope that holds his last connection to Maddie. As his head hits the pillow, he reaches his arm out and places the envelope back on the bedstand. Out of the corner of his eye, he notices a sliver of moonlight shining through a gap in the curtains. The ray reaches its thin beam directly onto the letters, as if highlighting the magnitude of each memory within, the memories which tonight lie heavily in his heart. Suddenly, he flips the covers off and makes his way out of bed and over to the closet. The dogs glance at him, wondering where he's going this late at night. Josh puts on his heavy robe and slippers, grabs the letters, then ensures Tootsie is doing well. Randy perks up; the others have returned to a sound sleep. "Okay, you can come."

Once downstairs, Josh gets Randy leashed and grabs a flashlight on the way out the door. The full moon is illuminating the night sky. Tonight, a flashlight isn't needed as he heads towards the backfield. Randy leads him to the special resting place of the Monkey's House pups, where Maddie's essence remains strong. Josh takes a seat on the concrete bench overlooking his family, with Randy sitting by his feet. The pond in the background is calm, except for the splashing from the fountain and the occasional croaking of a bullfrog. Josh flips on the flashlight and illuminates the letter.

"Maddie, I wrote you a letter. I wanted to for way too long. I just couldn't find the words until tonight."

My Love Maddie,

The past year has been unbearable without you. I've missed you so. Every night, I hold your letter close to my heart. I read it before my head hits the pillow. I hope it spurs dreams of yesteryear, and I believe it often does, bringing you back to me. However, it's also bittersweet. It brings back the great love we had, but quickly reminds me you're no longer by my side.

This letter is a long time coming. I'm sorry. I've been struggling with your loss, my confidence in caring for our dogs, and I'm ashamed to say, without you, I'm not as strong as I wish I would have been. In delaying writing this letter, I denied you were gone. Tonight, I realize you are not here in person, but I have you and God with me in spirit. Knowing this has lifted the weight of the world off my shoulders. I'm letting my fears fall through my fingers like sand, into the hands of those who will always be with me.

I'm smitten when I think back to the first day I laid eyes upon your beautiful face. When you stepped through the barn door, I prayed something special might happen. How comfortable we felt together on our ride. Your spunk captivated me as you took off back to the barn, leaving me in the dust. At the end of our blind date, I could see clearly, you were the one for me.

I miss you from the time I wake up, knowing you won't be on my daily journeys. From the simple trip to the veterinary office, the beach outing, or Santa's visit. From our early years, with our Sunday morning snuggles, to the more recent snuggles surrounded by our family. Being an early riser, I loved watching you sleep after you scooped up Buck, Tiggy, or one of our other babies into your arms. You always looked so content holding a dog. All was right in our little world.

It warmed my heart to read you loved our walks together. Please don't be sorry for not going on them all. Like horseback riding for you, walking with the dogs is my great stress reliever. My utopia was walking with you, hand in hand. The memories of our walks on the beach with our furry children, strolling into the sunsets, always brought a smile to my face.

My skin still feels your gentle touch, my lips taste your moist tender kisses, and with each recollection of our bodies as one, my heart races and my breath deepens. I realize now you are here. You're on the path every dog takes, but most of all, you're leading me through my journey, my final chapter.

Maddie, I know where I'm needed now. You can rest assured; I'll carry on with our mission as you care for our family in heaven. When I dream, I will dream of walking hand in hand with you along the beach with the sounds of waves and water washing across our feet. We'll witness the most amazing sunset, yet it will all pale at the depth of our love, deeper than the ocean itself.

Until we're together once again, my love.

PART 3

The Journey

BACK IN THE PRESENT

Southern Comfort

An orderly makes his way over to Josh and Kaitlyn, introducing himself. "Howdy Mistah Kelly, aah'm Raymond, but y'all can calls me Ray," he drawls as he points to his name tag with a big grin on his face. He's a young man with a strong, calming, deep southern accent, fitting for his large stature. Josh, who's now anxious about what lies ahead of him, squints his eyes, straining to see the name tag. Yep, that's what it says—"RAY," in all caps no less, along with a yellow smiley face sticker attached to the side.

"Ray, did anybody ever tell you you're one cheerful guy?"

"Mistah Kelly, aah try to bring a li'l 'Ray' a sunshine where evah it's needed. Aah love mah job. Who else gets tah meet new folks ever' day, good ol' folks like y'all, who appreciate whatcha do for 'em? Even if it just transportin' 'em 'round the hospital, aah'm happy tah bring 'em a little joy, takin' their minds off their troubles. Aah only have a short amount a time with 'em and found a big ol' smile and a cheery disposition do the trick."

Josh can tell Ray loves to talk; he may have finally met his match. "Well, you put a smile on my face, Ray. Please call me Josh."

"Okay… aah'll call you Mistah Josh. Mah momma taught me the value of respectin' others, especially mah elders… no offense." He winks and puts his large hand on Josh's shoulder in a reassuring way. "She said tah always use their proper names when addressin' folks. Aah think Mistah Josh sounds proper… what y'all think?"

"I like your momma's philosophy; she sounds like a wise woman. Mr. Josh sounds proper, but with a personal twist. I like it." Josh changes the tone of his voice, making it raspy, city like. "I can calls you Ray?" Josh and Ray laugh heartily as they both know the reference to an old 70s beer commercial, "You can call me Ray." It must have been decades before Ray was even born, but he explains how he'd seen the clips on YouTube many times before. Ray points out he has a fascination with the 70s and 80s, especially the music and commercials, spending hours watching old video clips nightly.

After the laughter wanes, Josh realizes he hasn't introduced Ray to Kaitlyn.

"Ray, this is my great niece, Kaitlyn." He remembers not to introduce her as Katie.

"Howdy, Miss Kaitlyn, let's finish gettin' y'alls uncle all squared away and down tah the OR." Kaitlyn smiles and nods politely. Ray's such a friendly, gentle soul. He's right where he's supposed to be, putting patients at ease when they are under intense worry. She can tell his jovial banter with Josh certainly helped his demeanor.

Betty walks towards them with a syringe. Ray looks at

her, glances over at Josh and winks, then turns back to Betty. In a deep voice, he inquires, "Aah kin calls you Betty?" This reopens flood gates of laughter so lively they are both on the verge of busting a gut. Betty steps back, letting them get whatever this is out of their systems. Kaitlyn wears a simple grin, one that indicates she has no clue what they are talking about, but it doesn't bother her. She's pleased to see her uncle relaxed before surgery, and the laughter eases her own tension, too.

Josh finally stops laughing long enough to shout out, while slapping the mattress, "I can call you Betty." He launches into another state of hysteria. Ray is bent in half, laughing so hard he can't straighten up. Two strangers, who will likely never see each other again, have connected, and enjoy these few special moments together, as if they've been friends for years. Nurse Betty stands with an inquisitive look on her face while Kaitlyn continues to smile.

Finally, curiosity gets the best of Kaitlyn and she asks, "Explain the Betty reference. I've heard the Ray one before, but never the Betty."

"Paul Simon had a huge hit song in the 80s called 'You can call me Al.' A verse in the song had a line, 'I can call you Betty.' Find the video on YouTube. It stars Chevy Chase along with Paul Simon. Maddie and I loved that video—sort of dry humor, but so funny."

As the laughter quiets down, Betty can finally give Josh his sedative to help him relax before going into the operating room. Ray looks at his watch, eyes wide, and he quickly turns and glares at Josh. Suddenly they all realize his surgery is scheduled to begin, like... right now. He effortlessly pushes the gurney Josh is lying in down the hallway as Kaitlyn walks alongside with a firm hold of Josh's arm, her eyes narrow as wrinkles appear between her eyebrows. Josh has a knack for being able to read people's emotions by their expressions and mannerisms. What might be written off as intuition was more accurately the combined insights of a man in his late eighties—one who's lived long enough and seen enough countenances to understand. The heart and mind are seen through outward expressions. Whatever the source, he knows Kaitlyn is worried about his surgery.

As they continue briskly down the hall, a bum wheel on the gurney makes itself known. It wasn't noticeable at normal speeds, but since Ray is now whipping along with Josh's gurney, every few feet it pulls slightly to the right. Under normal circumstances, this would have driven Josh nuts, but today he doesn't seem to mind it. Maybe the sedative is kicking in, or he just doesn't want to upset Kaitlyn more than she is already.

Josh takes his other hand and puts it on Kaitlyn's forearm. "All is going to be fine, although this wheel is freaking me out," he assures her with a big smile on his face.

Ray also wants to keep it light, which is part of what makes him ideal for this job. "Well, Mistah Josh, we wuz short a gurneys, so aah had tah makeshift a few outta some local grocery carts." The atmosphere's a bit more at ease when they finally make it to the operating room.

To Josh's surprise, Dr. Sena is waiting at the entrance. In his typically gentle tone of voice he says, "Josh, they have your good luck charm ready to give to you inside. You won't see me after surgery, but I'll come by tomorrow on my rounds and see how you're doing." Kaitlyn leans over and lands a peck on her uncle's cheek. Ray pats his shoulder as the operating room team wheels him in through the doors. As Kaitlyn and Dr. Sena are ready to go their separate ways, unbeknownst to them, Ray has clasped his hands in prayer. As they hear Ray start reciting a brief prayer for Josh, they both stop in their tracks, turning back towards Ray and bowing their heads.

"Lord, as Mistah Josh goes in for surgery, we ask y'all tah look over our deah friend and protect him. Grant y'alls peace tah the surgeons tah work with y'alls spirit tah bring resto-ration. Lead him through the darkest a times and into the light. We'all know when he's most vulnerable, y'all be with him, that y'alls love, resto-ration and grace will hold him safe. Ah-men."

The prayer brings Kaitlyn back to her first Sunday morning church service in college, and seeing Carson in the congregation. They'd met the night before at one of those awkward, freshman meet-and-greets sponsored by their dorm complex. California was a fresh experience for a young girl, born and raised in the mid-west. Her roommate, Madison, convinced Kaitlyn to attend the event. Since she didn't know anyone at the school, Kaitlyn figured it would give her a chance to meet some of the other students in her complex.

The gathering brought together a peculiar mix of students, ranging from extroverts like Carson, who would most likely run for student council and become president, to the introverts such as Kaitlyn. She quietly observed the crowd, studying their personalities. Kaitlyn wasn't looking to make lifelong friends at this first event. She was trying to figure out who she would risk saying "hello" to, or who may approach her.

Kaitlyn admired those who easily mingled with a large group of strangers, talking like old friends. She remained on the perimeter with the other wall-flowers when Carson caught her eye. Tall and handsome, with an athletic physique, it surprised her when he walked right over and introduced himself. They talked about what brought them to UCSD and their hobbies. They agreed to meet up again at a future gathering because of their mutual attraction.

Little did she know, she'd see him again the very next morning. After the service, Carson asked her to breakfast, which led to a wonderful relationship. She soon knew she'd found the love of her life. However, four years later, after the accident, her dreams of living a life with Carson were gone.

~⑨

With Josh now on the operating table, the room is abuzz, as the staff is readying for a successful surgery. The cardiothoracic surgeon, Dr. Ng, reassures Josh all will go smoothly while he introduces the operating team. "Hi Mr. Kelly, how are we doing this morning? Dr. Smits will be your anesthesiologist today. You're in skilled hands. She's our best. Dr. Klein will assist me, and we have nurses, Elizabeth and Arthur as well. Over there, in the corner next to all the equipment, is Richard, our perfusionist. He's our technical wizard, ensuring your heart doesn't miss a beat during surgery."

With a grin, Josh gazes over at Richard and softly says, "Ham and cheese on rye, please." He's the only one laughing. Everybody else has a puzzled look on their face. If they didn't know better, they would have assumed Dr. Smits had started the anesthesia already. Josh's statement was a little odd. But in fact, it's a memory he has of Maddie, a question she answered years ago during his original heart surgery. Although Josh is a dog person, his biggest trait matches that of a cat: curiosity. Maddie called it being nosey. When he asked her what schooling a perfusionist goes through, she said they have special training and are certified. Of course, Maddie jokingly added they may have been making hoagies at Wawa, the local convenience store, a few months ago.

"We'll be getting underway shortly, and I'll turn it over to Dr. Smits in a minute. You'll do great... it's going to be the best day of your life." Dr. Ng gives Josh a wink as he heard him give this quote to Dr. Sena earlier.

"Monkey's leash, where's Monkey's leash?" Josh fixates on his good luck charm. The spirit of not only Monkey, but mostly Maddie. He needs her with him at this moment.

Elizabeth steps over to Josh and rests her hand on his arm. "I'm not sure what you're looking for... a leash?"

"I have it right here, Mr. Kelly." Arthur rushes over and places it in his hand as Josh hastily wraps his fingers around it, forming a tight grip.

Dr. Smits is now positioned up by Josh's head. She lets him know it will be a few more minutes before they begin the procedure, and how once they administer the anesthesia, he'll quickly fade into grogginess and fall fast asleep. Upon waking, he won't remember a thing from the few hours of the surgery.

"Mr. Kelly, I'm aware of Monkey's House and love your mission. Thank you for all you do for our four-legged friends. We adopted a little Toto dog, a terrier-yorkie mix three years ago. Her name is Trixie, and she's the love of my life."

"We've had terriers and yorkies over the years. However, there was one who stood out, Crazy Eve." Dr. Smits clearly sees the impish smirk on Josh's face as he thinks about Eve.

"Would you like to tell me about Eve, or should I say Crazy Eve?" That surely was an invitation for Josh to talk about this family, and he obliges, telling her all about Eve's antics.

"Out of all the dogs we've had over the years, Eve had to be the most mischievous. She was definitely the wackiest, bringing her comedy act to Monkey's House daily. Maddie called it the 'Eve bat-crap-crazy hour.'"

Eve was a little yorkie, and when she made her way to the Kellys, she had a long list of aliments: blind, emaciated, kidney and liver issues, with uncontrolled diabetes. After being on a healthy diet, supplements, and insulin injections, she turned around. As Eve gained weight, her kidney and liver values normalized and she could have a dental procedure to remove all her rotten teeth. Four teeth were all that remained. Once healed, she was full of joy and committed with her whole heart.

"Oh, did I mention Eve was crazy?" Josh says with a grin.

Dr. Smits laughs. "You've described her as crazy a few times. What do you mean?"

Josh is in his glory, continuing on about Eve. "She tried to kill our vacuum cleaner."

"You're kidding, right?"

"Nope. One morning, Maddie woke up and heard growling. Worried a fight was imminent, she jumped out of bed to witness Eve in an all-out attack on our poor, innocent, unsuspecting... vacuum cleaner. It was able to stand its ground until Maddie stopped laughing long enough to pull her off."

Although Dr. Smits is wearing a mask, Josh can see a big smile shining through her eyes. "Well, to be honest, I don't like housework either. I've been known to rough up my vacuum from time to time, too."

"Have you ever had a dog that was too smart? She's one of those dogs. Like a rebellious teenager who makes you want to pull your hair out. Yet the one who sets up your remote or smartphone in a minute."

Dr. Smits continues to prep for the procedure, yet carries on with the conversation to keep Josh's mind distracted from the pending operation. "I have two teenagers; I know exactly what you mean." She'll be able to administer anesthesia in a few minutes. "Mr. Kelly, do you have any other stories about Eve?"

Josh obliges. "Eve was glued to Maddie's hip and was always on the couch with her. When Maddie got up and left her iPad behind, Eve changed the language settings. Once to Portuguese, and another time to what I believed to be Korean."

"How did you get it back to English?"

"It wasn't easy. I'm sure Eve got a good chuckle watching me struggle to get it switched back. I could have used your kids."

"Mr. Kelly, I'll be starting the anesthesia now. We'll see you again when you wake up. This is when I normally ask patients to count back from 100, but you can continue with your stories. I'm enjoying them. Remember, you'll feel groggy soon. That's normal."

Josh smiles dreamily, continuing with his stories. "Eve loved her life at Monkey's House. She thoroughly enjoyed all the field trips and any type of adventure. Her favorite trip was to the Jersey Shore. She loved walking in the water and all the exotic ocean smells. On one trip, after loading all the dogs back onto Waggin' One, Eve wriggled her way out of her crate and jumped into the driver's seat... Luckily, her legs didn't reach the pedals... yet somehow... she hit the automatic door locks... and..."

Anticipation

Kaitlyn senses worry, hope, and despair as she enters the waiting room, each person on their own journey as they wait to hear of their loved ones' conditions. She notices an empty sofa in the far corner and heads towards it. On her way, she passes a couple in deep sorrow. The young man is comforting his partner. She's clinching a little stuffed pony as whimpering turns into streaming tears.

Finally, she takes a seat only to find out the sofa is hard as a rock. No surprise: its typical hospital furniture: sterile, red, vinyl-covered, lacking adequate cushioning. She tosses her backpack upon the small coffee table shared between her and another sofa. Its occupant doesn't look up. The middle-aged woman is intensely praying, as she twists her wedding band.

Kaitlyn is thankful she's gotten the last empty seat in the waiting area. It's in an excellent location with a view down the hallway towards the operating rooms. She's passing the time on her smartphone, yet any little movement within the hall finds her jerking her head up and twisting to the left to scan for a doctor or nurse coming her way to give any shred of an update on her uncle's surgery. Directly in front of her, mounted on the wall, is a monitor listing all the patients and the stage of the procedure they're in—pre-op, surgery, or recovery. It doesn't display names because of privacy and HIPPA regulations, so a unique code identifies each patient so their loved ones can follow their progress.

Kaitlyn likes that those waiting could pick the unique code to identify their loved one, comprising of two letters along with four digits. Kaitlyn hesitated a few seconds when the receptionist asked for a code. Her face relaxed, and a smile appeared as she told the receptionist, "PR0614". It was perfect. The "PR" stood for the splendid memories from when she was a young girl, without a care in the world, spending summers with her aunt and uncle at their little beach house, Paws & Relax. The number 0614 was from the story her uncle told her this morning. The day of their first date, which began the life they shared for decades.

It's approaching three hours since Josh went into the operating room when Kaitlyn looks up at the monitor. "PR0614" is still in surgery. She knew this was going to be a long day. Aortic heart value replacement takes well over three hours, and sometimes upward of six. This is an operation requiring painstaking precision that can't be rushed. However, since this is Josh's second replacement, the doctors warned her of the potential for complications that would most likely cause the overall procedure to be longer than a first-time valve replacement.

Josh's initial replacement surgery was twenty-six years ago. Open heart surgery was the norm back then. He's told Kaitlyn more than once he thankfully wears the "zipper," an eight-inch scar, attesting to its success. However, today, Dr. Ng will perform the common transcatheter aortic valve replacement procedure, which is known as TAVR. Dr. Ng will access Josh's heart through a blood vessel in the groin. Through a tiny incision, a catheter is inserted and guided by imaging technology to the heart and the affected aortic valve. Kaitlyn is relieved to know her uncle's surgery will be less invasive this time, but reminds herself a second replacement procedure has a greater potential for complications, which does little to ease her growing anxiety.

Holly arrived at the hospital a few hours after Josh and Kaitlyn. She'd have come sooner, but had to prep the morning meals for the dogs while Tracey and Bob handled the serving process. The two of them would also manage the after-breakfast walks and whatever chores needed to be done throughout the day.

Kaitlyn notices Holly walking down the hall towards the waiting room and quickly waves her arms and calls out, "Holly, over here." Before Josh and Kaitlyn left the house this morning, Holly told her she'd be there for Josh, but equally, to lend emotional support to her.

Anyone can sense an immediate sigh of relief in Kaitlyn as she pushes herself off the couch. Being alone and worrying in a hospital is an even more stressful combination for Kaitlyn. The circumstances of her accident, the recovery, and mostly the loss of her love have been on her mind; not to mention the worry for her uncle. There's angst in Kaitlyn's face as Holly gives her a caring hug. "How did things go this morning? Did you hear anything yet?" They both sit down.

"It's too early to know much. He went into surgery two and a half hours ago. I'm hoping to hear something soon." Kaitlyn points to the monitor, "Uncle Josh is 'PR0614' and as you can see, he's still in surgery. From what his doctor told me, he'll probably be in for a while. Everything went fine with pre-op this morning... well, almost everything."

"Why, what happened?" Holly's eyes bulge out.

"Sorry, I should have stated it differently. Everything went fine. Uncle Josh was a little perturbed when his nurse almost didn't let him take Monkey's leash into surgery with him."

Holly's eyes roll as her voice elevates. "Oh, boy. Josh planned for this in advance. Sure he didn't take too kindly to her."

"Don't worry. His cardiologist, Dr. Sena, quickly got it all squared away. In fact, I don't believe Uncle Josh had time to get upset."

"Dr. Sena is such a caring doctor. When I brought Josh here for his pre-surgery checkup, I met him. Did you know your Aunt Maddie used to work with him years ago? I think that's another reason Josh likes him so much."

"Uncle Josh told me. It's always a plus to have a good relationship with your doctor."

"So true. Maddie always said you should want to hug your veterinarian. Guess you should also want to hug your doctor."

Kaitlyn is uneasy discussing medical issues. Rightfully so, considering the enormity of the impacts her accident had on her life. The surgeries and rehab she endured, dwarfed further by the challenges she's faced over the past few years, still make it difficult for her to talk about any medical topics. She sits quietly for some time.

Holly cuts through the awkward silence. "Okay, so what stories did your uncle tell you on the ride over?"

"He told me about sweet LA. Actually, their entire trip to see Oprah. Sounds like Aunt Maddie and Uncle Josh had a romantic trip to Los Angeles. They even came home with a dog."

"LA was the only dog they ever brought home on a flight, or should I say, a private jet. LA took to Josh; he was her person."

"I could tell he loved LA. He also enjoyed telling me all about Hooch and his banana fetish."

"What a character Hooch was. He loved the beach. I remember on one of our beach trips, Josh brought along a banana…"

Kaitlyn quickly jumps in, "To bury it in the sand for him to find, right?"

"That's right. But there was another beach trip involving Hooch. Ginny was walking him when she lost her grip on his leash. Hooch ran into the ocean and swam into the surf. He was determined to reach England. Josh jumped in after him. The water was freezing and the waves unusually high for New Jersey—probably more like your waves in California. Josh finally reached Hooch at the height of a wave and the next thing you know, it caught both of them."

"What! You're kidding me, right?" Kaitlyn is sitting on the edge of the couch.

"If I didn't know better, I'd swear they surfed that day. Not gracefully. But surfed." Holly chuckles.

"Wow, what a story."

"Wait, there's more. As they got closer to the beach, we noticed Hooch had a banana in his mouth. It came out of Josh's pocket during the rescue. Hooch looked thrilled; it might have been the best day ever for Hooch. Josh, not so much." Kaitlyn laughs at the imagery of the story.

Kaitlyn's smile fades and her eyes sharpen. "On a serious note, I found an official letter from the local zoning board. It appears they will close Monkey's House and take the property. What do you know about this? I mentioned it to my uncle. He said very little, and I didn't want to upset him on this day, of all days. What do you think?"

"Josh has been fighting them off for over ten years. Sadly, I've seen it take an emotional toll on him. He doesn't show it; he keeps it bottled up inside. But I believe he thinks he's failed Maddie."

Kaitlyn's jaw tightens, "He did not let Maddie down, or the dogs."

Holly nods in agreement. "I know he didn't. But I can't tell you much else... except it doesn't look good."

They sit quietly for a while, waiting, wondering, and praying. They hope Josh will be out of surgery soon.

After sitting with Holly for an hour, Kaitlyn notices a medical professional walking down the hall towards the waiting room. She assumes it's a doctor from the operating room; the blue foot covers and operating smock give it away.

She's approaching Kaitlyn, whose body suddenly becomes ridged. Forcing herself to relax a bit, she rolls her shoulders back and takes in a deep breath. Holly notices Kaitlyn's reaction and looks towards the hall, seeing what has drawn Kaitlyn's attention. The doctor makes her way over to Kaitlyn and Holly.

"Hi, I'm Dr. Lea," the young doctor announces. Kaitlyn and Holly quickly introduce themselves and are eager to hear what she has to tell them about Josh's surgery.

"Mr. Kelly, he's your uncle, I understand, correct?" Dr. Lea is a first-year resident whose tone is clipped and is meticulous in her approach. She clearly could use some work on her bedside mannerisms.

"Yes," Kaitlyn cautiously answers. The way Dr. Lea is talking is worrying her.

"Mr. Kelly is doing well," Dr. Lea goes on, explaining they are performing open heart surgery after all. The catheterization part of the TAVR procedure did not work as they had hoped. She states that the major difference in the procedures was recovery time. Obviously, with open heart surgery, Josh will have a longer period of recovery.

Kaitlyn's emotions shift back and forth quickly: worried about the invasive procedure and the recovery time, relieved they could proceed even though the first option didn't work. Her anxiety level lessens but she speaks urgently, "Is the surgery done? I now see why it took much longer than expected. When will I be able to see him?" She is spitting out questions, rapid fire.

Unfortunately, Dr Lea offers too much detail on the surgery without noticing the impact it is having on Kaitlyn. Being her first year as an intern, hopefully Dr. Lea will develop more empathetic mannerisms. She clearly could take a lesson from Dr. Sena, who would have calmed Kaitlyn's anxiety with his gentle voice, assuring her everything would be fine and she'd see her uncle soon.

The surgery is taking longer than expected, but they are in the final stages. Holly had planned to stay with Kaitlyn longer if there were complications, but after hearing Josh's surgery status, everything appears to be on track now. She should have left thirty minutes ago to help care for the dogs and prepare their dinners.

Holly politely interrupts, "Kaitlyn, I'll stay a little longer to keep you company." Holly goes out into the hall and makes a quick call to Tracey. She tells her she is going to be late and gives instructions on preparing dinner, then makes her way back to Kaitlyn.

After a few minutes, Dr. Lea goes back towards the operating room. Holly, not a skilled storyteller like Josh or Maddie, decides now's a good time for one, especially after the awkwardness of the doctor's visit. "Would you like to hear how I became part of Monkey's House?"

"Sure, I'd love that. It may help ground me a little too." Her mind calms and the worries fade slightly. "What gave you the inkling to volunteer at Monkey's House? I mean, I love senior dogs, helping them out. But for many, the idea of losing a dog is too much to volunteer at a dog hospice."

"I'm a huge dog lover and have a small dog walking and boarding business. Shortly after Monkey's House opened, customers started telling me about an amazing sanctuary the next town over. I looked it up on social media and found myself intrigued with the approach your aunt and uncle took caring for hospice dogs. It was groundbreaking. I witnessed spectacular results and knew I had to be part of their exceptional organization. I even started fostering Monkey's House dogs at my house."

"Now you're the lead caregiver, along with Uncle Josh. I guess you can say you're surely a part of it now."

Holly smiles. "Maddie was so knowledgeable; I learned volumes from her. Honestly, I've probably only picked up a third of what she knew, and they consider me the expert now. Josh taught me determination, dedication and how to be efficient. Did I include efficiency?" They both chuckle, knowing how he hates wasting a second of time.

"To Josh's defense, I agreed with him ninety-eight percent of the time, but never let him know. Initially, I would overlook those little inefficiencies until Josh had to point them out to me. He'd make me so mad, because then they would start bugging me too."

"Like what?" Kaitlyn wants to hear more about her uncle. She witnessed it firsthand but assumed it was only her, a young girl he was educating in life.

"One day, I went into the garage, getting ready to prepare the meals. Josh walked over, holding a bolt cutter in one hand and the other full of metal latches, well the ends of the latches."

Most of the dogs eat in the garage in their own crate to ensure there's no "sharing" of food. Typically, they get their medicine and supplements served in with their meals. All the crates have two latches. Only one was needed. Volunteers would latch both, even during cleanup, with no dogs in them.

"More than once, I would hear Josh mumbling with his hands full of dogs, trying to unlatch the crates and open the doors." Holly laughs. "He put an end to that."

Holly then transitions the conversation to show how Josh has a great heart, how he built a strong bond with her son Justin over the years. Much like the relationship Kaitlyn has with her uncle.

When Holly started volunteering at Monkey's House, Justin was only four years old. He was too young to bring to their house, but a little over a year later, Justin became a regular fixture, coming along with his mom to visit and play with the dogs. He would even help his mom, walking dogs down the lane with her.

Dogs are noble companions for children, which was evidently true with Justin and many of the dogs they fostered for Monkey's House. Their relationships were much more than your normal dog and child companionship. Justin has autism spectrum disorder (ASD), a neurological and developmental disorder which affects how a person acts and interacts with others, communicates, and learns. When Justin was younger, dogs became an important part of his world. They were his best friends, not passing judgement—just pure love between two kindred souls. He was ecstatic at only having dogs as brothers and sisters.

Kaitlyn asks, "Wait a minute, he wouldn't be the boy who was crazy about Spiderman, would he?" Josh mentioned Justin in his Spiderman costumes to Kaitlyn when she was nine years old, on her first trip to North Cape May. She was going on and on about Wonder Woman and even had a Wonder Woman bathing suit.

"You got it. Justin was Spiderman, and Josh was Superman."

They hit it off, and Josh became like a grandfather to Justin. The debate about who was the greatest superhero went on for years. The pranking began when Justin gave Josh a Superman figurine. They took turns hiding it around the garage, seeing if the other could find Superman. As Justin got older, he would mow the grass and do odds-and-ends around the farm. Josh liked his company, as they often worked together.

Once Maddie and Josh purchased their beach house, Holly and Justin were regular occupants. However, rarely when Maddie and Josh were there, as one of them had to be at Monkey's House. Holly and family would head down when Paws & Relax was vacant. Eventually, Justin would go down with Maddie and Josh on short weekends to enjoy the beach and play in the water. Justin would bring one dog they were fostering; his favorite was Bugsy.

Bugsy was a cross between a Boston terrier and a pug—a "bug", thus the name Bugsy. He was Justin's private guardian, his rock. Frequently, when Justin was having one of his sensory overload episodes, Bugsy would come to the rescue. He'd go to his side and rest his head on his hip. Justin would slowly release his hand from his ear to rest it on Bugsy and gently pet his head; shortly after, his other hand would come down.

Maddie and Josh even witnessed Bugsy calming Justin on their trips to the beach. Bugsy had no training on how to comfort a child going through sensory overload; he did so intuitively. He was not the only dog with special talents. Josh and Maddie witnessed many of their dogs' unique super sensitivity time and time again, realizing dogs are much more in tune with their surroundings than we give them credit for.

When fun was to be had, Josh would join Justin in their ocean kayaks or navigating the shoreline of the bay on paddle boards. Occasionally, Maddie would join them, packing lunches and taking the kayaks over to the New Jersey Blueway for adventures on the back bays of Cape May. It was a birdwatching oasis with a wide variety of waterfowl, so they'd compete for who would see the largest variety of birds. Justin would often shout with excitement, "I don't know what it is, but it's one of them."

Maddie was the angler in the family and taught Justin all about saltwater fishing and crabbing. Josh quietly stood in the background, picking up her pointers. He wished to be a fisherman, but he didn't have the stomach for it. When Maddie and Justin went out on a deep-sea charter excursion, Josh quickly volunteered to stay with the dogs at Paws & Relax.

He'd never forgotten the day-trip early in their marriage: they were vacationing with Maddie's family on Long Beach

Island and they ventured out on a half-day fishing party. The old mighty sea goddess was angry that day and the rough seas had everybody on board sick, everybody except Maddie, that is. Never again, Josh swore, so he was perfectly happy minding the pups at home.

Kaitlyn says, "Justin must be in his thirties now."

Lifting her head high, Holly's eyes soften, "He has a family now. I have two wonderful grandchildren, Abby and Tommy, and a grand puppy named Zippy. Justin runs his own plumbing business."

The Other Side

With a concerned look on her face, Dr. Smits once again checks the instruments. For the past few minutes, her primary focus has been on the monitors, which are showing a rapid drop in heart rate. A pulse of thirty-eight was forty-five only twenty seconds ago. This coincides with his blood pressure dropping, now at eighty over fifty and continuing to decline. Dr. Klein pauses in closing. He'd just begun, yet now awaits direction from Dr. Ng. Analyzing the situation, Dr. Ng can tell it is going south and calls out for 1 milligram of adrenalin to be drawn up in case it's needed. Elizabeth now has it at the ready. Heart rate and blood pressure continue to drop critically low as Dr. Ng injects the adrenalin into Josh's heart... then it happens. The monitor shows he's flat-lined; the entire room buzzes, quickly jumping into action.

As the internal defibrillation paddles charge, Dr. Ng places them alongside Josh's heart. Once fully charged, he states, "Clear!" The jolt causes the heart to jump up slightly as they wait long seconds for it to restart. There's no response. Dr. Klein massages the heart, manually pumping the blood through Josh's body as Dr. Smits is pushing air into his lungs. Dr. Ng has the paddles charging and, once again, places them on Josh's heart. A few seconds later, "Clear!"

Up on his feet, Josh is extremely dizzy and his legs wobbly. Crashing to the ground seems like it's a good possibility at the moment, so he takes a few deep breaths to help stable himself. He puts the palms of his hands against his face, rubbing his forehead, eyes, and cheeks a few times. Josh is trying to figure out what's happened to him as he blinks his eyes hard, hoping to make sense of it all. *I'm in surgery, I'm sure of it,* he thinks to himself as he frantically reaches for the IVs in his arm, but his hand runs down his arm, freely gliding across smooth skin—no ports or tubes anywhere. He notices the pleasant temperature, nothing like the ice-cold operating room. *Could the anesthesia be playing tricks on me?* he wonders.

"Hello, is anybody there?" There's no reply. He takes a few moments to compose himself and scan his surroundings. A short distance away, he sees what appears to be an outline of a dog, but he knows he's not back at Monkey's House. Perhaps he's hallucinating or dreaming, but it seems all too real.

After a short period, the fogginess in his mind clears and he notices a faint light streaming from afar. He shakes his head and blinks a few more times, hoping it will help adjust to the darkness encompassing him. This reminds him of dusk, when it is hard to see clearly. Finally, he realizes the outline he saw is indeed a dog lying on the ground a few feet away. Josh believes he recognizes her from years ago.

He calls out, "LA, LA is that you, girl?" There's no answer at first. His head spins from side to side as he reaches into the hazy darkness, aimlessly grabbing for a bit of reality. His mind seems to be playing tricks on him until he hears a response.

"Dad, it is me... LA."

Grasping the moment, trying to understand the spectacle in front of him, Josh's body tenses, bracing for whatever lies ahead. As he takes cautious steps towards the dubious image, he calls out, "LA, it really is you." He kneels down and pats her head in disbelief. "What are we doing here?"

"I've been waiting for you." She gazes into his eyes as her tongue licks the back of his hand.

Josh is sure he's dreaming. How else is he able to hear LA talking back to him? Talking dogs aren't real. He ponders. LA's lips aren't moving, yet he understands every word she's saying. "I'm not sure what's happening, LA. I was in the hospital... now I'm here with you."

"You'll find out soon enough."

"How can you be talking to me?"

"I've always been able to communicate with you. Now, you're able to understand me better, to actually hear me."

"Are we in heaven?"

"Almost. We have a short walk to get there."

The questions, out of confusion, come rapid fire. "Why are you here to meet me? Where are Maddie and the other dogs? Who are these other dogs lying nearby? I don't recognize them."

Through the years, Josh has forgotten some of the dog's names, but he never forgets a face. He's sure they're not Monkey's House dogs; he doesn't sense that special connection deep within his gut that's now flaring up ever so strong with LA by his side. The other pups look to be in their prime, yet LA is still an old broken-down dog, much like the day they sent her off to be with the others. "Why do the others look so healthy, yet you're just the same as that last day you laid across my lap?"

"Many of the dogs only come here for short periods to see if their person arrived. See Patch over there? She's been waiting like me. She will transform to her younger self once her person finally comes home to meet her." Patch's age was clearly noticeable from her grey muzzle and frail body, much like LAs.

"Why did you wait for me? You could have been young and healthy, enjoying your youth again?"

"I had a hard life until you and Mom rescued me. You did everything possible to give me a wonderful home with many brothers and sisters. You showed me there was a thing called unconditional love. I loved lying on the front porch, no matter what the weather, waiting for you to come home. Mom would always make me so comfy, with blankets and heating pads when it was cold, or a portable fan and cooling pads during the hot weather. She believed I liked the warmth of the sun to nurture my achy body. I did, but what warmed my soul was greeting you home from a hard day at work. I wanted to be the first dog to get your attention. This is no different; I've been waiting for you to come home, to be the first you'd see when you arrived."

Josh has tears in his eyes. "I've missed you." He gives her a big hug. "What do we do now?"

"We go home." LA tries to get up but can't seem to get her frail body off of the ground. She has been laying here for decades, yet a fraction of time in eternity.

Josh remembers a day when they went to the Jersey shore; the dogs were down by the surf except LA. She couldn't make it across the long sandy beach to the water's edge. He picked her up in his arms and carried her down to be with her family. She enjoyed sticking her paws in the surf, but it was the ride down in her dad's arms she loved the most. That was over thirty years ago. Josh is no longer the man he was back on the beach that day, at least not physically. Yet, he's determined to reenact that moment, getting LA to a happy place. As he bends over to pick her up, he can't be sure what's crackling more, his knees or his back. He slowly lifts LA's fifty-pound body in his arms. "You ready, girl?" He takes a deep breath and heads towards the light.

The first few steps are agony. He is sure he's going to tumble and is concerned for LA's safety, but as he continues step by step, it's a little easier. Josh's sore joints aren't as sore anymore, and he notices his gait is less wobbly. He's regaining a bit of his strength. Josh notices LA is squirming in his arms, feeling more solid as her body starts restoring muscle. After a couple more steps, he put LA down, seeing she's now able to walk on her own by his side. It is getting brighter with each step, and as they get the closer to the light, he can clearly see how LA's body is transforming back to her youth. One of the oldest looking dogs they'd ever taken in looks like a healthy three-year-old. As they approach the end of the tunnel, the light gets even brighter. LA runs off to meet the others, gleefully announcing their father's arrival. Josh is stronger, too, but he hasn't had the same transformation as LA. He is still an old man, just not the exceedingly frail senior on the operating table.

As Josh emerges from the darkness into a kaleidoscope of color, he stands in amazement at the beauty before him, and the calm flowing over his soul. His worries and anxieties, the baggage he's carried through life, dissipate into thin air. Only once before had he experienced this sensation—on the day of his baptism. He's mesmerized by the impact of what's happening and the vastness of all that's right in front of him.

They walk together towards a bridge spanning a small bubbling creek. Josh stops; LA halts by his side. He appears to be inspecting the bridge. "It's a beautiful bridge, LA. Blue, red, green, well, every color of the rainbow, but it's rather small. I guess I was expecting something spectacular."

"It's not about the Bridge. It's how you lived your earthly journey and those waiting for you on the other side." LA walks over the Bridge, followed by Josh.

It's merely a half-dozen steps to the other side. On the last step, as Josh's right foot hits the ground, he freezes in awe of what's appearing in front of him. Across the horizon, hundreds of dogs are running to welcome him home. Dogs of all shapes, sizes, and breeds, all Monkey's House pups. They are all young and healthy, nothing like their earthly conditions. Although their appearances don't resemble the old dogs he knew and loved, he immediately recognizes each one from afar. Their bond, a special connection only a dog and their person have together. His eyes focus, taking in this scene that seems familiar. The sheer number of dogs is familiar of course, but also the transition from sadness and difficulty to joy and comfort that each of these dogs experienced in his and Maddie's home. The broken dogs were welcomed into Monkey's House, given the gift of love, and lived out their final chapters in ways they never imagined, before making their way here.

With LA still by his side, he glances over at her. "You're right. It's not about the Bridge. It's what's on the other side."

The army of dogs is pushing closer and closer to Josh and LA, leaving little space to maneuver. Josh kneels down to get to their level and meets his long-lost pups. He loves getting reacquainted with the dogs in the front, when he notices a commotion coming from the back of the pack. Still on his knees, he can't see over the dogs, but his heart is pounding as he thinks it has to be Maddie making her way toward him.

He stands up slowly and sees the crowd of dogs parting like the Red Sea. As the dogs make way, he realizes it's not Maddie but none other than Monkey, the little dog who inspired it all. He's making his way up to the front to be reunited with his dad. Monkey is why all these dogs gather here today. Without him, who knows if Maddie and

Josh would have ever started a dog sanctuary? Monkey is obviously their symbolic leader here. The dogs understand if it weren't in part for Monkey, none of them would be in this amazing family.

Upon making his way to the front, Monkey jumps into Josh's arms, kissing him all over his face with his little pink tongue. "Dad, I've missed you so. We have all been waiting for the day we would unite again. I imagine it's a little overwhelming to see so many of us here all at once."

"You should be proud. We smothered all these rescued dogs with love in your name, Monkey."

"You kept me pretty busy all these years, teaching the newbies the ropes up here. Actually, there aren't many rules. We just need to respect one another."

Monkey turns to the crowd and tells them to go about their daily activities. Dad would spend special moments with them in due time. He was the first to spend time with his dad, making up for those lost years, while guiding him on his heavenly journey.

The dogs disperse happier than ever. Josh looks down and sees a pile of leashes at the edge of the Bridge he just crossed. Leashes in the colors of a rainbow; some appear brand new. They bring back memories of Maddie, reminding him of the mailbags filled with thousands of leashes sent in memory of her. His mind takes him back to the day he spread Maddie's ashes, reuniting her with their family. His last gift to her was a bunch of leashes he buried among the dogs they loved and lost. He picks a red leash off the pile. Looking it over, he sees a dog's name embroidered on it: "Buddy." He hesitates and stares into space; it's like déjà vu as he believes he's held this leash before, but he can't place when or where.

Monkey notices Josh's puzzled gaze. "Don't worry about those. We don't use leashes in heaven. Let's take a walk."

Josh's mind is blown. The dogs are asking him to take a walk. Monkey wants to show him around, to meet up with the others. Josh is excited to see all the dogs; however, he has one thing on his mind—Maddie. Where is she? Why didn't she meet him along with all his furry children?

The air is fresh, with a crisp, blue sky overhead, a shade of blue he's never witnessed before. The breeze is moving the flowers like they are all dancing in sync, reaching towards the sun and soaking in its rays. Their fragrances fill the air as the birds sing in harmony. Everything is happening so fast; Josh's head is spinning. "Can we sit down for a bit?"

"Sure, over there's a nice shade tree we can sit under." A smirk appears on Monkey's face. He snickers, "Just don't sit too close to the trunk, if you know what I mean."

"What, all the male dogs taking lessons from Mr. Peebody?" Mr. Peebody came to Monkey's House with his bonded partner, Lucy, on the day they opened. As his aunts and uncles walked him and Lucy around the farm, it became clear he had no concept of personal space. He would pee anywhere, including on a pant leg. This is how he earned his name, Mr. Peebody. Peeing on anything and anybody was his signature.

Josh turned his focus back on Maddie, still troubled that she wasn't the first to meet him upon his arrival. Monkey tells him all things happen in heaven in due time. Josh doesn't understand, but he trusts Monkey, leaving it be for now, even though her absence remains an unanswered question in his subconscious.

Despite his excitement in meeting the dogs, Josh's head droops and back slumps; he craves meeting the love of his life again. Monkey attempts to ease his pain. "We spend time with Mom every day. There are many things to do here… anything you desire." He makes his way over to his dad and nestles into his side. Josh caresses a hand down his back and onto his belly. Monkey lets out a big howl, "Now this is what I call heaven."

"What is it like here?"

"Heaven is a place of 'no mores.' No more tears, no more pain, and no more sorrow. The blind can see and the deaf can hear. Those who couldn't walk or were missing limbs cast their wheels aside and run like the wind. You're never hungry, thirsty, or tired. The weights of worry lift away, and fear fades. Best of all, you're surrounded by loved ones."

Even with the beautiful account Monkey gives his dad, words don't do it justice. "Dad, you have to experience it to fully understand it, and that's what we're about to do."

Hang Ten

The vibrations of crashing waves echo through the valley. Josh finds it strange hearing the sounds of the ocean as he's walking through a meadow of daisies. Stacked field stone intertwined with dogwood trees and lilac bushes make up a beautiful hedgerow. How fitting: a couple of his favorite ornamentals are blooming. The fragrance of lilac reminds him of his grandmother. She had the most flourishing bushes growing next to her old farmhouse. As a young child, Josh loved that smell almost as much as the odor from his well-oiled leather glove. The sweet aroma of lilacs would let him know little league baseball was just around the corner. With each turn of his head, he notices another dog. One is rolling in a flowerbed full of colorful tulips; his grandmother would have had a fit. Another is running along the wall with its nose to the ground on the scent of a bunny or chipmunk. A couple are playing tug-of-war with an old piece of rope. There's also a group playing what looks like the dog version of tag.

"Monkey, look over there." Josh points out Clover, a Jack Russell running on top of the wall, jumping the gaps where time had been unkind. "This would be it, if I could choose what heaven looked like."

"Heaven's unique for each person or dog. It's everything you could ever imagine. It is what you've chosen. The greatest thing is you bring the best of yourself, and you see the finest in others. No personal demons here."

Josh continues his trek, with Monkey by his side. As they make their way up the hill, he continues to be drawn towards the sound of breaking waves. Josh assumes Maddie is just over the hill and down by the water. The ocean, walking along the beach was always their happy place. As they crest the hill, the bright sun is hanging high in a sky. It's shining down on the water, with the reflection directed right into their eyes. Raising his hand to his brow, like the brim of a cap to block the sun, he focuses for a few seconds until he clearly sees dogs on the beach. There appears to be a surfer in the water.

"It looks like... Hooch?" Josh is puzzled. "How is Hooch surfing?"

"Like I said, anything you can imagine."

Josh shakes his head and shouts out, "Hang ten, Hooch!"

"Look closer, what do you see?" Monkey flips his nose towards Hooch, who is now coming out of the water with his board.

"Wow, how did I miss that? A yellow surfboard shaped like a banana. Let's go down and meet him and the others."

Hooch, Eve, and dozens of other dogs are running up the beach to meet Josh and Monkey. Josh was sure Maddie would be here. After scanning the horizon, he realizes she's not. His eyes drop as his exhale takes the winds out of his sail.

This is all new to him, and he doesn't know what to expect. He figures there must be some reason behind this. "I was expecting to see your mom." Gazing back up, his eyes transition, opening wide, he's eager to hug Hooch and the others.

"In due time. It will happen when it's meant to," Monkey reassures him.

Hooch and the other cheerful dogs reach their dad. Hooch, now in his prime, spins in circles and jumps into Josh's arms. He staggers to regain his footing while keeping a solid grip holding a soggy, squirming dog. He's not surprised to feel Hooch's youthful energy flowing into his soul. Hooch hops back onto the beach so Josh can lean over to pick up Eve and the others, one by one, as they wiggle in closer to welcome their dad with kisses.

Once all the pups reunite with their dad, Hooch directs him to his destiny project. "Look over there. That's my banana grove." He's excited to point out how well the plants are growing with plentiful, never-ending harvests.

Josh walks through the rows of banana trees, with Hooch by his side, as the others follow. "I never imagined there would be bananas here."

"Didn't Monkey tell you? Anything is possible in heaven."

"Yes, he did. With all I've seen so far, I assume it's possible." Yet, there is still a hint of doubt in Josh's voice.

After touring the grove, they all gather around a little bonfire on the beach. One dog barks out, "We built this for you, Dad." Another chimes in, "We don't normally have a fire, just treats." They have plenty of treats, yet not your normal dog treats. Josh hopes for some marshmallows to brown over the fire, but no luck. They make all their treats out of bananas, served any way you want. So, Josh puts one on a stick and tries it roasted.

As they sit around the fire, they all seem to have a story about their Monkey's House days. All their stories feel embellished to Josh, their memories nothing like the way Josh remembers them. He enjoys hearing how they loved their time with Maddie and him, nonetheless. Rocket, an English bulldog, barks out, "Tell us a story about Hooch." Hooch is the prince of the beach, and as much a character here as he was on earth. Josh doesn't let them down.

"Hooch almost didn't make it to Monkey's House. He was a street dog in Philly. Dog catchers were after him for over two months, with no luck catching him. He was too clever for them, even though they tried everything. Hooch was always one step ahead and enjoyed making them look like fools. He'd bark 'Hey, I'm over here' and sneak around a few buildings and bark again. The neighborhood dogs thought he was so cool."

"What happened? How did they catch him?" Rocket asked.

"Rumor has it a bushel of bananas in a trap snagged him."

Hooch, wearing a guilty smirk says, "There's only so much a dog can take. I'm so glad they caught me. I ended up in paradise."

After a short stint of silence, Josh's desire to reunite with Maddie is weighing on his heart and it's clear to all.

Hooch breaks the silence, "Tell us a story about you and Mom, something we don't know."

"The ocean reminds me of the wonderful times we had at our house at the beach, Paws & Relax. Since most of you spent time there, I'll tell you a story from way before we started Monkey's House, all the way back to our honeymoon."

Josh and Maddie had been planning a honeymoon to the Florida Keys. However, in checking airline fares, they stumbled upon an unbelievable deal, offering a much cheaper rate to Hawaii. They discussed it and realized they may never get another chance to visit the aloha-state, they quickly changed their plans for a ten-day getaway. They split their honeymoon between the islands of Oahu and Maui. It was the trip of a lifetime. Not a day went by when they weren't on another excursion, exploring the rainforests, snorkeling with the sea turtles, or simply enjoying time together in paradise.

Josh starts the story, "I remember on Maui we decide to drive the sightseeing road to Hana. It was a scenic, yet frightful, drive."

The drive was four hours one way, hugging the coast of the island. Their route took them on a road that was on the high cliffs overlooking the ocean. Josh was white knuckling the steering wheel and Maddie would close her eyes each time locals whizzed by in the opposite direction. One of their goals for this excursion was to hike up to the Pools of 'Ohe'o, also known as the Seven Sacred Pools.

Thankfully, they made it there in one piece. Excitement overwhelmed them once they jumped out of the car and located the trail marker. The trek into the rainforest began. It lived up to all its hype, especially the magnificent falls. However, getting to the falls and back was a challenge. Maddie wanted to turn back more than once, though Josh wasn't sure which natural barrier gave her the most consternation. It may have been the fast-running stream, which turned out to be a mini river. Waist deep, Josh held his arms overhead to keep his wallet, camera, and Maddie's pack out of the water. She held onto his belt with both hands. If one of them went down, they would both be floating downstream together.

Triumphant over the first hurdle, they continued on, albeit soaking wet. Up next came mucking through four inches of mud on a narrow path through ten-foot-high bamboo, and of course, they were wearing flip-flops. What topped it all off was coming upon a family of gigantic spiders.

Josh throws his arms up, palms wide as he wiggles his fingers. "They even frightened me, with bodies the size of the palm of my hand and legs longer than my fingers." Seeing the dog's reactions was priceless, so he added in a little campfire folklore. "It surprised me to see the spiders in the forest. From what I understand, they live on sandy beaches, much like this one. I'm told they love heat."

The dogs' eyes widen, and they shuffle closer to one another as they look around the campfire. Their eyes are going back and forth, scanning the beach for spiders. Their dad's story has them shaking, imagining those long-legged creatures crawling around on their beach.

"Relax, I'm joking about spiders being here." Josh laughs.

Despite the challenges they encountered, it was an adventure of a lifetime. On the way back to the parking lot, Maddie noticed a big warning sign right by the trail marker, directing them hours earlier. It stated the hike up to the Seven Sacred Pools was for experienced hikers only, and that proper hiking gear was required.

Josh gazed upon Hooch, "Now that I think of it, hiking without proper gear sounds like something you would do: jumping into action without thinking through the consequences."

Hooch snickered, "Yeah, but in the end, I have a banana in my mouth. So, all ends well."

After a few more stories, Monkey walks down the beach and joins the group. After a short time, he nudges Josh and tells him they need to continue their journey. Meeting the beach crew brought back such wonderful memories of all the pups. Witnessing Hooch surfing reminded Josh of his youthful days, body-surfing the waves at Long Beach Island. His body now feels rejuvenated and he believes he'd be able to ride the waves again, this time on a surfboard.

About a hundred feet off the beach, on to the next leg of their journey, Josh stops. "We need to go back." He turns and heads toward the ocean while Monkey gives him an inquisitive look. He's not sure what's up, but follows along. Once they arrive at the water's edge, Hooch sees them and surfs all the way in to see what his dad needs.

"Okay, you got an extra board?" Josh has a spark in his tone.

Hooch lets out a big howl. "Everything you need is the shed over there. Remember, the trick is... if you believe it can happen. It will happen."

Josh heads into the surf on a standard board, nothing like Hooch's banana board. Side by side, they lie on their boards and paddle out into the waves. Josh is having a hard time keeping up. "Hooch, slow down. How are you paddling so fast?"

"I am a cocker spaniel with four webbed feet, doing the doggy paddle on a surfboard." He stops for a few paddles and lets dad catch up. "You know, I said to be a surfer. But now, be a spaniel. Back to a surfer when we get there." They both laugh, although Josh must have taken his advice as he passes Hooch, and they now sit upon their boards, waiting for a perfect wave.

Truth is, every wave here is a surfer's dream. "Look at me, I'm a crazy surfer dude, Hooch," Josh says as he rides his first wave all the way in until it breaks onto the beach. Time and again, they ride the waves. Any onlooker would swear Josh has been surfing since he was a kid, and in Hooch's case, a pup.

After catching a dozen rides, they're both waiting for one special wave to take them back to shore. Josh is ready to see the other dogs. There's catching-up to do. Most importantly—his desire to find Maddie. As they sit enjoying each other's company, Josh sees a shark fin out of the corner of his right eye. At this moment, he realizes he can see out of his right eye again, the one he lost vision in over sixty-years ago from the jet crash. Excitement of having full vision fades at the concept of being eaten by a shark.

Barely able to speak, in a whisper, he's able to get out "Hooch... Hooch, there's a shark on my right."

"Don't worry. We don't have sharks here."

Hooch's reassurances aren't calming Josh as the fin comes closer and closer. "Stay still, don't move." The fin comes within reach of Hooch, who bends over and pulls it out of the water... with Eve attached, snorkel and all.

With a sigh of relief and a bit of annoyance, Josh laughs. "Eve, I wouldn't have expected any less from you. You got me good." Eve beams with pride.

Back on the beach, Hooch sits with his signature head tilt, wearing a big smile. "Do you now assume anything is possible?"

"No, I don't," he replies, hesitating for a moment to witness Hooch's expression. It does not disappoint; the smile has disappeared. "EVERYTHING is possible! It's not every day I'm riding a ten-foot wave like a pro and shooting out of the pipeline with my best friend close behind on a banana surfboard." Hooch's smile was back, bigger than ever.

The waves may have lifted his surfboard, but it was the love of seeing his family that lifted his spirits. After some wet, sandy hugs, he's off again with Monkey leading his dad to what lies ahead.

Chimes of Liberation

Josh and Monkey walk through the valley as a refreshing breeze blows against their faces. It carries beautiful music from the far ridge. As they crest the knoll, they see thousands of wind chimes in the distance, dancing in the breeze and striking out a lovely, harmonious melody. Sunshine reflects off individually polished pieces of metal, giving an appearance of diamonds levitating in the sky. As Josh and Monkey approach, the awesome sight mesmerizes them. If they didn't know better, they'd swear it was nighttime. The chimes glitter like stars in the clearest of skies.

Live in the moment, Josh remembers Maddie telling him, *always live your Dash*. He stops, closes his eyes and listens. The music is soothing his soul. "This is amazing. What is this?"

"Wait, you'll see when we get closer." Not another word is spoken as the beautiful tones entice them to make haste.

About to enter the field of dancing stars, Monkey has a tear in his eye. "This is hallowed ground for many. Of all the places in heaven, I get emotional here."

Walking further into the midst of all the chimes, Josh falls to his knees, his body tingling as uncontrollable tears stream down his cheeks. These are not sad tears, but tears of joy, tears of triumph. Josh immediately realizes the chimes have special meaning, not your traditional wind chimes. They are made from parts of dog wheelchairs, carts, and wagons—any contraption the dogs once used to assist with mobility on earth. The chimes, once part of a symbol of disability, are now instruments of liberation. They've broken free of their chariots, gracing the dogs with independence. Much like the Bridge, these chimes are purely symbolic and Josh can barely contain his joy as he sees those same dogs now running on an agility course down in the hollow; that's the miracle.

Lifting his gaze to the sky, he closes his eyes and crosses his hands in prayer. "Thank you, Lord, for renewing these dogs' bodies, allowing them to run and jump once again under their own power."

Josh feels a cold nose in his ear and he knows it isn't Monkey's. It may have been ages ago, but he thinks he recognizes that wet nose. Opening his eyes, he sees Dozer standing right in front of him: a strong, broad-shouldered German shepherd. Any signs of the Degenerative Myelopathy (DM), which consumed his body on earth, is now gone. Dozer was a handsome short timer at Monkey's House, but during his brief time, he received the love of a lifetime. When Maddie and Josh sent him on his last journey, he knew love more than he'd ever believed possible. They only knew Dozer when DM took over this entire body, but it never took away Dozer's spirit or his love for them.

Still on his knees, he throws his arms around Dozer's neck. "It's so good to see you, Dozer." As Josh hugs his beloved friend, healing energy flows from Dozer into his body. By now, most of his aliments, aches and pains are gone.

"Dad, I'm so happy to see you. You won't need to pull me around anymore. Maybe I'll pull you now."

"You're one healthy boy. No more wagons or carts for you." It thrills Josh to see Dozer whole again.

"Nope..." Dozer flips his nose over toward a large, shiny metal chime hanging magically in the sky. "They gave me the ability to take walks with you and mom. I was grateful for it, but now I love the music they make." Dozer pushes his shoulder into Josh's hip as he gives him a hug.

"They make great wind chimes," Josh says with tears still in his eyes, returning his gaze to the pups below.

"It looks like you guys have an obstacle course. In fact, it looks pretty extreme, like a Ninja course for dogs." Josh is in awe of the course. Even more so, he's delighted beyond belief seeing dogs, once in need of mechanical help to get around, running the course like champions.

"We are pretty intense. Once we get our bodies and our independence back, there's no stopping us."

Dozer leads his dad and Monkey towards the course. As they get closer, the dogs on the course stop in their tracks, turn and run up the hill to see their dad. Josh notices Monkey slow down to make way for his dad's reunion with the others.

Josh pets Legend, Fletcher, and the others as he falls to the ground in laughter amidst all the happy, wriggling pups. They are so excited, each trying to get their dad's attention. Licks, wiggles, and cuddles... are even better here in heaven, with dogs in restored bodies. Once things quiet down a bit, Josh notices their sweet little white poodle, Ariel. He's surprised to see her; up until now he has met none of "Maddie's pack." These were dogs who would never leave her side at Monkey's House. They were the likes of Sora, Buck, Daisy Mae, and so many more, but especially Ariel.

"Ariel, look at you with all your legs. You look as glamorous as ever. I see you're still wearing your bling."

Before he's finished speaking, she darts forward and leaps into his arms. "I'm always by Mom's side. But I couldn't wait for you to see how fast I can run and jump on my own."

Josh lovingly embraces Ariel. "I can't wait to see you pups conquer the course. For most of you, I never saw you walking without assistance." The dogs, eager to show off for their dad, dash off to the starting line. Dozer takes a seat next to him, both looking down the small slope. It's a great vantage point for watching the dogs' triumph over their earthly disabilities.

"Dozer, this course is like dog agility meets mountain biking. Why is it designed like that?"

"Years ago, you loved biking, and we wanted you to join us when you were ready." Dozer looks over toward the edge of the course. "That bikes for you, no helmet required." Josh notices what looks like his favorite childhood bike, yet larger. The adult version of the Schwinn Sting Ray, the same bike he'd ride on makeshift obstacle courses with the neighborhood kids.

As they ready to watch the dogs take turns, Dozer lies down with his head across Josh's lap. First to go is Bambi, a tan, slender Italian greyhound who looks like they shot her out of a cannon. She's avoiding all the obstacles on the course, just flat out running.

Josh scratches his head. "Bambi is so fast, but she's ignoring all the obstacles. I don't understand."

"Heaven gave her the ability to run again; it's what she loves, her unique gift. Running all out is also her way of showing her appreciation for something as simple as the freedom of movement, given back to her. In her case, she shows it through speed."

Next up is Dolly, a little white mutt covered in black and brown spots. When Josh last saw her, she was missing her left front leg along with a paralyzed hind-end. Off she charges with all four legs in harmony, ducking her head into the smaller tunnel, only to shoot out the other side in a flash. She goes in and out of the weave polls, like a downhill skier tackling the slalom with her side pushing into each pole. Over a few jumps she goes, followed by the seesaw, up and over, sprinting to the finish. The other dogs bark and howl; Josh joins in with a few howls of his own and a big smile on his face. The howling reminds him of Maddie and their Sunday morning snuggles from years ago.

"I don't see a pause table. Don't dog agility courses have one?" Josh asks.

"We replaced it. We paused our crippled bodies on earth longer than we ever wanted and don't need to rest anymore. It feels so good to keep moving."

"What did you replace the table with?"

Dozer looks towards the edge of the course, where a runway leads to a long pool. "We have our own version of a Dock Dive. Our pool is a hundred feet long."

"Why so long? The world record is around forty feet."

"World records are insignificant here; we soar on the wings of God. We are all beating earthly records every day. My best so far is over sixty feet."

"Did you know when your mom and I were younger, we competed in a race that was basically an obstacle course? It was called The Cape Mud Run. This kind of reminds me of that, except this is much cleaner."

Josh, who was more athletic than Maddie, enjoyed new physical challenges. He coerced Maddie into the Mud Run. It must have been the way he described it: a fun, minor event along the coast, after which they would take a stroll on the beach and grab a seafood dinner along the boardwalk. He made sure to never mention the word "race." They trained together for several months. Josh even setup a little course in the backyard with obstacles he assumed they might encounter. Josh soon mastered each one he built. Although it wasn't graceful for Maddie to get over, around, or under them, with practice, she managed.

The big day for which they'd prepared for months was upon them. As they pulled into the parking lot, Maddie realized this was much bigger than the "little fun thing" Josh promoted. When she noticed how muddy everybody was, she turned to Josh and gave him a look that said, "what did you get me into?" Reminding her they had trained for months, he convinced her to compete since they were already there. They should just do it and have fun. It would be an adventure they could tell all their friends about.

"How did you and Mom do?" Dozer asked.

"Well, we finished. Your mom might have been the muddiest racer. She finally talked to me again halfway through our walk on the beach. By the time we sat for dinner, she was laughing. But kept saying 'never again' over and over."

Dozer loves the story of his parents doing a course much like what they had here. They refocus their attention back to the course, watching one after another dog, big and small, running and jumping with gusto. Josh recognizes everyone, except the next one up, a beautiful white German shepherd. "I don't know that dog, or am I just not remembering her? She looks as fit as you."

"That's Sammie. You're right, she wasn't part of our family. She had DM too, but now we push each other to see how fast we can finish. We always go for our personal best." Dozer playfully pushes his head into his dad's side. "I'll tell you a little secret. Every day here, we are at our personal best."

"How did you meet Sammie, and why am I meeting her now? My journey has reunited me with our dogs. She's the first from outside of our sanctuary."

"She has a connection with us. Her mom, Sarah, was friends with Mom. You probably remember her. She partnered with Mom on educating folks about Degenerative Myelopathy. Sammie and I were the poster dogs."

"I remember her as Sam. Wow, look at her destroy the course." She looks like an Olympic champion going for the gold.

Ariel, who you couldn't miss as her collar glistened in the sun from all the bling, is next up. She looks up to her dad, "Watch me go!" She takes off with excitement, proudly showing her father the skills she's mastered. Her energy is like the thrill of a little girl on her bicycle, without training wheels for the first time, after her dad releases his grip on the saddle. Ariel's glitter is like those little girls' tassels blowing in the wind from the ends of their handlebars. She's killing the course today and is heading toward the finish line, when she suddenly veers off towards the pool.

"She's not... she's going to do the Dock Dive!" Josh grins ear to ear. Approaching the pool, she lets out a cheerful yelp and leaps, flying through the air, hitting the water at about the forty-foot mark. Josh jumps to his feet and runs down with Dozer to meet her. When he gets there, all the dogs have gathered around Ariel, making a fuss over her.

"Congratulations. This is a personal best for you," Dozer says.

"I did it for my dad." Looking into her dad's eyes she continues, "There is one thing I want from you, Dad. Join us." Ariel flips her nose to the corner of the course. "There's a bike so you can have some fun with us, like you weren't able to do for decades."

Picking up Ariel and hugging her, Josh disagrees: "I always had fun with each one of you, in whatever capacity we could. I loved our time together." He kisses Ariel on the head. "But I understand what you mean. This is a different kind of fun… now let's get that bike."

Josh sits on the bike, ready to tackle the course, with all the dogs anxiously waiting behind him. Rusty, a little red Pomeranian, remembers the many times he rode with his dad in the canine backpack, whipping through trails in the Pines. He is excited to be running alongside his dad this time, as are all the others. The bike takes off as he pushes down on the right pedal. It feels as though he's just done this yesterday, not the many decades ago when he was last on his bike with his cycling team. However, this time, his crew members are four-legged and furry.

Zipping through the large tunnel, he's able to ride up the sides, sweeping back and forth, side to side from the momentum. He hears the pounding of hundreds of paw-steps right behind him. As they stream out of the tube, Josh looks like a shooting star with the pups trailing along behind him. He travels so fast, it's hard to recognize the dogs behind him, but spots Ariel easily. Her shiny bling gives her away. They glide in and out of the weave polls, like a dragon weaving through the streets of Chinatown on the Chinese New Year.

Jump after jump, up and over the seesaw they race; next, Josh heads for the dock dive. As they reach the edge of the pool, he pulls up on the handlebars and flies with the dogs. He lets go of the bike and hits the water first. Ariel and Rusty land close by as more and more dogs splash into the surrounding water, even Bambi. Josh pops his head above the water and sees Dozer and Sammie flying overhead, both landing all the way at the other end of the pool.

His ride with the dogs fills Josh's heart with joy as he witnesses the miracles bestowed upon them. Spending time with them has rejuvenated his soul. Glancing up the hill from the course, he notices Monkey coming his way; it is time for them to go. He says his goodbyes for now and they walk back the same way they came. At the crest of the hill, he turns, looking upon the dogs with a smile on his face. They're at it again, the young pups on a mission to crush the course.

Approaching the wind chimes, Josh stops and listens. "If it's possible, the music sounds even sweeter now."

"Dad, now you know the true source of the beautiful music. It's not created by pieces of glistening metal, but from renewed hearts and rejoiced souls."

Having Courage

Off in the distance, Josh notices a person walking in their direction with a large dog by their side. They are traveling on the same dirt path, walking directly toward them. Josh is at a loss for words, thinking it has to be Maddie. He's puzzled why he hasn't reunited with her by now. The butterflies in his stomach are flittering away. All he wants is to be with his long-lost love again. Anticipating it's Maddie with her soul dog, Sora, his heart is pounding as he picks up his pace to a point where Monkey needs to run to keep up. As the gap closes, Josh slows his pace; Monkey's stride goes back to a brisk walk. His grin fades to a frown, pulling pain down across his face. Like a window shade blocking the sun, the realization shades his soul. It's not Maddie. A man he doesn't recognize is approaching. His eyes lower to the dog, straining to remember the pup, but he can't make out who it is. They are still too far away.

As they get closer, Josh finally recognizes the dog and shouts out to her, "Major, is that you?" Stooping down to be at her level, he firmly slaps his leg. "Come here, girl." Major readies to take off but hesitates, looking up at the man by her side. Once he nods, Major runs with all her might to meet Josh. He can sense this man is her special person, her companion before she made her way to Monkey's House. She is a strong Belgian Malinois in her prime, a state she was in long before she ever made her way to Josh and Maddie. When they knew Major, she was a tripod, nothing like the dog in front of him now. She was missing her right hind leg, right ear and eye, with scars covering her entire right side. The shelter told them they heard she was a military dog who saved somebody in the Afghanistan war. Maddie and Josh doubted the Afghan story. They couldn't believe a military hero would end up in a shelter, scheduled to be euthanized. As Major and Josh hugged, he felt the might of her essence flow from her body, further bolstering his strength and reinforcing his desire to once again be with Maddie.

As the young man approaches, the military story clicks into place. Clean shaven and sporting a buzz cut, he's dressed in an army green t-shirt, camouflage pants held up with a black belt, and is wearing black military boots. The ultra-fit man stops and comes to attention as Major runs back to his side. He salutes. "Sir, Sergeant 1st Class Tucker Burns and NCO Courage. It's an honor to meet you, sir."

Josh snaps a salute back without hesitation; once a Marine, always a Marine. "At ease, son." Josh reaches out and shakes Tucker's hand.

"Please call me Josh." His attention goes to Courage. "So, your name is Courage. What a noble name for such a beautiful soldier." Looking back at Tucker. "Sadly, we didn't know her name when we got her. We don't get the names of the dogs or their history. We named her Major since we were told she was in the Military."

Tucker smiles. "Major is a fitting name, but she didn't have such a high rank, although she was an NCO, a non-commissioned officer. Military dogs are always ranked higher than their partners, commanding our respect for our dogs. It's also meant to prevent handlers from abusing or mistreating their dogs." Tucker looks down at Courage and they lock eyes: the sacred bond between them is crystal clear. "If I could, I would have named her General; she's never failed me. I cannot always say the same about people." Tucker jokes.

They take a seat under a large maple tree with ever-stretching branches shading the lush, soft grass they sit upon. As a gentle breeze ruffles the leaves and the bluebirds chirp, Courage lies across Tucker's lap. She's keeping watch, still protecting him, even today. "You're the first person I've met here. Do you know why I'm meeting you and not my wife, Maddie?"

"Be patient. All things in due time."

The sadness in Josh's eyes reflects the ache in his heart.

"I've seen Maddie and thanked her for all you did for Courage. Josh, I can tell you she's thrilled with her furry family… and so proud of how you kept Monkey's House going. Every time a dog crosses the Bridge, she's waiting there ready to welcome them home. After giving them a hug and loving on them, she always asks how you're doing. She wants to know everything about you and what's new at Monkey's House." Tucker dips his head, pauses, then looks back up. "She's sad when they tell her you're so lonely, missing her."

A tear runs down Josh's face. "If not for our mission, for the dogs, it would have been unbearable all these years." Josh takes a deep breath, composing himself. "Can you tell me more about Maddie? When we'll be together again?"

"Sorry, Josh, I know nothing else." Tucker leans forward, putting his hand on Josh's shoulder. "She's where she needs to be, tending her pack." He perks up his tone. "But I can tell Maddie can't wait to be with you again... you'll be together soon."

Josh shakes off his mixed emotions, his drive to see Maddie. For now, he wants to find out more about Tucker's relationship with Courage. "Please tell me all about Courage, where you met, how you've become so close?"

Tucker tells his life's story, how he was born and raised on a farm on the outskirts of Winterset, Iowa. It's known for their covered bridges; in fact, the movie, *The Bridges of Madison County* gave the little town its fifteen minutes of fame. He loved playing shortstop for the Huskies high school baseball team, even helped take them to the state championships his senior year. In the off-season, when not working the fields with his dad and brother, you could find him quail or pheasant hunting with Scout, his treasured Brittany spaniel.

After graduating high school, Tucker enlisted in the Army. He spent his first two tours in Iraq, in the infantry. Upon reenlistment, he requested to become an elite Army Ranger and went through rigorous training; they sent him on his third tour, this time to Afghanistan. Being stationed with military dogs in his battalion made him realize how much he missed his old friend Scout, reinforcing his love of dogs. After witnessing these dogs working and the bond they built with their handlers, he hungered for a canine relationship again.

Prior to his fourth tour, he applied to be a military dog handler. The response to his request seemed to take forever, but eventually, he got his dream assignment, partnering with Courage. She was right out of military training school at four years old, a little older than most military dogs starting their careers. Her extensive training covered all aspects needed for warfare support, including bomb sniffing, particularly improvised explosive device (IED) detection. Tucker and Courage quickly bonded, and shortly after, found themselves in Afghanistan. They became totally devoted to one another all the way through his last tour.

One day, their squad of five, along with Courage, found themselves in a predicament in a small village twenty klicks south of Kandahar. A grenade launched from a rooftop struck their armor-plated Humvee, blowing the left front wheel completely off. Exiting the vehicle, they found themselves pinned down, taking fire from Taliban fighters. To say it was a chaotic scene wouldn't do it justice. Shots rang down on them from rooftops, through windows, and doorways. Bullets hit all around, seemingly from every direction. What appeared the safest way out of the barrage of bullets was through a narrow alleyway a few feet to their right. However, Courage didn't seem to agree and wouldn't follow Tucker's commands, instructing her to head down the alley. Courage's training kicked in. She was skilled in the many circumstances a soldier might encounter, including a situation like this. They should have listened to her, but with hell raining down upon them, Gunner Tommy Smith convinced the team the alley was their best choice to get to safety. Waiting for the cavalry wasn't an option, since fellow platoon members were at least ten minutes out. Held down as they were, they all assumed their chances of survival were slim, so they proceeded down the alleyway.

As gunshots continued to hit all around them, one bullet caught Rex in the shoulder. However, getting shot wasn't what stopped him from his exit. Courage did. She ran out in front of the team, barking franticly, doing what they trained her to do, which was letting them know this was not a safe extraction route. When they kept advancing, she fearlessly ran full force out in front of them, triggering an IED: miraculously, she survived the blast, but she incurred major injuries. If the team had hit the explosive, as tightly bunched as they were in that narrow alley, they all would have been severely wounded, if not killed.

"Courage saved soldiers on many missions; the guys loved having her on our sorties. On our last one, she once again saved my team. That's why she was all messed up when you guys finally rescued her." Tucker hesitates; Josh senses the memories of that day are hard for him.

"Thanks to Courage... Dallas, Rex, and Chuck all have families now," he says with conviction.

Dallas has a wife and three daughters. He held a few odds-and-ends jobs here and there until he met Cindy, his wife. She helped him get grounded, and he finally found his true calling. He became the minister of a little church in San Antonio. It caters to the poor, those in need of prayer and sustenance, through his soup kitchen and shelter. He no longer goes by Dallas, but is now Chris, from his given name Christopher.

After Rex's shoulder healed, he ended up back in Afghanistan for two more tours. Besides receiving the Purple Heart that day, they also gave him the Silver Star for gallantry when he risked his life, saving fellow soldiers a year later. Over the years, he's advanced in the Pittsburgh police department, now holding the rank of lieutenant. His wife passed in childbirth with their second child, Elizabeth. He's proud of his daughter, who's now a Pediatric Surgeon, performing life-saving operations—on newborns no less. His son Dan is following in his footsteps, albeit in a different branch of the military. He's in the Navy on an aircraft carrier.

Chuck took advantage of the educational GI bill and went to college. He received a bachelor's degree, BS in Biology, and continued on for his masters, receiving an MS in Climatology. He's currently a Climatologist for NOAA, the National Oceanic and Atmospheric Administration and his team is researching methods of tornado early detection, striving to develop an early warning system which will give residents of the Midwest more time to prepare for oncoming storms. Chuck and Betty adopted two girls and live in Boulder, Colorado.

Tucker is running his hand down Courage's back. "Courage. You made all of that possible." Courage lifts her head off Tucker's lap, licks his face, then nestles her head into his chest.

Tucker continues softly, "She also saved Tommy... I see him from time to time." He takes a couple deep breaths as he continues to stroke Courage's thick coat. "Sadly, the horrors of war were too much for him."

"I'm so sorry about Tommy," Josh says. He can still feel Tucker is not telling him everything but doesn't push it, letting him decide whether to open up.

After a long pause, Tucker continues with his eyes focused downward on his best friend. "No soldier left behind... I ran back, grabbed Courage in my arms and got out of there as fast as I could. It wasn't fast enough. Three bullets stung me in the back, hurting like hell but I didn't stop... I had Courage. Last thing I remember, my team was pulling both of us into a Humvee, telling me to let go of my Courage." Tucker is now firmly holding onto Courage, lifting his head with a heartfelt smile to Josh. "Thank you for caring for my best friend until we were ready to be reunited once again."

The Playground

Monkey continues to lead them along the path when Josh abruptly stops, looks back from where they came and notices the trail is empty. Tucker and Courage have vanished. His forehead scrunches and his eyes narrow. "I could communicate with Hooch, Dozer, and all the others, hearing them talking back. But I couldn't hear Courage. In fact, I don't remember Sammie talking either. Do you know why?"

"They were talking, but you're not their person, so you couldn't hear them. Tucker is Courage's dad and Sammie, well, his mom and dad, are not here yet."

"Now I understand." They continue on their journey. The trek is getting hilly, and the trail has many curves traversing the mountain. Josh is trying to see what lies ahead, but peering around the next corner isn't possible. The path is shady now, as large swaths of trees line the trail, blocking out the sun. An occasional ray of sunshine pierces through gaps in the branches directly into their eyes, confusing their vision. They soon find themselves in a peaceful setting, walking through a deep forest, listening to birds softly chirping and leaves twisting in the wind. Suddenly, Josh hears some strange, out-of-place sounds and scans the woods, trying to pinpoint the origin.

Traveling around a sharp bend, he notices the footing has changed from the soft bed of leaves and pine needles. There's some kind of hard material mixed among them. At first, he assumes they're stones, but quickly rules out gravel as they have a little give to them. He looks down but notices nothing peculiar. Understandably, the forest is thick and dark, hard for his eyes to focus. Josh is glad when the forest's canopy thins out. The surroundings are getting lighter, making it easier to see.

Upon his next step, a loud squeak accosts his ear. Stunned, Josh quickly looks down, solving part of the mystery. Hundreds of little plastic squeakers are everywhere—noise makers he's well familiar with from dogs pulling them out of stuffed toys at home. He picks up a few. Looking closely, he detects teeth marks on the plastic, most of which are torn into pieces. Focusing back on the path, he sees them strewn everywhere. Shaking his head in puzzlement, Josh wonders where they've all come from, yet he continues on. Questions run through his head as he looks around, trying to solve the remaining piece of the puzzle.

Around the next bend, he sees a large basin full of dogs. Josh stops as Monkey continues forward towards the other dogs. A detour takes him to the left as a huge, colorful pile of snow draws Josh's attention. After all, a snow bank amidst the warm weather and beautiful summerlike landscape is clearly out of place, let alone one peppered with many colors. As he approaches, it doesn't take him long to figure it out. He's seen remnants like this before, but never a quantity of this magnitude. It's not snow at all, but white polyester stuffing which once filled dog toys, along with the remnants of the toys themselves.

Josh bends over and picks up what once was a cute bunny toy. The squeaker had been "surgically" removed, no doubt from a skilled dog like his precious Darla. She's always after those treasured little round pieces of plastic—the noise-maker. Looking a little closer, there were toys that lacked the expertise of a squeaker surgeon. Instead, they showed evidence of the more high-spirited destroyer. He also spotted a lot of tennis balls in the pile. Most of them had the fuzzy exteriors chewed off.

The squeaking becomes deafening as he steps further into the field full of dogs playing with stuffed animals. However, once they see their dad, the noise stops as they drop their toys and rush to greet him. In the pack's front is Archie, a one-hundred-pound blockhead golden Labrador retriever. He jumps up, placing his front paws on Josh's chest, knocking him to the ground with joyous laughter.

Archie doesn't realize he has his dad pinned to the ground as he licks his face all over. "Dad, I'm so glad to see you. We all are." He finally lets Josh sit up as he lies next to him while the others make a fuss over their dad.

"Wow, you look great, Archie. I see your painful limp is gone."

When Archie made his way to Maddie and Josh, he had a horrific limp. They were told he had bone cancer in his leg. It didn't help he was twenty pounds overweight, either.

Through healthy eating, the extra pounds came off, and after many visits to veterinary specialists, thankfully they determined the limp was not because of cancer after all. Archie had suffered a major break in the joint when he was younger and it became arthritic, causing an excruciating limp. With physical therapy, including the underwater treadmill, his leg got stronger, and the limp subsided, so he no longer needed to live at Monkey's House. He had officially become an "Imposter" and was soon looking for his own family.

Aunt Karen took Archie to her house to prepare him for his forever family. It was a normal home setting, as he was sharing a home with her two dogs and cat instead of the twenty plus dogs at Monkey's House. Karen knew how Archie loved to tear apart stuffed animals, so she'd researched dog toys that were supposedly indestructible. They were no match for Archie, who quickly made confetti out of them, strewing the remains across her family room. To be fair, it took him fifteen to twenty minutes versus the normal five minutes he took to destroy "normal" stuffed toys.

A wonderful family adopted Archie. It thrilled them to have him join their household. He had two young teenagers to call his own, another dog to play with, and a cat to torment. Archie was living large. However, life had other plans. He found himself back at Monkey's House because of a tragedy within his new family. Maddie and Josh welcomed him back with open arms, where he was meant to be. Archie eventually developed another form of cancer, which led him to the Bridge.

Archie is relishing the long strokes of his dad's hand against his fur. Josh is now watching dogs gather in the valley, moving closer to the middle as they appear to be looking outward towards the perimeter of the field. Their bodies tense up and the tail wagging ceases—something special is about to happen.

At the Rainbow Bridge, Josh witnessed what's possible, but is still curious about what's coming next. Archie remains seated with his dad, while the others are just too eager and run out to join their buddies. All of a sudden, the sounds of barking and howling echo loudly through the valley.

"Wow, something roused them up. What's going on?"

"Wait for it." Archie would be in the middle of the pack, juiced up like the others. Today, however, is all about his dad and he's right where he wants to be. Tomorrow he'll be back at it with the others.

A whistle sounds and the dogs become quiet. They take a stance, readying to sprint into action at any moment. Within a few seconds, tennis balls fly towards the dogs from the edges of the field, some coming fast while others are lobbed. Arcs of balls are flying through the sky at all different heights. Balls in every color seemed to come out of thin air. A medley of color streams through the sky, forming a rainbow as the balls make their way to the dogs.

The colorful flight of the balls hypnotizes Josh. When he finally looks back down at the dogs, they're running about, jumping and catching them. These dogs could barely move when he knew them. Their enjoyment only came from chewing on the balls. Now they are racing and leaping two, three, even four feet into the air, catching them. They scamper to the perimeter of the valley, drop the ball, then rush back into the middle of the field to catch another.

In the center of the pack, he recognizes Matt, the handsome yellow Labrador retriever rescued by the humane police that became their farm dog for a short period. Josh remembers when Matt felt better, he'd grab a tennis ball and pull it by his side, yet he was too weak to actually play with it. Today, he's vaulting into the air, catching a ball, darting back and readying for another.

Suddenly, there is a break in action. The balls stop, yet the dogs are still anxious and in position, waiting for something evidently coming next. The whistle blows in two short bursts and stuffed toys fly out to the dogs. They are especially for dogs who love to play with, and eventually tear apart, their stuffed babies. Moose, a bulldog who looks like he could have played linebacker for the Pittsburgh Steelers, is tearing into his stuffed toy, which resembles a quarterback.

"Look at Moose over there." Josh points in his direction. "He sure is showing Tom Brady who's the boss today."

Archie cocks his head to the side. "Who's Tom Brady?"

"Right, you wouldn't know. He was one of the great football quarterbacks in his day. They called him the GOAT."

"Oh, I love tearing apart goat stuffed animals, too, although they are a rare find." Archie grins, showing Josh his teeth, making it obvious why he's called the "Destroyer." Josh laughs and gives Archie a big hug.

A few more rounds of balls fly to satisfy those fetch loving pups, while the toy destroyers continue tearing and ripping away.

Josh's forehead wrinkles and eyes squint as he looks into the sky. "Where are the balls coming from?"

"Focus… feel it in your soul and you will see."

Goosebumps cover Josh's arms, and a tingle runs through his body. He sees it clearly now. Lining the rim of the valley are teenagers. They are throwing the balls; most are using various sporting equipment to send them high into the air, streaming down for the dogs to catch. Tennis rackets, baseball bats, lacrosse sticks, golf clubs, hockey sticks, even a large slingshot a couple of kids made are launching balls.

"What's with the kids and sports equipment?"

"Nothing goes better together than kids and dogs. So, we get together every day to play and show affection. Many of the kids loved sports, too, so they use the equipment associated with their favorite activity. They switch from time to time."

The kids are welcome to come and play fetch with the dogs. After the balls stop flying and playing is over, the dogs make their way to the kids. Now it's time to share love between a boy or girl and a dog. Belly rubs for dogs, and licks for kids—a beautiful symphony of sharing love all along the rim of the valley.

"I think I know the boy with the hockey stick over there. His name is Cory. I'm good friends with his parents. Am I allowed to go talk to him?"

"Sure, you can go over. I'll wait here for you."

Many years ago, Josh worked with Cory's father, Jim. They became good friends, much more than your typical work acquaintances. They had a lot in common, especially cycling, and they enjoyed riding together through the hills and valleys of Mercer and Hunterdon counties on many weekends. Josh and Maddie got to know the family well and became lifelong friends. Jim and his wife, Jerri, would occasionally go to dinner with Maddie and Josh or enjoy a picnic together. Cory, the youngest in the family, loved animals. Once Josh saw all the kids throwing or hitting the balls, it did not surprise him to see Cory among those playing fetch with the pups. His hockey goalie outfit seemed appropriate, as he loved playing ice hockey and had been a great goal tender in his junior league.

Cory was also active in his church, having a soft spot for the needy. While raising money for the homeless on a charity bike ride, he was involved in an accident that took his life. He was only fifteen. He is proud of the way his parents and brother, Jeromy, took the tragedy and turned it into something positive. They established an annual memorial bike ride, in his honor, to raise money for college tuition. His memorial event provided scholarships to underprivileged students, helping them further their education in fields geared towards the community. They presented more than one hundred scholarships in his name over the years. Nurses, social workers, and even a doctor are now helping others, in part thanks to Cory. The event ran for decades to continue his legacy and the impact he had on others.

Josh finally makes it over to Cory, who's petting both a golden and Labrador retriever. The dogs look like they're best friends. He knows the one, Matt, but doesn't recognize the golden. "Hi Cory, do you remember me?"

"Of course, I do. Thank you and Maddie for making a heaven on earth for these dogs, giving them all your love before they came here. I'm also grateful we're welcomed to come and play with all of them, along with my dog, Troy. He's made a best buddy in Matt." Cory is content petting both dogs.

"It looks like a lot of kids come to play with the dogs. I remember growing up with dogs in our family. I always loved that they would play along with us."

"You know, we call this field 'The Playground'; it's our favorite place here."

"I saw your dad about a year ago. When we worked together, I remember him telling me his family was full of centenarians, and he, too, expected to live to be a hundred. He's passed that milestone and is still living his life to the fullest. In fact, last I saw him, he was planning a trip out west to see his great grand kids, your great nieces and nephews. I have to be honest, he's lonely without your mom. I understand his pain."

Cory stops petting Matt, who runs up to Josh and pushes his head into his body, a sign of affection Josh is familiar with from years ago. "Dad, it's so nice to see you. Did you see how well I can catch?"

"I did, Matt. It's wonderful seeing you as a young pup having fun out there."

Matt looks into his dad's eyes. "Thank you for bringing me back to rest with the other dogs on the farm."

"My heart swelled with joy when you came home for the holidays. It was the best Thanksgiving your mom and I have ever had."

The memory of that holiday brings Maddie front and center in his mind. He hesitates at first, not knowing whether he should ask, but he does anyway. "Cory, have you seen Maddie? I'm wondering when I'll be able to be with her again."

"I have seen her many times here playing with the dogs. She even joins in with us sometimes, throwing the tennis balls."

"Is she happy?"

"Happy doesn't even begin to describe her emotions. Maddie misses you dearly, but knows you'll be joining her soon enough. We are all surrounded by love, but I think she may have the most with all your dogs by her side. She's thrilled Monkey's House is still thriving, giving those in need of love all they could ask for on earth before you send them up here to join your family."

"I'm delighted to see you and know you're happy. Give my love to your mother; tell her the last time I saw your dad, he couldn't stop talking about her."

Josh heads back to meet Archie when he hears Cory call out, "Josh... I think you need to come with me."

Turning back towards Cory, he replies, "Where are we going?" He's sure it's seeing Maddie, or at least he hopes.

"You need to witness it. Having me explain it won't do it justice. Besides, one of your dogs will be there today—Bullwinkle."

Josh realizes he's probably not meeting Maddie, but he's sure going to love seeing lovable, goofy Bullwinkle. Cory leads Josh down a long walkway, passing through a kiddie fantasy land full of young children on rides, games, even a petting zoo. They enter a large building and see hundreds of small children sitting on the floor in a circle around a stage. From Josh's vantage point he can't see who's on the stage, but whoever is talking is holding the children's attention. Cory leads Josh to the other side and they finally see who's in the center. It's Bullwinkle. Josh goes to call out to him, but stops. He doesn't want to distract him; the kids all seem mesmerized by him.

Bullwinkle is wearing a funny-looking top hat and bowtie. It's no surprise to Josh he's sitting in a chair way too small for him, part of his comedy act at Monkey's House. A large coonhound, he was constantly squeezing his enormous body into a little chihuahua bed. Of course, his head and legs hung out of the bed, yet he seemed comfortable sprawled across the family room floor. Josh and Cory quietly take a seat on the floor behind all the children as Bullwinkle stands and shows off the beautiful brown and black spots covering his white fur base. Three of his spots are unique, in the shape of hearts. He highlights them to the audience of kids. There's a tiny brown heart on his chest, another one on his hind leg, and a large spot dons his entire side.

"Why is Bullwinkle talking about his markings and coloring to the children?" They're very young, between two and five years old and totally engrossed in what Bullwinkle has to say.

"Look again at the children: what do they have?" Cory points to a child close by. All the children have finger painting kits equipped with every color of dog fur: many shades of brown, tan, black, white, yellow, and many more. "In a few minutes, we'll help a child paint."

"Paint what?"

"Where did you think Bullwinkle's spots came from? Somebody was creative when they painted those hearts. Remember, today's theme is fun, much like the comedian, Bullwinkle."

Josh remains confused about what the kids will paint, but notices very young puppies running among those sitting down. They are plain-looking puppies, all white, brown, or black. Suddenly, teenagers come in, each grabbing a puppy and partnering up with a child. Josh recognizes some teenagers from the playground. The scene is wonderfully chaotic.

As Josh is taking it all in, he notices a lone little boy who doesn't have a teenage partner to help him paint a puppy with those special markings of love. He gets up and heads to the one puppy still roaming the floor. He grabs the little beagle in his arms and heads over to the boy. When he gets closer, he realizes it's his nephew, Eric. Josh assumes Eric doesn't know who he is, and it doesn't matter. He'll see how Eric is doing and enjoy some time together.

"Hi, I have a puppy to paint, but I've never done this before. Would you help me? I don't think I'd be good at it, but I'll bet you are."

"Sure, I'm good. I paint lots of puppies."

"It's good to know you've done this before. What's your name?"

"Eric. Mommy brings me here, stays in back. Not today. She said I'd be fine."

"Eric, you can call me Uncle Josh. What spots and colors do you want on this puppy? Once she's born and grows up, she'll have those marking forever."

"I know Uncle Josh—love spots." Eric digs his fingers right into the paint and rubs them on the pure white puppy. He makes her ears black and puts a brown and black mask on her face. Bullwinkle must be an outstanding teacher as Eric draws a heart on her hindquarter, along with large spots across her side.

"Eric, she looks beautiful. Are we done?"

"Not yet. I like kiss freckles." Josh doesn't understand Eric, but soon finds out. Eric puts his lips into the paint and kisses the puppy all over the remaining white areas.

"You know, your Aunt Maddie would tell me every time I would kiss our beagle Lucy, she would get another freckle. Lucy had lots of freckles. Now I understand where they came from."

"Eric, if I come back again, will you help me paint another puppy?"

"I'd like that, Uncle Josh."

Reunion

The surroundings seem familiar. He can't pinpoint it, but swears it's from his childhood. As Josh and Monkey navigate their way through the woods, he believes it's the trek he used to take from his parent's house to his grandmother's a couple of miles away. Sounds of nature are all he can hear, and he realizes it's been this way since his arrival. The background reverberations of life on earth, the hustle and bustle of daily living, cars, phones, computers, planes, televisions, you name it... they are all gone. The beautiful silence along with the unblemished hum of the wind, movement of water, the chatter of birds, or the pit-ter-patter of the dogs' footsteps, are sounds helping calm the mind and warm the soul.

Monkey leads Josh through a forest as the aroma of pine dissipates, replaced with an even stronger scent of honey-suckle. He hears the buzzing of bees working the bushes in the hedgerow, going from flower-to-flower, completing their day's work of pollination. As Josh makes his way into the narrow, lush green valley, Monkey is no longer by his side. In fact, he's nowhere in sight as Josh scans his surroundings. He goes to call out for him but stops. Monkey has been leading him all along the journey, but when they're about to meet the next group of dogs, Monkey steps back, allowing him and the others time to reunite.

Josh can't stop thinking about Maddie. His journey has taken him to meet many of the dogs, but she is the clearest thought in his mind, like a laser beam in the darkness. He's wondering who's next. Alone in this meadow, not a soul is in sight. He strolls through the center and comes upon a small stream; his mouth pulls up at the edges. This is indeed the way to his grandmother's house. Once he gets to the dirt road, he only has a quarter-mile walk and he'll be there.

Something about the water running over the rocks catches his attention. Many times, his sisters would tag along on the journey. They always stopped at the creek to get a drink of cool water, followed by searching for crawfish to catch and show their grandmother. The rushing water looks as fresh as it was seventy-five years ago, still cleansing itself over river rocks and carving through the bedrock as it has done for centuries. He notices the same rock formation he discovered as a child. It's shaped in the image of his childhood dog, Cheeta. She often went along on the walks, and on one occasion while drinking from the stream, the kids noticed that image of her etched in the stone below.

Although he isn't thirsty, he yearns to get a drink—not only for a taste of his youth, but he longed to be reminded of times with his loving grandparents. Lily pads are floating in a small, calm pool, blooming in varying colors causing him to reminisce. Besides being loving, grandmothers are also wise, and he remembers her advice about drinking from a stream. *Find where the water is running the fastest across rocks; there you'll find the purest.* So, he makes his way downstream to the rushing water.

Carefully stepping on a protruding rock, he plants his left foot, then stretches his other leg to the edge of the creek as water rushes below. Assuring his footing is on solid ground, he balances himself and bends over, cupping his hands. Josh hesitates, staring into the water in amazement. It takes a few seconds to recognize the reflection; the young man he always felt himself to be within his soul gazes back. Through the years, the dogs of Monkey's House garnered their strength from Maddie and Josh. Now, as Josh meets each dog, they return the favor, bringing him back to a youthful man. He is seeing the man who met a beautiful young woman ages ago. That day at the stable, the start of it all.

Lowering his hands, he brings up water and takes a drink. It never tasted so fresh. Bending over again, he pulls the end of a large rock, lifting one side to see if there's a crawdaddy underneath. Nope… nothing there. He lets the rock slap back down, creating ripples as it rests on the bottom. He's focused, waiting for the water to settle, so he can see the bed of the creek, looking for a little nook housing what they used to call mini-lobsters. Now like a sheet of glass, he's startled as there is another reflection in the water, his grandmother's. She's standing over him. Grandma Sandy rests her hand on Josh's back. "Josh, don't be frightened. I'm so happy to see you again."

"Grandma!" Josh exclaims as he gives her a big hug. "I love you."

"I love you, too," she replies. At one time, it wasn't easy for her to say those words. Josh's family was not one to express emotion to one another, at least not loving ones. It was Maddie who first got Josh to express himself, to say he loved her—of course—but to express these emotions to others, too, like his grandmother. The first time Grandma Sandy heard Josh tell her he loved her, it surprised her. She enjoyed hearing those words, and shortly after, became comfortable expressing her love to Josh and Maddie.

Grandma Sandy hooks Josh's arm. "Let's take a stroll." After college, Josh ended up living with his grandmother in her big farmhouse. Six of her ten grandkids lived with her at some point in their lives. Sure, she had plenty of room in her old house, but it was the love that brought many of them there. That was especially true for Josh, and after Maddie became part of the family, Grandma Sandy always welcomed her, too.

Grandma Sandy would cook dinner, while Josh would set their places at the old, metal kitchen table from the 50s. They always had a pleasant conversation to accompany their meal. After eating, Josh would wash the dishes while his grandmother dried. The enjoyable part of the evening was after the dishes were washed and put away. Candy and Smiley, her two dogs, would be waiting patiently by the door for a relaxing stroll down the back country road.

Now, his grandmother leads him down a dirt road he doesn't recognize. The road is not curvy and the neighbor's farm is missing. Josh realizes they're not going to her house after all. Along the road, they are picking up dogs. The number continues to grow the farther they walk. Josh senses something special is about to happen. Coming around a bend in the road, in front of them is a beautiful lake filled with majestic Tundra swans. Those same swans Maddie and Josh looked forward to seeing every winter in the state park.

"Grandma, this view is magnificent." Josh and his grandmother stand along the bank with hundreds of dogs by their sides. Suddenly, Josh's heart explodes. It's no surprise his grandmother is coming through for him again. She's reuniting him with Maddie. In the distance, Maddie is walking towards them with her pack, Sora, Ariel, Buck and many others. Monkey's also with her, which seems odd to Josh. Monkey had been with him just moments ago, leading him here.

Josh runs to meet Maddie with the dogs in lockstep; of course, they let their dad take the lead. They blissfully fly into one another's arms, reuniting with grateful tears and powerful hugs. Their bodies collide, but it's their souls that relish most in being united once again, two beings meant to be together, separate for so long. It's been over ten years in the making, yet hugging Maddie is so familiar to him, like it was just yesterday they embraced. They are now within each other's arms, where they belong. Sora, Buck and all the dogs push in closer and closer, making one of the largest group hugs on record. Grandma Sandy is making her way into the group, too, rejoicing in their reunion.

"Maddie, I love you. I've missed you so."

"Welcome to paradise, sweetheart."

As they take a seat, the dogs gather all around. This is the first time all the dogs and Maddie are together with Josh. At a loss for words, he sits quietly and turns his head side to side, witnessing the wonders of it all. Grandma Sandy is no longer with them, which doesn't surprise him. She was the one who led him back to the love of his life. Throughout his childhood, she was one person he could always count on, and in this moment, she knew he needed time alone with Maddie.

Josh has never felt contentment like this, sitting quietly within his heart and soul. He's at a loss for words; the enormity of his journey, and now this, has left him relieved yet speechless.

Maddie takes his hand in hers. "Sweetie, it's a lot to take in. I always expected to be reunited with our dogs when I came. But I never imagined the wonders here." She spreads her arms wide.

"I don't know what to say. This is so dreamlike."

"The beauty you've seen. Us being here with you isn't a dream... it's heaven."

"Getting through a day without you was difficult. Let alone running Monkey's House... It's been challenging without you by my side. I'm happy we're finally together again."

Maddie can see the journeys he's been on today, along with their reunion, have overwhelmed Josh. She gently coaxes him to lie down with his head on her lap. As he gazes into her eyes, he sees the young girl from their first date—that spunky, beautiful brunette with high cheekbones and plump lips. The woman he's loved for a lifetime, laughed and cried with, and created their own world together.

Josh reaches into his pocket and pulls out Monkey's leash, the wonderful gift she gave him their last Christmas together. "When you gave me this, you said to carry it with me. I have since the day you left. I still remember the words you said, 'When you need it most, Monkey will lead you.'"

He looks at the worn leash, places it in her palm, and closes her fingers around it. His loving hands are wrapped around hers. Josh missed touching her, feeling her warmth. "I don't need this anymore. You were right. Monkey led me through difficult times in the past. Today, he led me on my journey and brought us together again."

"I'll hold this for you." She puts it in her pocket. "I hope you realize the leash has no magical powers. It only reinforced what you knew deep down. It helped you see what's important, to live life with love in your heart."

"Honey, was your first day like mine? LA welcomed me. From there, Monkey had me meeting many of our pups. We met Hooch and his beach crew, heard the most beautiful music from the chimes of liberation. We witnessed miracles seeing broken dogs not only walking again, but running and jumping around an agility course. We came across genuine heroes, Tucker with his partner, Courage. Then there was 'The Playground' where I witnessed the connection dogs have with children, and I spent time with our nephew, Eric."

Maddie combs her fingers through his thick, sandy brown hair. "Monkey also took me on my first journey. It was amazing. I know your head must be spinning. My day was much like yours."

"Who met you first? I'll bet it was Sora."

"It was Sora. I'll tell you more about my journey later. For now, let's be in each other's arms."

"I haven't seen Goldie yet. Is she here?" She was the spark who got Maddie thinking about a sanctuary, making a difference in sick dogs' lives.

Maddie spots Goldie and calls out. "Goldie. Come here, beautiful."

Years before Monkey's House, Maddie and Josh fostered dogs with medical challenges. One such dog was Goldie, a twelve-year-old emaciated golden retriever, with a large tumor on her abdomen. They fostered Goldie, hoping she'd gain the needed pounds before her planned surgery. They tried everything, but Goldie was not gaining weight. Her lack of progress led Maddie to believe the tumor was cancerous.

They quickly learned to foster a dog for a shelter meant you used the shelter's veterinarian and went by their diagnosis. However, senior dogs with medical issues are the last to get attention, let alone adequate funding.

Maddie took it upon herself to take Goldie to their own veterinarian. The diagnosis was indeed cancer. Goldie had only weeks to live. Maddie turned to Josh and said they had to adopt Goldie. He was confused as they were already fostering her. Maddie insisted Goldie was not going to heaven without a family. They adopted Goldie into the Kelly family and, shortly after, assisted her to the Bridge. Since Goldie, no dog they ever cared for made their final journey to the Rainbow Bridge without becoming a Kelly first.

"Here she comes, sweetie." Josh sits up and sees a stunning golden jogging their way. Her long hair blows in the wind, bouncing with every stride.

"Wow, she looks great. She's filled out like we had always hoped."

Goldie licks her dad's face. "It's great to see you, Dad."

Josh wraps his arms around Goldie, giving her a hug. "It's good to see you, girl," he says, petting her silky coat.

"Sweetie, there is one thing I've been waiting to do together. Let's ride Zeus and Brit on the beach, taking in a sunset. Just the two of us."

"I'd love to ride together. It's been ages since we went horseback riding, but I assume it will feel like yesterday, based on my other experiences here."

Maddie kisses Josh. "The ride will give us a little quiet time. Just the two of us. This evening we have a big event, a celebration. The dogs, aunts, and uncles are excited to show you the wonders of life."

Second First Date

They're alone now… well, almost. Sora is by Maddie's side as she walks hand-in-hand with Josh into a lush, green field where horses are grazing to their hearts' content. All these magnificent animals are part of their family. Suddenly, Zeus and Brit come trotting over. They're excited to enjoy time with their parents on this special occasion.

"Wow, these guys look great. I never saw them in their prime." Josh reaches way up and pats Brit's neck. He's close to seventeen hands, much taller than the average horse. A thoroughbred draft cross, Brit sports a shiny chestnut coat with a reddish mane and tail. In his heyday, he was a champion cross-country eventer. By the time he came to be Josh's steed, the previous owners put a lot of training into him, hoping to turn him into a dressage horse. He never took to dressage, so they gave him to Josh for trail riding. Brit was so well schooled, you could glance right and he would head in that direction. Reading the rider's body was his specialty. If only he sensed when Josh wanted to stop. Pulling back on the reins meant little to him. Josh had to be prepared to let him run until he wore himself out. Although halting was a problem, Josh sure loved the power-steering and to experience the pure energy under him when Brit took off in a full gallop.

Zeus nudges Maddie's arm. "Yes, we're going there today," she says to him.

"Where are we riding?"

"Do you remember where Zeus loved to ride?"

"Yeah, it was the Pine Barrens or the beach. He loved both."

Maddie is tickling Zeus's nose. "He wants to go to the beach. Don't you, big boy?" Zeus is a draft horse, a Suffolk Punch. While the breed is typically a shorter, stockier version of a Belgian, Zeus is clearly a big horse weighing in around a ton. After a nasty accident, Maddie was told she would never ride again because of her lingering injury and pain. It devastated her, but after a year without a horse, she took a chance on riding Zeus, a big, calm fellow. He's a gentle giant who wouldn't hurt a fly. Much like her, he suffered an injury while pulling a carriage in Cape May, and had to be retired. They bonded immediately, and shortly after, Zeus became part of the family. Like in her college days, she spent any spare time with Zeus. She especially loved it when Josh could join them on a trail ride in the Pines with Brit.

Josh looks around for the tack, but there isn't a single bridle or saddle in sight, let alone helmets or chaps for them. "I take it we don't need riding gear in heaven."

"You're learning." She smiles, giving him a peck on the lips, followed by a poke in the ribs. He missed her playfulness, which inspires him to grab and tickle her.

"Payback for tickling the big guy's nose." They end up embracing, looking into each other's eyes and culminating in a long kiss. "I've missed your aroma, the taste of your lips, and the silkiness of your hair," he says in almost a whisper, stroking his hand down her long, thick tresses. "I love running my fingers through your hair."

No mounting block needed. Zeus and Brit buckle their front legs, lowering themselves towards the ground as Maddie and Josh climb onto their mounts. Once aboard, the horses rise and off they head on a slow walk. Josh grabs a hold of Brit's mane. He's ridden bareback many times in his youth, but never without a bridle. Reins in his grasp let him feel like he had some control, so he's unsure of himself at this moment. Maddie is a natural, sitting comfortably on Zeus, which is easy to do. Zeus's back is wide and soft, almost like sitting on a couch.

Josh hears excessive howling breaking the stillness of the day. "What's all the barking about?"

"You'll see in a minute. We're almost there." As they crest the side of the hill, Josh sees a pack of excited dogs. Lucy, Mr. Peebody, Sunshine, and Shark, along with many other dogs of varying hunting breeds gather, waiting for the games to commence. They are giving PeeWee, a little chihuahua dressed up in a rabbit costume, a head-start. The costume also smells like a rabbit, a key ingredient of the game. PeeWee is so fast on his paws, and his tiny stature lets him speed through small gaps in a fence or in and out of holes. The game is definitely challenging when PeeWee is the rabbit.

"Looks like a game of hide-and-seek. Except there's only one hiding and the rest are seeking." It's amusing Josh as the seekers sniff the ground, and off they charge.

As they continue their ride, Josh notices the agility course in the distance. The dogs mastering the course filled his heart with joy and eyes with grateful tears, not to mention the excitement of biking for the first time in decades. A clicking sound comes out of the side of Maddie's mouth and Zeus takes off, heading straight for it. Josh's eyes widen; he only has a small clump of mane to hold on to. Then, he remembers the pups telling him anything is possible here. Upon witnessing it many times, he regains faith, and with a little pressure from his heels on Brits' flanks, off they go. In no time, they catch up to Maddie and Zeus, even passing them like they're standing still. Brit runs all-out, and Josh settles onto his back as though they're one.

Brit slows down a bit to let his buddy Zeus come along-side. In a nice canter, they're heading straight for the agility course. The horses are looking to join the dogs running through the obstacles. This realization results in a look of fear on Josh's face. Maddie notices it right away. "Just go with it. They've done the course hundreds of times. Relax and have fun."

As they approach, the dogs scatter, forming a line around the edge, readying to cheer them on, especially their dad. He mastered the obstacles on a bike, but this is a unique experience where he has to depend on Brit to do the work. His job is just to stay on, to be as one with Brit. Josh is fully aware of Brit's physical capabilities as a cross-country event horse, however, Josh himself was a trail rider, so he's still a bit skeptical.

The horses take the course in a different way, with a lot more jumping over objects. They head into the weave poles, twisting in and out like a western rider in a pole-bending competition, only Josh doesn't look like a competitive western rider. He's wide-eyed and tightly gripping Brit's mane. As for Maddie, she places her hands perfectly on her thighs, allowing her to bend and push into each pole. Front legs tuck as they jump over the seesaw and head towards the Dock Dive. Suddenly, the dogs get super excited, barking and howling even louder.

Right in front of him, Josh notices the large pool of water. He's not sure he's ready for this, but reminds himself of the dog's telling him all is achievable here. Readying for the plunge, he's about to close his eyes when Brit takes a wide right turn, swooping back around. He finds himself facing the pool from the side. The width of the pool has to be twenty feet, and Josh wonders what's up since Maddie and Zeus have stopped near the ramp of the Dock Dive.

"Hang on, sweetheart."

"What do you mean, hang on? Aren't you and Zeus following us?"

"Zeus is too large to jump. Don't worry. Brit makes it once in a while," she smiles.

Josh is wondering if he should jump—off of Brit's back, that is. Brit is off before he can make a decision, as if he's charging out of a Kentucky Derby gate. Legs wrapped as tightly as possible around Brit's flanks and with a white knuckled, grip of his mane, they race toward the edge. As Brit leaps into the air, Josh closes his eyes and hears the dogs cheering him on. Flying. They seem to be soaring through the air, then make it across with plenty of room to spare, landing on solid ground. His flight reinforces those words he's heard all along... "anything is possible."

Maddie guides Zeus over to Josh. "I'm so glad he made it today. Many times, he ends up in the pool." She smiles and gives him a wink.

"He doesn't make it most times, huh?" He gets Brit to rump bump Zeus. "Remember our first date? You had me dripping wet from Nosey splashing in the creek, and you guys left me in the dust, sitting on Thunder." With a quick tap of Josh's heels, Brit takes off. "Karma baby!"

Maddie gets Zeus turned around and heads off after them. With a bit of pressure from his left leg, Josh has Brit lined up with the ramp to the dock dive. Brit's canter turns into an all-out run. Zeus tries to keep up but is lagging. Suddenly, the dogs take off, following Zeus. Brit hits the end of the ramp and off they soar, landing in the water around the middle of the pool. Within seconds, Maddie and Zeus hit the water. With Zeus, it resembles more of a cannonball as water is flying everywhere. Before they know it, there are scores of dogs jumping in all around them. Zeus and Brit plant their hoofs firmly on the bottom of the pond. As good sports, they are now being used as springboards with their backs cresting above the water. Not only were Josh and Maddie climbing on their backs and jumping off, but the dogs also joined in on the fun.

Maddie takes Josh's hand. "We seemed to have veered away from our relaxing ride together. But this is fun." Both are sitting on Zeus's back as they embrace and kiss. "How about we get back to our relaxing ride, just the two of us? I have some special places I want to show you."

"Yeah, I'm ready for a little downtime, for sure." Josh jumps off Zeus, swims over to Brit and gets aboard. Maddie takes the lead, making their way on to their next adventure.

The landscape transitions from open fields to patchy forests, to where they are now. If he was back home, he'd swear this was the Pine Barrens, although it wouldn't surprise him if it was since he's learned heaven is whatever you can imagine. Your favorite people, animals, and places will make up your personal heaven. Walking side-by-side, relaxed from the gentle swaying of the horses, they cut their way through a dense stand of pine and oak trees, making their way to a lake. A beautiful lake reminds him of their lake, the one they visited so many times. It was the last time Maddie was in the Pines, on their little New Year's Day excursion.

Today, the waterfowl are out in plenty. Swans and Canadian geese float gracefully while a blue heron stands majestically along the edge. There are also many species of duck gently rocking on the water. The calls of all the different fowl create a musically peaceful setting. Maddie and Josh reminisce about all the adventures they had in the Pines, their favorite slice of heaven on earth. They always had at least one animal within their stories, either horses or dogs, sometimes both.

After enjoying time together, Josh brings up a subject he wished he didn't have to, one which has been on his mind all day. "Honey, I'm afraid Monkey's House will be lost. The developers are going to take the property. We're out of money, and I've gone down every legal avenue I could." Josh pauses. "I'm so sorry. I let you and the dogs down."

"You have nothing to be sorry about. I'm proud of the way you ran our hospice. Besides, there's always hope our little haven will survive."

Josh interrupts the conversation, pointing to the far shore of the lake. "Look, there's another horse and rider. Who do you think it is?"

As the rider approaches, Maddie answers. "It's somebody imperative to all of this, or at least to our relationship."

Rita, their friend who arranged their first date, is riding her horse, Tally. She makes her way down a path to meet them. "Hi Maddie, nice to see you today. Welcome to paradise, Josh."

"Hi Rita. It's been such a long time. I agree with you; this is paradise."

"Rita, Josh got here today. He's taking in an awful lot so far, so I brought him out for some quiet time."

"It has blessed me to see the love between you two over the years, plus all you've accomplished with your dog sanctuary.

Well, I'm grateful I introduced the two of you—to have been a tiny part of your magic."

Josh gets Brit positioned right alongside Zeus, reaches over and holds Maddie's hand, giving it a loving squeeze. "Through the years, Maddie and I would often mention you. Actually, thanking you for being so forceful in getting us to take a chance on your matchmaking. We'd laugh and wonder what took us so long to agree. No matter—we're both glad we gave in to your relentless efforts."

Rita points Tally toward a trail. "I'm taking off. Letting you enjoy time together." Rita gives Tally a command and off they trot.

Maddie leans her head onto Josh's shoulder as they take in the majesty of their view ahead. There are only a couple hours of daylight left, so they decide they'd best continue on their excursion. Before they know it, they're walking the horses on the beach. Josh recalls how Zeus loved the water, and it's no different here as he wades knee deep with the calm waves brushing against his enormous belly.

Zeus heads off to the right, knowing the way to Maddie's oasis here at the beach: a little cove where the water is as calm as a sheet of glass. The horses break into a trot with Brit on Zeus's heels, leaving deep hoof prints in the virgin white sand lining the cove. Slowing to a walk, a monarch butterfly lands between Brits ears and rides with them for a while. After some time, the butterfly slowly flaps its wings. With each stroke, its tickling Brit's ears, making him wiggle them. Josh finds this comical. Halfway around the horseshoe inlet, they stop. The horses bend their front legs, taking themselves closer to the ground to let Maddie and Josh jump off. The horses canter off to the lush grass past the sand.

Maddie takes a seat and draws a big circle in the sand right next to her. "Here. Come sit right here."

He wonders why she drew the circle in the sand. Once he sits, he feels as though he's on a soft cushion. "How is this so soft? Why did you sketch out a circle?"

She reaches her arms around his waist, pulls him close, and kisses him. "How many more?"

"How many more what?" He doesn't know what she's asking.

She kisses him again and puts her index finger on his lips, keeping them closed. "All is possible here. You've seen it time and time again. So, how many more times do you need to witness it to believe?"

"It's hard to accept, I guess."

"This is not your ordinary cove. What you'll see here, well, you've seen before."

This inlet is a spiritual harbor, a place where aspiring angels come to learn and eventually carry out good deeds enabling them to get their wings. Now, laying on their backs looking into the sky, Maddie and Josh are enjoying each other's company. No serious conversation is had, merely simple talk and splendid memories. The loud croaking of a bullfrog interrupts the faint noise of the horses chewing grass. Josh pops up to a seated position. "I hear one big frog." Josh's eyes narrow and his head tilts, "How can bullfrogs be at the beach? They're always near fresh water."

Maddie doesn't address Josh's question directly. "Remember how we would get the small frogs on our front porch during the summer nights? They would come and eat bugs gathering from the porch light, nabbing those felled to the cement floor."

"Yeah, I remember those cute little toads. They came nightly, squeezing through the narrow wire we put up to keep the dogs in."

"Sweetie, the night Dozer passed, do you remember what was on the porch? A giant bullfrog. For twenty years, we never saw one there. It wouldn't fit through the wire. In fact, you had to take it back down to the pond to release him."

Maddie continues, "The colorful hitchhiker who landed between Brit's ears? That was the butterfly who came to visit us in The Cottage after Bullwinkle passed. It would land on the floor right where he liked to sleep. It wasn't frightened off and stayed for days."

As Josh contemplates what Maddie is telling him, he notices a deer walking along the edge of the water, then grazing with the horses. This deer is unique, a button-buck with a white hind leg. Thinking back, he remembers a special walk in the park with his buddies, Violet and Carbon, two of their dogs who loved to take hikes in the state forest. Josh enjoyed spending time in nature and the way it nourished his soul. He always took a dog or two to tag along, and made those walks adventures for them.

After Tequila passed, he needed to clear his head. A walk in the park would do the trick, so he grabbed his two companions and off they went. On the walk, they saw a deer standing in the middle of the trail. The dogs were interested, as was the deer with them. He found it strange the deer didn't seem the least bit leery. It sauntered off into the woods and they continued on their way.

Josh was a regular in the Pines. He spent decades there riding horses, walking, and biking. To his recollection, he'd never seen a deer during all his time in the forest, and was pleased to see one that day. There's barely anything for them to eat in the woods. They normally congregate near farmland where they have a plentiful food source.

The following week, on a different route with Violet and Carbon, they once again encountered the deer. He knew it was the same one as it had the unique white hind leg he noticed on their last hike. Again, the deer seemed interested in them.

Eventually, the deer jumped into the woods and was gone. As Josh approached where the deer went off the trail, he noticed it was flooded with a foot of water lining both sides of the path from spring rains. He thought to himself, *no ripples*. It made no sense, as it was a large flooded area. *There must be ripples.* As the sun shone through the Pines, it glistened off the water, creating many colors—blues, greens, and shades of red. It looked as though there was a film on the water, but as he got closer, a spectrum of colors appeared only when viewed from a certain angle.

He always believed the deer was telling him Tequila was with their other Monkey's House dogs who made their way to the Rainbow Bridge. Don't lose heart, all was fine.

Once he's confident in his realization, he pipes up, "Honey, they're the signs they gave us when we lost a dog, telling us they're fine at the Bridge." He points towards the deer grazing with the horses. "That's the deer who came after Tequila passed. The one I told you about in the park."

"I'm glad you can see it now." She gives him a big hug.

"Like the colors of the rainbow you saw on the water, when we really look, we become attuned to our surroundings and can see loved ones who passed, thanking us. They are telling us they're okay." Josh looks around as Maddie leans back into the sand, tugging his arm to meet her. Whether it's the lone daylily blooming on the beach or the bluebird perched upon a piece of driftwood, his acceptance of all of this is opening his eyes wide, and bringing peace to his heart.

As he lies backdown next to Maddie on the sand, he turns on his side and hugs her like he's done a thousand times before.

Tree of Life

Maddie throws down a little blanket in the middle of the field. There's a large tree perched upon a small incline directly in front of them. Josh isn't sure what they'll be viewing, but figures Maddie knows the routine, so this must be a prime location to lean back, relax, and take in the celebration. Upon taking a seat, Josh has the same blissful feeling as when they would sit together on the North Cape May beach—not a care in the world, just focused on one another.

Josh believes the tree is a Magnolia. it appears to be over a hundred feet high. It's towering into the heavens even deeper than where they sit. Its leathery evergreen foliage has a pyramidal shape and fragrant flowers. They appear to be the size of small dinner plates. It's a magnificent-looking tree.

Josh airs his assumption. "That's a Magnolia tree, right?"

"Yes, a Southern Magnolia. Similar to the ones we had in the front yard of our house. Although ours weren't the Southern variety, they were much smaller. This tree is special. It's sacred, containing magical powers."

"Magical powers, like what?" he reaches over and tickles Maddie.

"You'll have to wait and see." She giggles. The teasing

tickle becomes a young couple rolling through the grass in an all-out tickle fight.

For all the trees that could represent the wonderful souls here, the Southern Magnolia is perfect. Much like the dogs of Monkey's House, the Magnolia flower symbolizes perseverance, purity, love, gentleness, and immortality. The branches are flush with soft, white flowers, yet they are strong in appearance. Along with the flowers, the tree contains many buds waiting to bloom. Unlike on earth, once the flowers open and display their beauty here, they remain fresh and vibrant for eternity. Petals of the flower are cupped, like two hands holding water. On earth, they are inviting to the bees. Here, they portray the acceptance and giving of love.

Hannah Bear and her entourage set up their instruments at the base of the tree. It's the Monkey's House rock band, "Hannah and the Halos." As the sun goes down, more dogs arrive, some with their favorite aunt or uncle. Hooch, Eve, and the other beach pups are carrying sacks as they make their way to the refreshment stand. They brought some of their special dried bananas to go along with the regular treats, bully sticks and cod skins. They seem to be a big hit as pups are getting their treats and finding a nice place to sit or lie down, all facing towards the tree. On a little table at the end is Much Loved Bob, a cute little beagle, with his famous peanut butter pies. He'd never share them on earth, but after his arrival here, he's a changed pup and willing to give slices to his brothers and sisters.

As Josh scans the field, it brings back an ancient memory. In fact, he's recalling one of his first dates with Maddie. "Do you remember our first movie together at the Ringoes drive-in? This reminds me of that. Except the snack bar was candy, soda pop, and popcorn—not dog treats." He looks into Maddie's eyes and gives her a tender kiss. "I don't seem to remember the movie featured that night. Do you?"

"Well, I don't know how you would've. You were facing the wrong way, kissing me through most of it. Your enormous head was blocking my view."

"What, a little like this?" Josh leans over and passionately kisses Maddie.

"Mmmmm... by the way, Romeo, the movie was E.T., the perfect film for a drive-in, especially when Elliott's bike flew into the night sky with E.T."

Josh reaches over to once again to tickle her. "So, you saw the movie. I guess my fat head wasn't in the way after all."

The field is full now. Besides the dogs, aunts and uncles who loved the dogs through the years are sitting among them. Similar to a lunar cycle, they hold this event during a new moon when the sky is the darkest. Hannah and the Halos are poised to rock the crowd with their signature hit, "Life is a Dog Bone, Chew it all Day Long," a cute little song parody of "Life's a Highway" by Tom Cochran.

Eve starts the music with her first strike of the drums, quickly followed by Bullwinkle on the bass guitar and Hooch playing his yellow, 1960s Flying Banana Yamaha guitar. Pugsley, a chubby Pug, jams on the harmonica while tickling the plastic ivories on the keyboard. There isn't a soul sitting; all are up, wagging their butts to the beat. Three littles, Ariel, Bea, and Maisey, are the backup singers this evening. Pure harmony flows out of Hannah Bear and the crowd goes wild. They love her voice and music, and the lyrics are delicious.

Life's like a bone that you chew on
When one day it's here and the next day it's gone,
Sometimes you sit, sometimes you lay
Sometimes all you do is want to play
There's Monkey's House with an open door
Where people won't hurt you anymore
Where the love flows free and dogs soar
Come walk with me at the Jersey shore
We won't hesitate to break down the backyard gate
There's not much time left to play

Life is a Dog Bone
I want to chew it all day long
If you're by my side
I'm wagging my tail all day long

Through all the nooks and all the crannies,
It's in my mouth and licked all around
I love you now like I loved you then
This is the bone we've all dreamed about
From the neighbor's yard to old trash cans
Stealing bones is my delight

Take a break back in again
You're in my mouth. I'm not a lonely dog.

There's no bone I can't chew
Bone so tasty this I know
I'll be chewing till the sun goes down
Just tell 'em we're survivors

Life is a Dog Bone
I want to chew it all day long
Chewy chewy chewy
If you're by my side
I'm wagging my tail all day long
Chewy chewy chewy

During the last harmonica piece, treats fly up to the band. Tradition has it as the dogs enter the field, they grab two treats—one for themselves and another for the band members. Once they finish playing their signature hit, the audience will toss the extra treat up to the band. Pugsley loves this custom, as eight band members and hundreds of dogs mean a lot of goodies coming his way. He'll definitely be overdoing it this evening. Pugsley likes to compare himself to the singer Meatloaf, although he may actually be relating to the food, meatloaf.

This song always causes ruff-housing amongst the dogs, but they quickly settle when the lights wave in the sky. Tonight, the Aurora is displaying in many colors besides the normal pale green and pink. Shades of red, yellow, green, blue, and violet join in and the spectrum of colors appears like rippling curtains with an occasional shooting ray of light across the sky.

Maddie is sitting in front of Josh, between his legs. She leans back into his body as his arms wrap around her in a big hug. They have plenty of company as Sora, Buck, Randy and others snuggle in close to be near their parents. Maddie tilts her head back, giving Josh a kiss, and prepares him for what's coming. "The Aurora Borealis is also called the Northern Lights. Many cultures believed the lights were the spirits of animals and people. Well, this is what you're about to witness."

Josh isn't sure what she means, but acknowledges her, eager to see what will happen next. With the sky illuminated in colors, the tree stands out, like it's in 3-D, just as the Majestic Kingdom looked when they watched the fireworks from their balcony on their last trip together. The white Magnolia flowers are magnificent, with a glow about them. Maddie is right. Josh realizes something magical is happening to the tree.

While the grand tree entrances Josh, Buck is curious, "Mom, who do you think it will be... me?" It's an honor to be chosen. Surely, all the dogs want to be selected tonight, for their dad sits among them.

"You know by now we don't decide. It's up to the heavens."

Josh is hypnotized by the tree. Flowers are lighting up like a string of twinkling Christmas lights. Suddenly, the lights stop blinking and only one remains lit. The light coming from the flower streams into the sky like a shooting star heading in the wrong direction.

"It's Leo." Buck shouts out as a video of Leo plays above. The Auroral makes the perfect screen for the clip.

The first picture of Leo shows him dressed as Leo the Lion, one of his Halloween costumes. It continues displaying dozens of images of Leo, along with video snippets of him enjoying his time at Monkey's House. Who said dogs don't smile? He has the biggest grin sitting on one of his favorite laps, Aunt Trudy's. He's nestled in deep as she caresses his silky fur. Not sure who looks more spellbound? The video cuts to clips with Leo snuggling with many of the Monkey's House dogs, big and small.

The memories of Leo warm Josh's heart. He's thrilled to see him living his best possible life. He realizes it's not showing the condition Leo was in when he first made his way to Monkey's House. There's no sign of the initial struggles he had, those he worked so hard to overcome. Josh leans up and whispers into Maddie's ear. "It took Leo a long time to settle in after the trauma he endured from his previous person. Why isn't this showing any of that?"

"It shows them living their best life. What they need to remember. What we all should focus on... love and happiness."

Josh kisses Maddie's neck. "Leo was my favorite name you gave to one of our dogs. I'll never forget Leo the Lion, King of the Jungle."

"He was so frightened when he came to us. That's why I gave him a powerful name, hoping it would help him overcome his fear." It took a year just to touch Leo without him flinching. "What's important is he experienced love and compassion before coming here."

Leo loved the field trips, and the next clip was one of his adventures at the Jersey shore, strolling on the beach sniffing seaweed. The next photos show him on New Year's Day, walking in the Pines and hitching a ride in a carriage after he tuckered out. Leo's last image showed him sitting on Santa's lap, telling the jolly old man he's been a good boy and would love extra treats for Christmas.

Josh is stunned by all he's seen. "Wow, this is amazing. And I thought our Christmas tree was special. This tree takes it up a few notches."

Maddie's laughing, "Oh, you think?" She squeezes his leg. "I adored our skinny tree, telling stories to each other about our dogs. You always seemed to embellish them towards the end, turning many into memorable tales. If I remember correctly, I think a legend or two were born."

Josh notices Leo getting up and making his way somewhere. "Where is Leo headed?"

"Once the video ends, the dog or person will go to the one who helped them live their best life."

Leo makes his way over to Aunt Trudy and takes his favorite position on her lap.

The dogs wait patiently to see if the flowers twinkle again. There is no set number of souls it picks on any evening of the Auroral, although it generally features three. Tonight, the dogs are all hoping for another to highlight their story of the love they experienced in their lives, especially with their dad here to see it. The noise becomes deafening as the dogs carry on when they notice the flowers lighting up again. Once a flower is chosen, the light from its petals shoots up into the sky. This time for Violet, a black Labrador retriever mix, whose story is about to unfold.

As the pictures scroll, they reveal a dog excited to be traveling to a familiar oasis. For Violet, it's the New Jersey Pine Barrens. Looking out the window of the car, she anticipated familiar smells along the sand roads and trails she'd be traveling. The sounds of the waterfowl, as they'd pass by the old cranberry bogs, always drew her attention. Many of the images included her best friend, Carbon, a German shepherd mix who was the Kellys' personal dog. Carbon was a young, healthy dog, bringing playful youth into the house of seniors.

They can see the joy in Violet in a video walking with her dad, exploring the many trails in the forest. She had a strong pace, which put emphasis on her famous ear flapping. Violet's ears move up and down with her stride. With a slight bend in the middle, they're like the wings of a seagull flapping. Next up are selfie images of her and Josh using the lakes, bogs, or other unique aspects of the Pines as their backdrop. Carbon photo bombed his way into many of the pictures.

"I loved walking Violet. It made my weekend. I'm sure it made hers, too."

"You took her every weekend, except in the heat of the summer."

"Yeah, it was our three-season weekly adventure, for sure. Even the coldest of days didn't stop us, although a few times we had to cut them short." Josh's arms enfold Maddie, like he's picking her up. "I remember one day, it was freezing, and it hurt her paws, so I carried her all the way back to the car."

"You're the best dad." Maddie pulls his hand up to her lips and kisses the back of it.

In the last picture, you couldn't tell who felt more love, Violet or Josh, as she pushed her nose into Josh's face. Violet didn't lick to show affection. Her way of expressing love was putting her nose into your face. Josh learned her method and reciprocated. They would often sit nose to nose.

Thinking of Violet, Josh remembers his "Sweet Violet" passage near the end of his first book. It's so fitting now, he thinks.

Heading back from the park one day, we took a different route, the long way home, a scenic drive to do a little sightseeing. Violet glanced at me like, "Where are we going? Are we lost?" I told her, "We're not lost. Let's savor the time we have together. We'll celebrate this moment—the gift of borrowed time. Look around, there's beauty on this journey. Although we'll struggle at times, the view on this ride will be treasured forever." Hundreds of lucky dogs have made our home part of their journey, their "long way home." Their journeys are not always easy, but they celebrate life and make special moments count. I can only imagine the stories they take to the Rainbow Bridge.

As the video ends, Violet runs to make her way over to her dad, her Pine Barren hiking buddy. They embrace, bringing their noses to one another.

The flowers twinkle again and the dogs howl, wishing to be the one picked next. Surprisingly, two flowers stay lit and within seconds lights from both of the flowers shoot up into the sky.

"Sweetie, we're all in for a treat. We've never had two stories at once."

Maddie caresses his calves as they wait in anticipation to learn who the dual act will be. It's royalty, Princess Granny and Sir Cotton, both fluffy Pomeranians.

The first video shows Princess Granny and Sir Cotton looking stellar, sitting high in their royal carriage. However, instead of horses pulling it, their very own Aunt Karen is pushing them along the beach in their dog stroller. The silky hair of these two poms is flowing in the wind: Granny with her majestic golden orange locks, along with Cotton's stately white coat.

There's a picture of Aunt Karen scratching Granny's secret spot on her chest. It's causing her to melt like a stick of butter in the sun. When she's in Karen's arms, scratching just the right spot sends Granny into a backbend with her head stretching for the floor. The next image lets everybody see Cotton is not immune to tickling either. Cotton is upside down in her arms, and in-between belly rubs, is being fed with a spoon.

Dozens of photos display and videos play. In most, Princess Granny is wearing a tiara. She had five of them in varying colors to match outfits she might wear on any given day. Their last photo shows Princess Granny and Aunt Karen wearing matching tiaras, sitting on Santa's lap, along with their prince, Sir Cotton.

One would never guess from the photos and videos that Princess Granny was a puppy mill dog. Once she could no longer bear puppies, they discarded her. Old, blind, and deaf with significant heart problems, they tossed her like an old piece of trash. She ended up in a high-kill shelter. Cotton didn't have it much better. He had a broken pelvis earlier in his life, which severely atrophied his right hind leg. It gave him a fair amount of pain. When he came to Monkey's House, he was also in kidney failure.

Like the commotion around British royalty, the same happened with Princess Granny and Sir Cotton. Their loyal followers cherished them; they were truly loved during their time at Monkey's House.

Hannah and the Halos get ready for their next set. Three stories highlighted wonderful lives, actually four, if you count the combined stories of Princess Granny and Sir Cotton. Normally, there are two to three, so they assume it's time to get the dogs rocking and rolling again. Before they get to their instruments, the flowers are lighting up again, dancing among the branches. Unlike the last few times, the dogs are silent. They are in awe. Tree of Life has never gone past three stories. Also, the white lights have now changed to be every color of the rainbow. It's hypnotizing the audience, as they don't know what to expect.

Josh rubs his hands over Maddie's arms, which are now covered in goosebumps. "All the flowers are staying illuminated. What's happening?"

Leaning back deeper into Josh, "I've never seen this before. All the colors, and all the flowers are staying lit."

The flowers get brighter and brighter and the first light shoots up, putting an image of Maddie into the sky. Colored lights from the petals shoot up one after another, much like a Roman candle firework without the bangs. Images and video clips of the dogs, aunts, and uncles fill the sky. The images mesmerize the dogs, who are keeping a close eye on the hundreds of lights heading deep into the heavens, checking out all the images, waiting to see themselves among the stars.

When the tree appears to be done celebrating their lives, one bud on the tree is glowing. Still sitting between Josh's legs, Maddie twists at the waist and leans back to kiss him. Her eyes focus and jaw tightens. He can sense she needs to tell him something.

"Sweetie, I'd love to take a walk with you. You know, it's one of our favorite things to do together." Maddie extends her arm to help pull Josh off the ground. "Come on."

Making their way out of the field, the dogs know this time is for them. None follow. Walking hand-in-hand, they come upon a little bubbling creek and stroll along its bank. On this still and quiet night, the sound of the rushing water over the rocks has a calming effect on Josh. All is right at the moment.

"Honey, I have always imagined heaven would be special. We'd be together as a family, but never in my wildest dreams would I have envisioned this. It's incredible."

"It is an amazing place. Love, that's what it's all about. Love makes anything possible." She tightens her grip on his hand.

The Auroral lights are changing from the waving curtain to an arc of the colors of a rainbow. It appears the end of the rainbow is directly ahead of them.

"Wow, is this common? Have you seen this happen before?" Josh doesn't know what to expect. They see the arc touching down on the Bridge LA led Josh across.

Maddie stops in her tracks. Josh's arm jerks as she grabs it and pulls him closer to her, face to face. She wraps her arms around him, following with a long, passionate kiss. "I have to tell you something. It won't be easy for you to hear."

A knot forms in Josh's stomach; the colorful arc already had him concerned, and now this. "What is it? Is something wrong?"

Taking his hand, she places it over her heart and puts hers over his. "We're meant to be together; we have been since the first day we met. The buds on the tree are dogs who haven't made it here yet."

Josh's eyes open wide. "Then you were right, Monkey's House won't be lost to developers."

Silence fills the air. Finally, with welled eyes, Maddie says, "The glowing bud on the tree... that's you. You're not meant to be here. Not yet. There are more dogs to save. They need you. I need you to be strong. Strong for us. Strong for the dogs yet to come."

He freezes, his face grows long followed by tears running down his cheeks. "I want to stay with you and the others." He grabs her arm. "I love you."

"Sweetie, I wish you could stay. It's not my decision. Your job is not finished."

"My heart is here with you. I love you."

"I love you, too. We'll be together again soon." Maddie pulls Monkey's leash out of her pocket. "You gave this to me because you said you didn't need it in heaven." She hands it back. "Carry this with you. I'll always be on the other end guiding you."

"I will, but I don't need a leash to be close to you. You're always in my heart."

They share a final, extended embrace and kiss. With mixed emotions, Josh slowly makes his way to the Bridge. He looks back and sees Maddie flanked by all their dogs, his family. He holds up the leash. "I'll keep this close to my heart." Lowering his hand, he thumps his heart with the fist holding the leash. "All of you are in here. You'll lead me back here." Turning towards the Bridge, he maneuvers around a pile of leashes and steps onto the Bridge, crossing back over.

Letters of Inspiration

Time passes so slowly, and still, there is no news of Josh's progress. Holly should have been back at Monkey's House hours ago. However, she decided to stay until they got an update on Josh. By now, they have the waiting room to themselves. Josh's surgery is the only one still under way. Holly and Kaitlyn were expecting it to be over by now. They pace the room, staring into thin air. Before you know it, they are sitting again, followed by more pacing. Silence fills the air; they've been quiet for some time with Josh on their minds. They take turns gazing down the hallway. It's like they are taking shifts, wishing, no make that willing, for someone from the operating room to walk down and give them an update.

Suddenly, Holly turns her head towards the hall as she sees movement out of the corner of her eye. "Kaitlyn, here comes Dr. Lea again." Kaitlyn gets up and switches seats, taking a spot on the couch next to Holly. The memories of her time in the hospital, along with the apprehension of hearing how her uncle's surgery is progressing, are overwhelming her, and she needs to be close to someone who cares. As Dr. Lea takes a seat across from them, Kaitlyn grabs Holly's hand, squeezing tightly.

"Hi Kaitlyn." Dr Lea turns her attention to Holly. "Sorry, I don't remember your name."

"That's alright, I'm Holly."

Dr. Lea has the same emotionless look on her face as she coolly states, "Mr. Kelly had complications during the surgery."

Kaitlyn's heart sinks after hearing the word "complications" and she notices the anguish in Holly's face. Tears well up as they wait for more bad news.

She continues, with no genuine sense of compassion, "His heart stopped when we were about to close up… finishing the operation." Tears are now streaming down both their faces. "But wait, we got his heart started again. It took a lot of effort; we didn't give up on him. He's stable and they are closing now."

The emotional rollercoaster of this day, topped off with this brief, awkward conversation, has Kaitlyn breaking down as Holly holds her tight, telling her all will be okay. Once she delivers her update, Dr. Lea stands up and leaves. Holly tells Kaitlyn she'll stay another thirty minutes, giving her a reassuring grip on her hand. It's helping Kaitlyn pull herself together. Eventually, Holly heads back to Monkey's House to relieve the other volunteers.

Spending time with her uncle the past few weeks has been a blessing for Kaitlyn. His positive attitude has been rubbing off on her, and she enjoys listening to all his stories, many of which include her aunt. When they didn't actually involve Maddie, he seemed to angle the narrative in just the right manner to include her. Sure, he embellished the stories, but they highlighted the loving relationship her aunt and uncle had together. It seemed like a fairytale to Kaitlyn—a storybook relationship she wished she had, with none other than her beloved Carson.

The knot in Kaitlyn's stomach finally eases, then hunger sets in. There are vending machines in the far corner of the waiting room. Unfortunately, one is a soda machine, and the other is full of junk food. Suddenly, she remembers stashing a couple of granola bars in her backpack. Digging down deep into the pack, she pushes aside the large manila envelope containing the letters her uncle gave her to bring to the hospital. He never had time to read them in pre-op, as he'd hoped. Although she was sure he knew every word by heart, she assumed it gave him solace to have Maddie's letter close to his heart.

Uncle Josh told Kaitlyn about the letter her aunt wrote him, but she never actually read it. Over the past weeks, he told her she was welcome to read it, but she wasn't comfortable doing so. She was curious, wondering what words her aunt would have written to her uncle. However, Kaitlyn felt their correspondence was private. Now, she yearns to better understand the special bond they had; she pulls the large envelope out of the pack and peeks inside. It has a few items: two well-worn letters and a sealed envelope. She takes out the two letters, unfolding the oldest looking one first. It's the most worn-out piece of paper she's ever seen. It's obviously the letter her uncle reads every night before bed. Since Kaitlyn's been at Monkey's House, there hasn't been a day he didn't reference it in some manner. He calls it "Maddie's love letter."

Kaitlyn can see the love Maddie conveyed to Josh, as she finally allows herself to read the letter. Besides love, what comes across is the dedication they had for one another, the best of friends there for each other through the years. It melts her heart to read how Josh supported Maddie's passion for opening Monkey's House, making it his own life's mission. Maddie fears he may have sacrificed his passions for hers. Kaitlyn connects deeply with the last few lines. It reminds her of one of her favorite childhood memories with her aunt and uncle—walking the dogs on the beach. "I will wait at the Bridge with all our children, looking forward to the day when we can once again hold hands, walk amongst the angels and see the most magnificent sunsets, painting the sky bright with every color of the rainbow."

The letter flows with loving devotion, stirring Kaitlyn's emotions. Grateful to see the love Maddie had for Josh, it brings her back to the love she had and lost. She could have taken the same tone from the letter and written it to Carson. Much of how Maddie felt about Josh, is how she still feels about him.

As the last tear trickles down, she wipes it from her cheek. With a deep sigh, she decides she'll read Josh's final goodbye to Maddie next. His letter tells a story Kaitlyn always suspected, but was never sure of until now. Despite Josh's strong positive exterior, he's struggled terribly with Maddie's absence. Again, the love he confesses to Maddie brings back lost opportunities in Kaitlyn's own life; she blames herself for everything. She aches for Carson while reading the words her uncle wrote to her aunt. "My skin still feels your gentle touch, my lips taste your moist tender kisses, and with each recollection of our bodies as one, my heart races and my breath deepens." Kaitlyn's never stopped missing Carson, and she almost reached out to him the other day with coaxing from her uncle, but stopped.

As she reaches back into the manila envelope, she pulls out the remaining item. It being addressed to Katie brings a smile to her face, knowing this is his endearing name for her. She wonders what's inside. Wiggling her finger under the lip of the envelope, she proceeds to run it the length, opening it and pulling out a letter.

Dear Katie,

I have loved having you here with me for the past few weeks. It brought back splendid memories of our summers together; you joining Maddie and me at the beach. Honestly, it's so refreshing to have youth in the house. You brought fresh energy, ideas, and made things a bit more fun.

You have become a beautiful young woman, and you can accomplish anything you set your mind to do. Never forget that. Life is not always easy, but give it your best shot, and if you get knocked down, pick yourself up and try, try again.

Sorry I bent your ear the past few weeks. You know I love to tell stories and my favorite subject is your Aunt Maddie, followed by those of our pups. Yeah, I may exaggerate, but that's the fun of storytelling, and I think it's expected when you get to be my age. Putting emphasis on my relationship with Maddie, the love we had, I was hoping you'd realize it's time for you to find love once again. Carson and you were close once; I urge you to reach out to him again. You should find someone else to share your life if it isn't with Carson. Someone who can help you find and live your passions, or, as Maddie put it, your "Dash".

Don't be upset with me, Carson and I have kept in touch the past few years. He never stopped loving you. His baseball career took off. In fact, next year he'll be playing in Philadelphia for the Phillies. He's local now as he moved into the area. His contact info in case you want it: 215-555-9812 / CarsonBB17@email.com

Please give real consideration to attending the University of Pennsylvania Veterinary School. The school accepted you. I knew they would. You can stay with me and commute if you please. It's only an hour away. Hey, you can help run Monkey's House, too. You'll get the best of both worlds: traditional veterinary medicine along with non-traditional and alternative modalities. They make a brilliant combination, as you can see from our results.

You'll always be my little Katie. Thank you for all the joy you've brought into my life.

Love Always,
Uncle Josh

It shocks Kaitlyn to learn her uncle and Carson had kept in touch. She knew they hit it off at their college graduation, yet did not know they were still connected. Kaitlyn feels momentarily betrayed, but she also knows anything her uncle does is only in her best interest, or at least he believes so. Besides, today is not the day to send bad vibes towards her uncle, and in reality, she knows he's right about staying connected to Carson. It's a thrill to know that she can contact him. After this long, she assumed that Carson had moved on with his life.

After the accident, Carson put off joining the Dodgers for a year. He wanted to be there for Kaitlyn. Eventually, he signed with them. Shortly after, he reported to their Triple-A farm team, The Oklahoma City Dodgers. He was far away from Kaitlyn and attempted to contact her often, but he never received a reply. In his communications, he told her there was a ticket reserved for her for all the home games at the call window. Whenever he pitched home games at Chickasaw Bricktown Ballpark, he would search the stands as he took the mound, hoping to see Kaitlyn siting among the fans. Sadly, he never saw her.

Ever since her addiction, she felt ashamed and didn't have the nerve to reach out to the one person she loved the most. Now she's wondering if it's time. She has the means, but is she brave?

Reading Maddie's and Josh's letters affirmed the love and life they shared was exactly what she wanted for herself with Carson. Kaitlyn finds strength in their words, and the resolute to take a leap of faith. With new found confidence, she digs into her backpack, pulls out her tablet, powers it up, and readies to write her own letter. The power of those letters gives her the fortitude and desire to convey her love to Carson similarly.

She contemplates how to even begin her letter. "Dear" is too boilerplate, and something like "My Love," well, she feels she lost that right after avoiding him all this time. Carson, plain old Carson it is.

Carson,

I know it has been some time since we spoke, and I'm truly sorry. Over the past few years, I couldn't get you off my mind, even during my darkest days. My life was a mess. I wanted to save you the pain. Yet it seemed to cause more for me after I pushed you away. I dreamed you would pull me out of my nightmare, make things right again. You tried again and again, and I rejected your attempts. Knowing I rebuffed you made it harder for me to reach out. I knew I needed to break free, but I couldn't escape the addiction and horrors that came along with it. My journey was a struggle, but now I am on the right path. Once again, I'm the woman you met in college and fell in love with.

Time is the great healer; the accident and baggage associated with it are in my past. However, I've found the one thing time can't heal is the hole in my heart, and I have a tremendous hole from missing you. This may come too late, I hope not. My heart told me I had to reconnect with my true love, to see if you still have feelings for me, wondering if there's a chance to rekindle what we once had together. I can't imagine we'll pick back up where we left it. In fact, those last months were not my best. I would love to start over again.

I cannot stop thinking about the good times we used to have together, from the freshman gathering to our senior spring break, when we helped build a Habitat for Humanity home together. Those years with you were the best of my life. Being in your company made me a better person and boosted my confidence. You changed my life for the better. Every day spent with you put a smile on my face, and rightfully so, they were the best days of my life.

Since we've been apart, I have spent far too much of my time consumed by regrets. I constantly recount the wonderful times we've shared, and as the days passed, I have realized more and more I don't see a happy future for myself without you.

The last few weeks spending time with my uncle, hearing the love he had with my aunt, and now sitting here in the hospital reading their love letters to one another, have opened my eyes. It's helped me understand the importance of having someone special in your life who will not only love you, but support each other's dreams and ambitions through the years.

It may be too late. You may have found another, or don't want to see me. I pray that's not the case. Fate has ways of making things right. I hope this is one of those times and it gives us another chance at love. Patiently, I'll wait to hear from you. I'm looking forward to the day when I can hold your hand again. No matter the eventual outcome, please know how much you've meant to me and always will.

Love,
Kaitlyn

Within fifteen minutes of emailing her letter, Kaitlyn receives a call on her cell. It's Carson. "Hi Kaitlyn, I've been hoping you'd contact me for such a long time. I had to reach out right away. Are you still at the hospital? How is Uncle Josh doing?"

Stunned, Kaitlyn stays silent for what seems like an eternity. She's shocked he called her, and so quickly. Besides, how does he know her uncle is having surgery? And where did he get her cell number? Suddenly it clicks—her uncle, of course. She realizes now they stayed in contact more than the occasional Christmas card. "Hi Carson, I am at the hospital. Uncle Josh's surgery is finishing up now. It looks like I'll be here at least a couple more hours. I want to see him before I head back to his house."

"Happy to hear the surgery is finishing up. I'm in town today. Would it be okay if I stopped by the hospital?"

This is happening faster than she could have ever imagined. She wants to say it's not a good time, but what comes out of her mouth is a simple "sure." Carson tells her he'll come up to the waiting room. He'll be there in twenty minutes.

Kaitlyn's queasy. It could be several things bringing on this sensation. She'd love to attribute it to sitting hours-on-end in the waiting room, breathing in stale air with a faint aroma of antiseptic, or to worrying about her uncle, especially after hearing of the complications he's had. But she knows it's none of those… it's seeing Carson for the first time in years. Kaitlyn jumps up, she's got to get out of here; she needs some fresh air, and fast.

Earlier in the day, she remembers passing a small interior courtyard and now makes her way there with urgency in her step. The crisp fall air brings a bounce in her pace as she makes her way onto the patio. She takes in a deep breath, relishing the freshness of this space. The sun is shining strong, warming the walls surrounding the courtyard. Thankfully, it's warmer than she had expected. She sits on a bench next to a small Magnolia tree. The leaves are shriveling and dropping from the branches, preparing for the upcoming winter. The sun, fresh air, and the lonely chirping of a single bird create a much-needed sense of serenity.

Kaitlyn's able to see the hall which Carson will enter. Enjoying the change of scenery, she stays outside and does a brief meditation in this pocket of solace in the middle of the city. It's helping calm her nerves at the moment. Her meditation routine is doing its job until she notices Carson strolling down the hall. She waves to catch his attention, and he stops, turns and joins Kaitlyn in the yard. They are quick to embrace. Carson doesn't act like it's been years since they've been together. Kaitlyn is a little more reluctant. It's not Carson, but her. She's made a mess of their relationship, although she knows it was the side effect of the accident, the influence of the opioids. Carson's soothing demeanor lightens the conversation as he brushes off a couple of leaves sitting on her shoulder.

They make their way back to the bench, and sitting alongside each other, start catching up. Carson is doing most of the talking, filling Kaitlyn in on his movement through the minor leagues over the past couple of years along with attending law school in the off-seasons and online. The highlight is the exciting news of being brought up to the majors, onto the pitching crew for the Phillies. He moved into the area two weeks ago, into an apartment in the Fishtown section of the city. Kaitlyn is less eager to discuss her past few years. She does, however, tell him she'll be staying in the area helping Uncle Josh in his recovery and running Monkey's House while attending University of Penn's Veterinary program.

"I'll be helping Uncle Josh at Monkey's House as long as it's still open. Looks like he'll have to close. They are taking his property to build a high-end golf community."

"They won't be taking your uncle's property."

Kaitlyn's eyes widen, "What do you mean?"

He explains that Josh went to him, knowing he's in law school and his dad is a partner in a law firm. Carson recruited his dad pro-bono, but after thorough research, there was no getting around eminent domain. The Supreme Court held that general benefits which a community would enjoy from the furthering of economic development are sufficient to qualify as a "public use." The developers would claim a golf community would benefit the economy of their rural community.

Carson also brought it up with the major league's legal team to see if they could provide guidance. They couldn't but were impressed to know a player was getting their law degree while playing baseball. The commissioner got wind of it, and his connections were greater than those of the developers. The league bought the land and gifted it to the Pineland Conversancy to be preserved as wildlife for eternity.

"A few more signatures and it will be preserved Pinelands. Never to be built on. Monkey's House is safe." Kaitlyn throws her arms around Carson and kisses him. For the first time in years, she lets herself express her emotions wholly, without any hesitation.

Time is passing, and Kaitlyn suggests getting back into the waiting room. She wants to be there, hopes Dr. Lea will return to announce her uncle is in recovery and she can go see him. Before she heads home, she needs to see he's doing okay. She's also excited to tell him he no longer needs to worry about Monkey's House. But mostly, she wants to tell him how much he's loved.

Lucky Charm

In the hall outside of the operating room, Dr. Sena is talking with Josh's surgeon, Dr. Ng. "It became touch and go when we went to close. I can't tell you what went wrong. The replacement went exactly as planned. His stats were perfect, and the team had everything covered. The new aortic valve was working great. When Dr. Klein started to close, it happened. Suddenly, his heart stopped." Dr. Ng is visibly shaken; he was sure they were going to lose Mr. Kelly. He has had close calls before, but not when everything was going so smoothly. Issues more often arise with patients who already have complications coming into a surgery, or they are high-risk candidates. There's always a solid reason behind it, yet in this case, he's still scratching his head as to why Mr. Kelly flatlined. At least he considers the operation a success, even though he's gained a few more gray hairs.

Dr. Sena puts his hand on Dr. Ng's shoulder in support. "You still seem a little upset. I'll go talk to his niece; I have a relationship with the family." He makes his way down the hall towards the waiting room where Kaitlyn and Carson are sitting together on the sofa, catching up on the years lost. Kaitlyn notices him coming their way, and she tenses, wondering why it isn't Dr. Lea or the surgeon coming to give her an update.

Isn't that what's customary after surgery? This can't be a good sign. She assumes he's coming to give her bad news about her uncle. Her ridged stature is now shaking. However, she manages to get off the sofa and heads towards Dr. Sena. Carson is following closely behind, their pace speeding to a brisk walk. She can't read the doctor's expression. Is he readying to give her give her good news or bad? Kaitlyn stops in the middle of the hall, freezing where she stands, unprepared if it's bad news. She's had her fill of it over the past few years. Losing her uncle would be devastating for her.

Dr. Sena makes his way to where she's standing. "Let's take a seat in the waiting room so we can talk."

"I don't need a seat; I'm fine standing. Please tell me how things went with my uncle's surgery."

"Your uncle is doing fine, although he had unexpected complications during the surgery. At one point, his heart even stopped, but he's doing better now. In fact, he's out of the operating room and resting in the surgical ICU." Tears of relief stream down Kaitlyn's face. She turns and hugs Carson tight like they were never apart. Neither wants to let go.

Exhausted from the turmoil of the entire process, her thoughts are with her uncle. He has such a calming effect on her. "Can I see my uncle? I want to make sure he's okay."

Dr. Sena introduces himself to Carson, then turns his attention back to Kaitlyn. "Of course. Let me take you to him. I'm sorry, Carson, but only one person can see him right now. I'm sure you understand." Carson nods in agreement and heads back to the waiting room.

Navigating the hallways, Kaitlyn has many questions running through her head about her uncle's heart stopping. Does that mean he's at risk of it happening again? Did it cause any damage to his heart? When Dr. Lea first told her and Holly about the complications, she couldn't imagine life without her witty uncle. A few hours ago, he was happily talking about his years with Maddie, the true love of his life, and telling stories about their dogs. He was so full of life one minute, and in the next, almost gone. Kaitlyn remembered her uncle saying you have to live life and enjoy every moment, which was exactly what he did. But she wasn't ready for their time together to be over.

For the past few weeks, Josh has been Kaitlyn's rock. Sure, he is demanding, and like Holly says, he is indeed a "Machine." He pushed her to apply to veterinary school when she was uncertain about her path. During the little time they spent together, he helped her transition back to the old Kaitlyn. Structure, purpose, and love were once again in her life when she needed it the most. Her uncle is a breath of fresh air, and being around him and the dogs has been taking her mind off her turbulent past.

Dr. Sena leads her into the cardiac surgical ICU. It's a large room, yet somewhat empty, with only three patients. "It's next to the operating rooms, so please excuse the activity." Pointing to a door in the back of the room he says, "That leads to the operating rooms. Never mind the staff going in and out, as they are prepping for tomorrow's operations."

As they make their way over to Josh, it's surprising to them how active and alert he is already. Post-operative cardiac patients are typically tired and groggy. Kaitlyn cautiously approaches her uncle's bed, reaches out toward him and grabs ahold of his hand, pulling herself as close as she dares. Considering such a long operation, and the complications he endured, he looks well, not at all how Kaitlyn imagined. "I'm so glad to see you. How are you feeling?"

"Surprisingly, well, for what I just went through. Dr. Sena, I'm glad to see you here. I didn't think I'd see you till tomorrow morning."

Kaitlyn is thankful Dr. Sena is still in the hospital. He came back for an emergency consultation with one of his other patients. He places his hand on Josh's arm and jokes, "I'm always here when you need me, or, in this case, when one of my other patients needed me. Since I was in the hospital, I wanted to check up on you." With a soothing voice yet serious smile he continues, "You need to get some rest. Did anybody tell you your heart stopped during surgery?"

"They didn't have to tell me; I knew the minute it happened."

Dr. Sena's eyes widen and he takes Kaitlyn aside, "I'm very skeptical hearing out-of-body experiences from surgery patients that flatlined. They contribute the perceived phenomena to hallucinations associated with the drugs used during the operation."

Josh has a spark in his voice. "Katie, I met your Aunt Maddie in heaven, at the Rainbow Bridge. Not just Maddie, but I reunited with all of our dogs. I even saw Grandma Sandy, your great-great grandmother."

Josh is getting excited about his dreams, and Dr. Sena intervenes, "Let's let your uncle rest. You can return in the morning."

"Don't go. Katie, please stay here as I want to tell you all about it. I'm afraid I won't remember in the morning." He turns to Dr. Sena. "Please, ten more minutes."

"Ten minutes it is. We have to let you rest after that."

"It was magical, as you might imagine. Monkey took me on a journey where I met all the dogs. Do you remember the story I told you about Hooch, how he loved bananas and how he counter surfed them off the kitchen island? I went surfing with him, and he had a yellow surfboard shaped like a banana. We were riding the waves and shooting out of the pipeline like professional surfers."

Excitement builds in Josh's voice as he continues describing the journey: "Beautiful wind chimes led us to a dog agility course like no other. But it wasn't the course that made it special, it was the occupants. Our dogs that had mobility issues on earth, like Dozer and Ariel, they were all running and jumping with renewed bodies."

Josh's eyes well up. "There was also a playground, where teenagers played fetch with the dogs. Young children helped paint markings on puppies. It was such a beautiful sight."

Josh stops for a few seconds as he remembers meeting Maddie. "I finally was reunited with Maddie. It was marvelous. We even went horseback riding on the beach."

There's another thing Josh wants to tell Kaitlyn, but he can't remember. He notices something on her shoulder. A Magnolia leaf is stuck on her sweater. "That's it." He points to the leaf. "There was a big gathering at the Tree of Life. It was magnificent. It showed the wonderful lives our dogs had with us." His eyes and voice drop. "That was when Maddie told me I needed to go back. It wasn't my time." Josh pauses, "Katie, they're not taking Monkey's House to build the golf community."

Kaitlyn's brow folds and eyes narrow. Carson just heard today the land behind Monkey's House is now in preservation. "How did you know?"

"Maddie told me. Oh, and the buds. There were a lot of buds."

Dr. Sena pulls Kaitlyn aside and tells her the memories Josh is having are indeed dreams brought on by the anesthesia. Much of what he's saying makes little sense. The best thing is to listen like she's interested, but ignore the desire to ask for any details. He would forget them all by the morning and things would return to normal.

He turns his attention to his patient and friend. "These are only dreams, Josh. They are from the drugs. You were telling Kaitlyn stories about many of these dogs recently. This is an exaggeration of them."

"Uncle Josh, the stories you told me this morning, and on the ride here, are intertwined within your dreams." Kaitlyn aches for her uncle; his dreams were so vivid, and she's sure they felt real to him.

"I guess you're both right. It felt so real. Like I was with my family." Josh slumps back into the bed as his breathing weakens and eyes droop. As he blinks, a tear runs down his cheek. He needs to be close to Maddie now more than ever.

Suddenly, Josh begins to open and close his fingers, like he's grasping for something. "Have either of you seen Monkey's Leash?" It is hard to hear Josh. His voice is fading. The breathing tube he had during surgery must have dried out his throat. "It's my connection to Maddie," he continues as another tear trickles over his cheek.

Neither of them knows where the leash is. Dr. Sena asks Charlie, an intern, to check the operating room for his good luck charm. As Charlie enters the room, nurse Elizabeth rushes over to Josh carrying Monkey's leash, placing it firmly into the palm of his hand. She wraps both of her hands around his. "This certainly was your lucky charm today. Always keep it with you for good luck."

Kaitlyn remembers Ray saying a brief prayer before Josh went into surgery. She hasn't uttered a prayer in ages, but today is special in so many ways and deserving of one. Taking Josh's hand, she tells her uncle it's time to thank the Lord for getting him safely through the operation. Dr. Sena agrees and steps up as they join hands while she says a little impromptu prayer. As she's finishing up, the operating door in the back of the room slams open, getting everybody's attention. Charlie walks through with a confused look and tells them he didn't find the charm. Yet, he's carrying a handful of colorful leashes, holding them high, hoping someone will understand what on earth they're doing in the operating room. He's grasping the middle of the leashes, and as they drape over his palm, they resemble a rainbow.

Kaitlyn's eyes open wide. She gazes at Dr. Sena, who looks as though he's just seen a ghost. They don't know what to make of the leashes. Kaitlyn looks back at Josh and notices him lying with a huge grin on his face. Obviously, he understands. Kaitlyn meets Charlie and brings the rainbow of leashes back to her uncle, setting them at the foot of his bed.

Josh sits up ever so slightly, struggling to get words out. "Is the red leash embroidered?"

Kaitlyn flips through the leashes. "Yes, it has a name on it…"

"Buddy, right?" Josh finishes the sentence. An astonished Kaitlyn nods as she wonders how he knows.

With an inhale, breathing in the wonder of it all, Josh falls back into bed. He smiles up towards the heavens with a twinkle in his eye.

Dr. Sena is puzzled. "Kaitlyn, I don't understand. We only sanitized and sent Monkey's leash into the OR. Where did all these others come from?"

"I don't know," Kaitlyn replies.

Josh reaches over and grabs Kaitlyn's arm, gently pulling her close. He leans up, ready to tell her something, as she bends close to hear. With a gleeful tear in his eye, he whispers, "They don't use leashes in Heaven."

Epilogue

Kaitlyn walks through the door of Monkey's House after a full day of classes. She takes a seat on the steps as the dogs frantically greet her, vying for her attention.

"Welcome home, Kaitlyn." Josh laughs as the dogs somehow get her onto the floor and then into an impressive dog pile. "I wonder if Maddie's quote, 'you should want to hug your vet' applies to dogs, too."

"I'm not a veterinarian yet. Tomorrow's the end of my first semester. I have a way to go."

Josh is wearing his barbequing apron and holding tongs. "I'm grilling chicken and vegetables for dinner. It'll be ready in about thirty minutes. You want some, right?"

"Sure thing. As soon as I can get up, I'll go get changed and then be right back down."

A pleasant June evening finds Josh setting the table outside on the deck. Hearing birds sing and frogs starting their evening serenade, he glances around the farm, his eyes focusing across the pond to the sacred resting place of his family. His eyes soften and a smile forms. He's right where he's meant to be.

Sitting at the table, Kaitlyn takes her uncle's hand in hers. "Lord, thank you for all you've given us. For Uncle

Josh's health and giving me a second chance at... well, life. Please help the tests go well tomorrow. Thank you for this wonderful food and for the chef." They both smile. Kaitlyn has had very little spare time as the veterinary program she's enrolled in is the university's accelerated track.

Josh adds to the prayer. "Six months ago, you reunited me with Maddie and my family. The day I spent with them renewed my spirits and filled my soul, knowing I'll be with them once again someday. Thank you, Lord. Amen."

Kaitlyn, who hasn't eaten since breakfast, digs right in then pauses. "I noticed your bags by the door when I came in. You all packed?"

"Yep, probably over packed. I'm not sure what I'm going to need, or what's there."

"It's been a while. I'm sure everything is going to be great." Kaitlyn takes another bite.

"I'm not leaving till the afternoon, but tomorrow morning is my swearing in. It's going to be a busy day."

The Pineland Conversancy is having their official kick-off celebration for the preserve right behind Monkey's House. They included Josh in the ceremony; he's being sworn in as an honorary ranger. For the past three months, he's been tinkering on an old John Deere Gator, the four-wheeler ATV he purchased for monitoring the property. Josh made modifications to the rear bed to ensure its precious cargo, his dogs, won't fall out.

After a pleasant yet quick meal, they make their way through the sliding glass doors. Josh heads in first and stops in the middle of the family room. His eyes well up, seeing the montage of pictures covering every inch of the room.

"Everything okay?" Josh doesn't answer as he's engulfed with the emotional magnitude of what hangs in front of him. Kaitlyn rests her hand on his shoulder. "Uncle Josh, are you okay?"

"Couldn't be better." He reaches his hand up and pats hers, resting on his shoulder. "Katie, thank you for bringing down the pictures from the early years of Monkey's House. So many include Maddie. I love it."

"It was my honor to highlight Aunt Maddie."

"I like how you have the leashes from heaven incorporated, too."

"They are right where they belong, as a rainbow over Aunt Maddie and Monkey."

Kaitlyn heads up to her room to study. Tomorrow is her last day of school before the two-week semester break. Josh takes a seat, overflowing with gratitude as the images he's gazing upon show a full life, lived with passion. He realizes there's a lot to do before bed and loads Kaitlyn's car with his luggage, then spends the next couple of hours caring for and walking dogs. Before he knows it, he's walking up the stairs carrying Darla. Once the pups are all snuggled in their beds, it's time to be with Maddie. As his knees hit the floor and fingers intertwine, his heart soars. He starts with a brief prayer followed by telling Maddie the joyful day all the pups had, finishing up with a goodnight kiss, sent into the heavens. "Maddie's love letter" sits on the nightstand, but like most nights since his surgery, his heart is full just knowing it's there—no need to read it.

The slamming of the front door wakes Josh. Kaitlyn is off to the university at the break of dawn again. As he brews his coffee, Darla and Rocky are ruff-housing by his feet. It takes him back to the day of his surgery. "Hey guys, no fasting for me today. I'm making a hearty breakfast, like the ones my grandma would cook for me." The sizzling and aroma of the bacon has the dogs sitting at attention. "Okay, a small piece." Josh's eyes roll up toward the ceiling with a grin. "It's only a little bacon." Eating the over-medium eggs cooked in bacon grease brings a smile to his face. This is the way Grandma Sandy prepared them.

After cleaning the dishes, Josh makes his way into the garage. "Good morning, Holly."

Holly has the pups' food ready to serve. "This could be the best day of your life."

Josh's head tilts and eyebrows rise. "Hey, that's my line."

"Today's your big day."

"In more ways than one."

It's approaching noon and Josh needs to get the dogs ready so they can head to the ribbon cutting. He looks dapper in his ranger uniform. It's not as formal as his Marine dress blues, but he wears it with equal pride, knowing he saved Monkey's House and led the fight to preserve the natural oasis behind his property.

Darla and Rocky are wearing little orange vests that have "Ranger Dog" written across them. They relish riding in the back of the gator, barking out directions. As Josh wheels his ATV past the pond, a bullfrog splashes into the water and turtles duck under the surface. Moving through the field where the pack walked with Maddie and their pups for over thirty years has him puffing his chest and holding his head high.

As he arrives, he sees the celebration is small. Josh thinks it's fitting for a preserve—the fewer people, the better. Where you would normally have politicians clamoring for a piece of the limelight, none are in attendance. They wouldn't dare show their faces after hitching their wagons to the developers trying to close Monkey's House and take Josh's property.

Pinned on his ranger shirt is his honorary badge. The dogs have tiny ranger buttons affixed to their vests as well. Josh has a greater sense of relief from the symbolism the ceremony. Their sanctuary is now safe and will continue rescuing dogs for years to come.

After the attendees leave, Josh starts his ranger duties, journeying across the preserve in the gator with his two cohorts. The adventure takes them to every corner of the refuge, and before he knows it, he realizes he's running late.

Back at the house, Josh gets his clothes changed just in time as the car service pulls up. A twenty-minute drive isn't quite enough time for one of his long stories, but Josh still tugs at his driver, Michael's ear. At the high-speed line, he jumps on the train to Philadelphia.

Once at his destination, Josh glances at his watch; Kaitlyn should be here by now. He grabs food and a drink as time goes by.

Twenty minutes later, she arrives. "Sorry, I'm late. The final exams went long." She takes the seat next to him.

There is a long pause, then a smirk forms on Kaitlyn's face. Josh looks her way and squints. "Well, how do you think you did?"

"I think I aced them!" she says as she stomps her feet and shakes her head. She then transitions to what's in front of her. "What inning are they in?"

"Heading into the sixth. The Phillies are down by four runs."

"Do you think Carson will be called up today?" Kaitlyn clenches and shakes her fists. "I'd love to see him pitch."

"I would, too. They need him. The starter and the last reliever got hammered. I think they'll call him up next."

This is Carson's first opportunity to pitch in the big leagues. He did great during spring training in Clearwater, but in the last preseason game, he injured his shoulder. Now, after the two months of rehab, his pitching has never been better. At the top of the seventh inning, it thrills them to see Carson walking out of the bullpen towards the mound. He throws a few warmups, then before his first official pitch, he pauses, and looks up into the stands. His eyes appear to meet Kaitlyn's as he tips his head slightly.

"Did you see that? He smiled at me."

"See what?"

"Ah, come on Uncle Josh. You saw him look up here."

"I don't think he looked this way." Josh can't stop grinning as Kaitlyn elbows him in the ribs. "Ouch. Okay, okay. I saw it."

Carson is rewarded with his first win in the big leagues as the Phillies rallied, winning the ball game by two runs. Josh and Kaitlyn recall his every pitch to one another with excitement when she notices Carson coming out of the clubhouse. Her attention immediately turns towards him; running to meet her love, she throws her arms around him and gives him a big kiss. Josh congratulates him, and soon, all are about to hit the road in different directions. The Phillies will be off on a long road trip to the west coast while Josh and Kaitlyn are finally heading to Paws & Relax, to enjoy the beach together.

Out of the stadium parking lot, they jump on the Walt Whitman bridge into New Jersey. Josh points to the reddish horizon as the sun is setting in the distance. "We'll be looking at that from the beach tomorrow."

"It's been over ten years. I can't wait."

"I have some exciting news. Your place should be ready when we get back." Josh had renovations made to the house, adding an apartment over the garage. He felt she needed her own place. Kaitlyn never complained, but her uncle insisted. During the construction phase, Josh ordained himself the assistant foreman. Although he loved the entire process, he didn't get a good vibe that his oversight thrilled the crew.

"Wow, that is exciting. Thank you so much."

A few dogs will be waiting for them at Paws & Relax. Aunt Claire was down for a few days with Rusty, Sammy, Chuckles, and Smug. She'll head out when they arrive, leaving the pups to enjoy the beach with them.

A few miles into their trip, Josh asks, "Would you like me to put the radio on?"

Kaitlyn exhales and settles into her seat. She gazes over at her uncle with a smile. "Let's keep it off. I'd love to hear some more of your stories."

Thank You For Reading
Leashes in Heaven

If you enjoyed Leashes in Heaven, please consider leaving an honest review on the book's product page at the online bookstore where you purchased it. I will read them all. Thank you.

Recommend this book to your friends and family. Give a big shout-out on your social media platform.

For my dog-loving readers, check out Monkey's House and consider becoming part of the Monkey's House family:

Facebook: www.facebook.com/monkeyshouse.org

Instagram: www.instagram.com/monkeyshouse_doghospice

Monkey's House website: www.monkeyshouse.org

Acknowledgments

There are many I want to thank in writing *Leashes in Heaven*, helping me make it a wonderfully, inspiring love story:

Patricia Allsebrook, for being there from the beginning as a great sounding board from the first concepts of *Leashes in Heaven* to the final written word. You were my second set of eyes over the past year and with your constructive guidance and encouragement, I knew the journey of writing my first fiction novel was heading down the right path.

Christy Day of Constellation Book Services, for being so understanding about all my iterations for the book cover and interior layout. You helped me craft an inspiring, powerful cover and laid out the book wonderfully.

Thank you to those who read my manuscript and provided insightful feedback. You helped me fine-tune my story, ensuring it would resonate with readers: Vicki Masterson, Jim and Jerri Golis, Caitlin Bluem, and Tracey Mauro.

Thanks to my various coaches from my very first book *Where Dog Go To Live!*, to *Life's a Dog Bone Chew it all Day Long!*, and now *Leashes in Heaven*. You've all played a part in making this book possible: Geoffrey Berwind, Debra Englander, Cristina Smith, and Steve Harrison.

I would like to thank my wife, Michele Allen. Without her love and dedication to homeless hospice dogs, there would be no Monkey's House, the backdrop of this love story. With all my heart and deepest gratitude, a special thanks goes to the dogs of Monkey's House. Many found their stories intertwined with Josh's and Maddie's due to their strong and unique personalities, enhancing a heartfelt story. Writing them into this novel brought back such great memories.

Finally, my greatest thanks go to God. You've been crafting this story in my heart and soul since the day we opened Monkey's House. I could never have done this without your guidance and strength. I'm grateful to be your servant, giving dogs a heaven-on-earth before they rest at your feet.

About the Author

JEFF ALLEN is the cofounder of a successful nonprofit —Monkey's House Dog Hospice & Sanctuary. Living a life among twenty-five hospice dogs has inspired him to start telling their stories, which led to his first book, an award-winning bestseller *Where Dogs Go To Live!*. When he's not saving dogs, he's helping to improve peoples' lives as a manager in Human Resources at a global Biopharmaceutical company.

Monkey's House was established by Jeff and his wife Michele Allen in 2015. Their sanctuary, recognized for its outstanding work saving and caring for over 150 hospice dogs, was awarded Rescue of the Year in 2017 by World Dog Expo. The State of New Jersey—Senate and General Assembly honored them in a joint legislative resolution for their exemplary work through Monkey's House. They were both named 2021 USA Today AnimalKind award winners.

www.jeffallenbooks.com

Reading Group Guide

Discussion Questions

1. The opening scene highlights a playful ritual between Maddie, Josh, and their furry family–Sunday morning snuggles. At one point in Josh's life, this was his favorite day of the week. Speaking of favorites, what was your favorite scene in the book and why?

2. Maddie's passion and love for the dogs was the driving force behind Monkey's House. Josh adopted her passion and made it his own. Do you think it finally became his true passion, or was he doing it for Maddie?

3. Discuss the importance of letter writing in the novel. What motivated Maddie, Josh and Kaitlyn to each write one? What does each of their letters represent? Why did it take a year for Josh to write his and years for Kaitlyn? Was there a common purpose or theme?

4. What lesson does Josh learn on his journey through heaven, meeting up with his furry family members? Is there more than one lesson learned?

5. Tears streamed uncontrollably down Josh's cheeks as he knelt under the Chimes of Liberation. Which scene really tugged at your heart?

6. Kaitlyn suffered for years after the diving accident. Her addiction to opioids destroyed her relationship with Carson. Carson seemed willing to stay with her and help her though it, but she pushed him away. Did you think they would get back together?

7. Sora's pendant, the globes filled with family members' hair, and Monkey's leash all brought on loving memories and tears. What does Monkey's leash symbolize? Do you have a special keepsake, and if so what's the special meaning?

8. Maddie was inspired by Monkey to make a difference in hospice dogs' lives by opening Monkey's House. Has anybody, or a pet, inspired you to make a change, to make another's life better? Have you been the recipient of such a gesture?

9. Taking a walk together, especially strolling along the beach hand-in-hand with a beautiful sunset on the horizon, was Josh and Maddie's slice of heaven. Why do you think it was so special to them?

10. At a magical cove, a butterfly landing on Brits head, a bullfrog croaking, and a button buck grazing are all signs Josh witnessed before. Do you believe spirits of loved ones appear to let us know they are well as Josh and Maddie do? Have you been graced with a sign from a loved one?

11. In Surgical ICU, Kaitlyn's and Dr. Sena's jaws drop when they see the rainbow of leashes. Did you like the ending? Where you surprised?

12. Josh read the letter Maddie wrote him every night before his head hit the pillow. Yet, back home after his surgery, he rarely read it. Why?

Made in United States
Orlando, FL
21 April 2023

32308983R00190